Early praise for Hal Duncan's Scruffians!

"The Arthurian legend of the Fisher King, the myth of Orpheus, Shakespeare's *Tempest*, comic book superheroes, and *Twilight* are just a few of the tales that Duncan (*Ink*) deconstructs through a prism of queer sexuality, youthful rebellion, and rage against authority, in this thrilling, funny, and moving collection."
— *Publishers Weekly*
(starred review)

"Duncan's voice is uniquely grand, and the stories gathered here reflect his ongoing exploration of both queer experience and mythic/narrative modes of storytelling and meaning-making. Frequently sharp-tongued and a bit dark — I'd even say a little roguish, sometimes — these stories are delightful and provocative, and I'd certainly recommend picking them up for a read."
— Brit Mandelo
for Tor.com

"Inventive, disturbing, witty, and perverted. Hal Duncan is a queer devil and *Scruffians!* is his dirty little blessing."
— Jameson Currier, author of
The Wolf at the Door and *The Forever Marathon*

"Hal Duncan's stories enchant in every sense of the word. In language as magical as the street urchins that give the book its title, these tales conjure up a world in which myths and legends take on flesh, with all the attendant pleasures and dangers that implies. (And he throws in some pirates and fairies for good measure!) Tough, tender and deeply engaging *Scruffians!* dazzles and delights from beginning to end."
— Peter Dubé, author of
The City's Gates, Conjure: a Book of Spells and *Subtle Bodies*

Scruffians!

STORIES OF BETTER SODOMITES

Hal Duncan

Lethe Press
Maple Shade, New Jersey

Published in 2014 by Lethe Press, Inc.
118 Heritage Avenue, Maple Shade, NJ 08052 USA
lethepressbooks.com / lethepress@aol.com
ISBN: 978-1-59021-193-9 / 1-59021-193-6
e-ISBN: 978-1-59021-260-8 / 1-59021-260-6

A hardcover Deluxe Edition featuring an additional previously unpublished story, exclusive cover art, and full-colour photographic illustrations is available through the publisher's website.

These stories are works of fiction. Names, characters, places, and incidents are products of the author's imagination or are used fictitiously.

Credits for previous publication appear on page 199, which constitutes a continuation of this copyright page.

Set in Agmena, Myriad, Viva, Astonished, and Garvis.
Cover and interior design: Alex Jeffers.
Cover images: Rob Lorino (front); Yannis Angel (back).

LIBRARY OF CONGRESS CATALOGING-IN-PUBLICATION DATA
Duncan, Hal, 1971-
[Short stories. Selections]
Scruffians! : stories of better sodomites / Hal Duncan.
    pages cm
ISBN 978-1-59021-193-9 (pbk. : alk. paper) -- ISBN 978-1-59021-260-8 (e-book) -- ISBN 978-1-59021-394-0 (deluxe edition with illustrations : alk. paper)
1. Fairies--Fiction. I. Title.
PR6104.U536A6 2014
823'.92--dc23
                    2014010654

Contents

How a Scruffian Starts Their Story

—I was born under a bad signpost, says Foxtrot Wainscot Hottentot III.

— I was stolen from gypsies, says Puckerscruff of the urchins.

— I was raised by werewolves, says Flashjack of the hellions.

— I ran away from the circus, says Joey Picaroni.

— I bought me soul from the Devil, says Nuffinmuch O'Anyfink, king of the tinkers.

— I was a teenage virgin mum, says Bananastasia Roaminhopper, rightful Princess of Russia (allegedly).

— I took the King's shilling and died in all his wars, says Ratatat Dan. But not for the likes of you.

— You see, says Gob, a *Scruffian*'s story needs a *hook*.

They sit on the living-room floor of the Scruffian squat—their crib, they call it — in a rough circle round the old fireplace that's now shrine to a sound system. There's beer cans and bottles strewn between them, baccy packets, squishy black and gubbins scattered among the booze, chucked from here to there at a gesture or word — *skins?* The scamp, Foxtrot, is lucky if he looks eleven. Joey must be at least seventeen. Well, they all must be *at least* whatever they look, and then some. And then maybe *a lot*.

— You've gotta open with swagger, says Gob.

The Scruffian-to-be looks at them as if they're bonkers, thinking that he can't really *improve* much on his opener…and closer really:

I ran away from home cause my dad used to beat the fucking crap out of me.

The truth isn't *quite* as simple as that, he supposes, not quite. Maybe the word beat doesn't do justice to the fucker's repertoire of tortures, the physical and the psychological, like his fondness for holding a cigarette up to No-Son-of-Mine's eye, so close he could smell the singed eyelashes. And there's the whole issue of *why…*

2.

An early memory (he must have been even younger than Foxtrot—or younger than Foxtrot *looks*, of course, given what they've told him about Fixing): the boys' changing rooms at primary school; a smart-arse aiming to best him on street cred because this quiet, *sensitive* boy was an easy target, asking if he knew what a hard-on was; him saying he knew fine well cause he had one right now; a friend calling him a retard afterwards, telling him you never said that sorta stuff; him asking his Mum why; his Dad going ballistic. *No son of mine…*

Or a later memory, from when he was the age Puckerscruff is Fixed at, maybe younger – thirteen or so: looking at DIY porn on the Internet with his best mate, Harry, mostly the fucked-up gross-out stuff where hideous old freaks do the weirdest shit; the two of them laughing at each other's mugged horror and mock-retching; the *phwars* and nudges when they clicked onto the proper porn; and him knowing fine well it was Harry's reaction that thrilled him more than anything on screen, the thought of Harry hard.

And then when the actual fooling-around started…

—Don't *watch*, says Harry. Gayboy.

He can't help watching his mate going at it though. And it was Harry who'd fucking decided he was bursting for a wank anyway, while they were lying there in the tent, talking about the girls at school that Harry fancied, and the one he…thought was really pretty, Charlene. Whatever. It was Harry who was totally being the gayboy, pulling his jeans and pants down to play with himself, not even getting into the sleeping-bag first.

Gayboy? No, he's bi. Like that character in *Doctor Who*. He's just really picky about girls, yeah?

—Yeah, he says, fag smoke trailing out in practised exhale.

Dylan's a year older than him and hot, indie as fuck with his purple and yellow undies showing, jeans dragged down to his hips by the bullet belt. A bit emo maybe with the razor-blade scars on his forearms — the thin type that come from not cutting too deep — but that just makes Dylan think *his* cigarette burns are impressive.

He says he does it to himself, of course. Said the bruises round his throat were from auto-erotic asphyxiation.

He slips a hand into Dylan's waistband as they snog.

He's never really come out. Everyone just knows it—Sarah, Katie and Jennie, who think he's so cool because of his sexploits; Topher and Stevie, who're awed at how he can just hit on guys like that; all the straight boys at the parties or piss-ups in the cemetery…who know how much he fancies them because they couldn't really *not* know. It's not really an issue in social circles where everyone has a poster of Conor Oberst on their bedroom wall. He's lost count of all the guys who've said he gives better hand-jobs than their girlfriends.

He's never really been caught. It's not like his Dad ever checked the web history on the computer. It wouldn't have made any difference anyway; he's not a retard like Topher, whose mum had a Serious Talk With Him when he left Firefox open on fucking Gaydar. It's not like Dad found a stash of gay porn mags, or heard about him sucking off some schoolmate, cause who the fuck needs mags when you've got XTube, and like any of their parents have a clue the shit they get up to.

It's not like his dad *needs* the fucking excuse.

He kicks back on the swing, but lets his heels scuff on the rubber of the playpark's surface, drag him back to a rest. The chain is biting cold in his hand, the plastic wet under his arse, and it's getting dark; but so fuck? His ribs are still sore and he feels more like jumping in the river than going home. He sniffs, rubs a teary eye. It's just the cold though, yeah? That way a wind in winter makes your nose run and your eyes water. He wouldn't last long in the water at all in this weather.

He clocks a shadow over by the trees, knows straight off what it is—here, at this time of night. He just sits on the swing, gazing in the direction of the lurker, until the guy cruising him gets the message, starts strolling forward, unlit fag in hand.

— You got a light?

— Yeah, here.

— Cheers. You want one?

— Thanks.

A pause as the guy studies his bust lip, the bruise on his cheek.

— You scruffying, yeah? he says.

— Huh?

The guy seems to lose nerve, takes a hurried draw of his fag, looks away.

— Never mind. Sorry, I thought…you…

—You're no son of mine, the fucker says.

The fucker's hand is thick-fingered, big-boned, not podgy but meaty, like it was made for punching the shit out of him. The skin is rough and ruddy, skin that burns in the sun rather than tanning. It should be covered in black hair, like a fucking troglodyte's but it's more freckled than anything. Still, the sovereign rings and the DIY tattoo on the back of it — a crude, biro-and-compasses R.F.C. in block capitals — those give it the right thuggish quality.

It's weird what you focus on.

5.

It's weird how people just walk by him as he sits there on the bench, weird how they have no idea that he doesn't even belong in this *city*, never mind this park. He just got off a train at King's Cross, picked a direction and started walking, kept walking until he found a quiet place to sit down, and have a fag, and think; to them he's probably just another teenager bunking off school.

He trails a finger across the carved-up wood of the bench: names and insults; gang initials; band names.

He's never heard of the Scruffians.

—*Orphans, foundlings, latchkey kids,* the children down by the fountain are chanting.

The Scruffian-to-be takes a path curving off to the right and up the hill, towards a statue of a mutton-chopped Victorian gent that nestles in rhododendron bushes. But he keeps his pace to a stroll; the half-dozen chavs he's taken the turn to avoid aren't paying him any mind and the park's busy; no need to advertise himself as a target. It's just…because he's *trying* not to be noticed…he just knows…

— Oi! Check this gaylord out!

Fuck.

— *Urchins, changelings, live-by-wits.*

— Oi, you! Oi, gaylord!

He knows it's just giving them what they want, but still… He stops, turns, tells them to fuck off. He's just fucking had enough. Behind the chavs, the kids at the fountain stop their hopscotch game, nudge each other, point his way. Yeah, yeah, come see the show. Except…they carry on chanting.

— *Rascals, scallywags, ruffians, scamps.*

A group of punks his own age, sitting on the grass, clamber to their feet. Sweet. A whole fucking audience of —

They start unhooking chains, wrapping them round hands as they join in the chant.

— *Scoundrels, hellions, Scruffians STAMP!*

6.

He's not sure what's happening now; doesn't seem like the chavs are either, jeers turning to nervous aggro as they clock the chains. They must be off their home turf themselves. But if these other kids are some local gang, they're… a fucking weird mix for it. Shit, there's even a couple of skaters with them now.

All of them have weapons — chains, cut-throat razors and fucking — Christ, even the kids have Stanley knives. And all of them advance with slow menace, flourishing chains like nunchuks, thumping weapons against chests, stamping feet. Choreographed in perfect time with the chant.

As the Scruffian-to-be takes the spliff offered by Flashjack, he can't help studying the perfectly — impossibly perfectly — intact hand, the one the punk had raised when the Scruffians were only a few yards from the chavs, close enough that they could see this wasn't a trick. The one Flashjack had taken a pair of secateurs to, snipped off the pinky with an expression half grimace, half grin, all fucking madman.

That had sent the chavs running. He'd been too shocked to do anything except gape.

— Fuck me, that hurt, the punk had said. Should see your face though.

He passes the spliff to Gob.

That's just how his story starts, he thinks. I ran away from home cause my Dad used to beat the fucking crap out of me. I came to London and found the Lost Boys, these *Scruffians* who have some…*thing* they stole that makes you like them. Unaging. Indestructible. Fixed. He *tries* a more twisty opening, turns it over in his mind: I kissed the *boys* and made them cry…in ecstasy.

Yeah, whatever.

— You want my story? he says eventually. Fuck, it ain't even begun.

Gob grins.

— Now, that's *way* better, he says.

How a Scruffian Gets Their Name

1.

—Eeny, meeny, miny, moe. Catch a nipper by the toe. If he squeals let him go. Eeny, meeny, miny, moe. You are not...

Foxtrot's finger stops its bouncing.

— Taterdemulligan Jackanips? suggests Bananastasia.

The fresh-Fixed Scruffian — the Scruffian who's only just become a Scruffian, who knows *what* he is now but isn't at all sure about *who* — rolls the name around in his head awhile, tries to imagine himself answering to it. *Hey, Taterdemulligan! Yo, Tat, how's it going?* Not *too* bad, but...

— Nah, he says eventually. It's okay, but I dunno that it's *me*.

— Tain't you then, says Gobfabbler.

The fresh-Fixed Scruffian—who was just another boy up until two days ago, when Flashjack and Joey held him down, a folded leather belt between his teeth, and Foxtrot pressed the Stamp to his chest, and it ripped the very soul out of him, carved it on the surface of his skin — looks round at the seven crib-mates gathered for the ceremony by Foxtrot. Foxtrot Wainscot Hottentot III, that is.

Bananastasia Roaminhopper.

Puckerscruff Ragamuff.

Flashjack Scarlequin.

Joey Picaroni.

Ratatat Dan.

Gobfabbler.

And then there's him. And all he knows is he's not *No-Son-of-Mine*, not anymore.

—Eeny, meeny, miny, moe. Catch a nipper by the toe. If he squeals let him go. Eeny, meeny, miny, moe. You are not…

Again Foxtrot's finger stops, picking out another of the mob sat on the threadbare rug — Puckerscruff this time, who crosses his arms, gives a cold hard glower.

— Tadgerfluff, he says pointedly. Luckpusher Chancelot Tadgerfluff.

— Um… says the fresh-Fixed Scruffian.

— He didn't know, mumbles Flashjack, the Scruffian of the fluffed tadger in question. And you know I've got fuck-all self-control, babe…

He trails off as Puckerscruff's glare turns to him.

— Moving swiftly on, says Foxtrot.

—Eeny, meeny, miny, moe. Catch a nipper by the toe. If he squeals let him go. Eeny, meeny, miny, moe. You are not…

This time Foxtrot's finger points at the fresh-fixed Scruffian himself, the Scruffian who gave up his old name even before his old life, who has no sodding clue who he is now, really. A latter-day Lost Boy, sure, a full-fledged Scruffian, Fixed by the Stamp like his crib-mates; but even when he stands at the grimy mirror in the bathroom, staring at his soul carved on his chest…

— I just dunno, he says.

2.

—Dunno, mate, says the punk. I mean, they call me Flashjack Scarlequin, but I don't even remember who it was twigged me for it. I'm a hellion, see, fucking bodymods to the max, motherfucker.

The punk who seems to be leader of this *Scruffian* gang, the one who did the…*thing* with the secateurs, sent the chavs packing, this *Flashjack* stops beside the dumpster and turns, pulls up his sleeveless tee to show a chest hatchworked with black scars. Like some kid went mental with a black inky. A sharpened black inky.

— I sorta accidentally overwrote that memory. I think.

Flashjack shrugs, drops his tee and beckons him on. It's just the two of them now. As quick as it formed to rout the chavs hassling him in the park, the Scruffian mob disbanded, leaving just this spark-eyed Sid Vicious. Who'd slipped an arm round his shoulder — *cheer up, mate, it might never happen...again* — and led him off through the streets, away from a cold night on a park bench, away from kickings past and future, to something else, something he can't believe. A world of Scruffians who can spark flame from a finger-click, light a fag.

Used to be, Flashjack blathers, casual as if they were chatting about last night's telly, that getting Fixed with the Stamp set you as is for the rest of your unnatural — which is to say endless — life. But since the first Scruffian to get his Stamp nicked found it tweaked him, well, now they can be anyone they choose to be. That's how you get the urchins with their spikes, and the hellions — most of whom are a lot freakier looking than Flashjack.

Considering how fucked his Stamp is, says Flashjack, everyone's a bit flummoxed he looks even *vaguely* human.

At the corner, Flashjack flicks the butt away—the stump of finger not just healed now but sprouting — and points across the road, at an old brick tenement, its ground floor doors and windows all sealed with steel.

— This way.

They cut down an alley, over a wall into the backyard. More steel panelling.

— How — ?

But the word's barely out before Flashjack's running, jumping to a window-ledge, swinging up onto an extension's roof. Another jump to a drainpipe that he shins up, swings from. Within seconds he's crouched on a first-floor window-ledge, chucking down a rope-ladder.

3.

—I dunno, says the one who goes by Joey Picaroni. Like we need another mouth to feed.

— Don't pay him no mind, says Flashjack. He ain't the boss of this crib. That'd be Foxtrot.

Flashjack points at a boy who can't be older than ten, hunkered down in front of the Xbox, playing *Tekken 6* with a hot kid in a red windbreaker. *Any more pwned, you'd have the queen on you,* the latter's saying.

Caught by Red Windbreaker's grin, it takes him a full second to realise that the child fingered as the leader is wearing a fake moustache.

—I *am* a teenager, say Fox.

— You were Fixed at eleven, says Joey.

— Oneteen, Fox corrects him.

— There's no such number as oneteen.

— Of course there is, old boy. *Eleven's* just a silly groanhuff name for it. Same goes for twoteen, of course. *Twelve*, indeed.

— Joey grumps. Fox strokes his moustache, glances over at the stray still standing awkwardly behind Flashjack. It's like he can somehow wink without actually winking.

— But…look! Twelve's what *everyone* calls it, says Joey.

— Why is it twenty-one and twenty-two then, says Fox, not twelveen and twelelve? It's senseless, Joey, dear chap, senseless.

They're nuts here. They're all nuts—scamps, scrags, scallywags, scofflaws, all of them. Even their names are nuts. Joey Picaroni, Foxtrot, Flashjack — they all have these crazy Scruffian nicknames. He looks at the scofflaw, Joey, lounging sideways on the armchair. *Kind of a cuntfucker at times,* Flashjack had warned as he held the board aside, beckoned him in through the window. *Then there's Earwigger and Squirlet, Tolliver and Firepot…*

He'd lost track as the scallywag punk nattered on, distracted by the Scruffian crib, and all the eyes turning on him. Fox's now.

— Found him at Titchycoo Park, Flashjack proudly announced.

—That's how it goes, see, Gobfabbler prattles. Scamps like Foxtrot, scrags like Puckerscruff, scallywags like Flashjack, then scofflaws like Joey Picaroni what's barely still kids at all. Whether you calls it eleven or oneteen, Foxy was Fixed at that age afore a scamp turns to scrag. Whereas you'd be a scrag, for sure.

He only half-listens to the crib's fabbler, lost in his study of Red Windbreaker. Who's a stray too, it seems, not Fixed yet either, not a Scruffian. A hand claps his shoulder — Flashjack, his finger grown back fully now.

— C'mon. I'll show you where you're kipping.

4.

So maybe the handjob was a mistake. It's not his fault. He didn't know Flashjack was taken, and he was sure the scallywag was flirting with him.

— And this is one of the scrags' group rooms. That mattress over there's free; brung it in for the other stray, but Pipsquirt and Guddler started bunking last night, so he got Pip's, so you get this one, unless you end up bunking with another scrag too, eh?

He'd winked, made a point of Pipsquirt and Guddler both being guys, of how loads of Scruffians were queer — no fucking haters here.

Totally flirting.

It's breakfast the next morning, Joey at the cooker—*Yeah, we're tapped into the mains gas; power, plumbing, you wouldn't believe the shit Fox can wangle; or maybe you would if you knew how old he is, if any of us did* — turning out paper plate after paper plate of greasy fry-up for Scruffians who just keep coming. It's chaos round the table, as many standing as sitting, but the murderous silence of the green-haired urchin who's apparently Flashjack's squeeze cuts through it all. Seems Flashjack didn't even *think* not to brag to Puckerscruff about his emptied balls.

As he slinks through to the living room with his paper plate and plastic cutlery, Gobfabbler falls in behind him, whispering that he shouldn't worry, it'll blow over.

— He ain't usually this prickly, Puckerscruff. Leastways, not in the unfriendly sense.

Puckerscruff's an urchin in more ways than one, inch-long spikes radiating from each wrist. He'd thought it was rock-kid chic till the scrag unlatched one leather wristband at the table, and he realised the spikes were poking through holes in this disguise, stabbing out of the flesh itself.

— Him and Flashjack just been lovebirds since Ripper Vickie's day.

Through mouthfuls of grub, Gobfabbler is explaining that the world's first serial killer was, in fact, none other than Queen Victoria Saxe-Coburg, Defender of the Faith, Empress of India, and Popess of the Holy Aryan Templars. He stabs the last bit of sausage on his own plate, wipes up the last streaks of ketchup, pops it in his mouth. Over on the sofa Red Windbreaker is blowing on a mug of coffee.

He wants to ask Red Windbreaker his name, but the Scruffian-to-be doesn't have one either. For now, they're both just *mate* or *oi, you!*

5.

Stories are important here. There's the fable of Orphan that Gob told him, a myth of the Stamp's origin so clearly cribbed from Orpheus he doesn't believe it for a second. Is he really supposed to imagine that the *groanhuffs* got their hero's name as a corruption of a word in a language that didn't even exist back then?

— Believe what yer want, said Gob.

Then there's the story to be told by him, the personal history he's to share, if he does decide to take the Stamp, like the one Red Windbreaker's telling now, quietly, to just a few.

—Don't go in there just yet, mate.

— Why not?

— Storystarting. Tother stray, like. He's taking the Stamp, so they's blethering his baggage off. Yer wanna take the Stamp clean, like, fresh start; figger yer backstory, take the Stamp, pick yer name, savvy?

— I…guess.

— He's from one of em foster thingies, like Doctor B's — pfft! Hark at me 'splaining. You prob'ly knows that modern stuff fine, eh?

— Yeah, fostercare, I…should we be listening?

— I ain't called Earwigger for nuffink, mate.

— But isn't it private?

— Ain't nuffink private among Scruffians, mate…'cept moments, like. Yer just don't interrupt.

— Oh…okay.

In the living room, seven of the Scruffians sit in a horseshoe, audience to Red Windbreaker, who talks quietly enough that, from the kitchen door, the other stray can't hear much of what he says, just the odd phrase breaking loose of his mumble, some wry quip snapped with a toss of hair.

No, he thinks, not a horseshoe. Crosslegged on the floor, they're all turned to the stray as kids before a teacher with a storybook, but Bananastasia's tight to one side, Foxtrot to the other, tight enough to pass the joint with a raise of hand. A circle.

—So you're taking the Stamp? You decided?

— Yeah. You?

— Dunno yet. Maybe. But…I think I fucked up. I don't think Puckerscruff likes me.

— Oh, that. Lulz, yeah. Flashjack's fleshjack…he's less Ragamuff at the mo', more Raga*miffed*, eh?

— Ha. But still…
— You could always say at least he *knows* you're a wanker.
— Very funny. Thanks.
— Or tell him Flashjack said they could use an extra hand round here. You just took it a bit too far…
— Hilarious. Did your mum and dad die of laughter, foster boy — shit. Sorry. *Fuck.* I didn't mean…. It's just fucking *habit*…
— …It's okay.

6.

It's two scofflaws who bring the Stamp in from some other crib, arriving with a whistle in the dead of night-from the alley outside, a *wheedloo-WHUT* that takes him a moment to place: *Scruffians STAMP*. Instantly, the crib's a flurry of excitement pulling him in its wake upstairs, to the entry window, where the visitors are clambering in. Rebelladonna Scrapegrace and Ravewaif Snarker by name, they ignore almost everyone but Foxtrot, with just an exchange of mumphing nods between them and Joey — scofflaw mating calls, whispers Gob-fabbler.

Ravewaif wears a bulky backpack. Rebelladonna is hellion, and wears that.

Her eyes are red, like a fucking Terminator, glowing under the hoody she pulls back now to shake out what look like dreadlocks — for all of a second before he sees them writhe. Harlequined black and pillar box red, the snakes slither loose, raising heads to scent the air with a flicker of tongue, a hiss. The dainty little bows of pink ribbon worn as chokers by some only make it more disturbing. The Stamp's courier has one mother of an escort.

— Take a picture, fucktard, she says as she walks past. Won't last as long as the memory though.

—What do you think? he says.
Red Windbreaker and himself, the two of them sit at the kitchen table while the living room is prepped for their Fixings. They look at each other over mugs of cocoa, nervous. They've both been hearing the stories since they got here — Scruffian disappearances, whole cribs emptied overnight, Earwigger and Joey muttering that it's like the old days. Foxtrot's laid it on the line for them, no illusions: it could be that the Institute's back. It isn't a safe life they're choosing, not by a long shot.

— What do *you* think? says Red Windbreaker.

How a Scruffian Gets Their Name

It's scary. With a Stamp to tweak, he could give himself fucking Wolverine blades, put his old man's tattooed knuckles to shame. But he's not sure he wants to be someone's monster; he just wants to be *someone*. He had his own storystarting the other day, and he got what Earwigger meant, that it was preparation to become yourself. So maybe this is that story. If there's some Big Bad freaking everyone out, maybe that's the fight to *make* him someone. But still…

Under the table, the other stray kicks at his foot.

— I'm up for it if you are.

7.

Last night they got wasted on ecstasy together—all of them, strictly speaking, Flashjack arriving home from the hunt triumphant with a fuckload of pills swiped from a dealer, dishing them out in a club kid's communion, dancing from scallywag to scrag, popping pills into open mouths, a mother bird with a flock of scamps around him for his chicks, until, yeah, the whole crib was royally fucked, but with the two strays necking pills at the same rate as Scruffians ever springing back to Fixed sobriety, in the end, well, it seemed just the two of them really, together.

Everything was hilarious. Everything was love. He remembers explaining how Joey was totally just on the lookout for everyone, like always suspicious of everything because he wouldn't let anything hurt his crib-mates. He remembers babbling how amazing it was, how *epic* it was, that Flashjack and Puckerscruff had been together forever. He loved that he'd found this community, that the two of them had found it, at the same time just about. They were like cadets together; and when the other stray said *space cadets*, he'd laughed and said, see, he was the joker with a quip for everything.

The Velvet Underground were playing on the stereo, and they'd danced to "Foggy Notion" and kept dancing to "Temptation Inside Your Heart," prodding each other's chest at the refrain, lip-synching lyrics in each other's face, collapsing exhausted afterward, to lie with their backs against the sofa's base, arms round each other's shoulders, and make out through "One of These Days" and "Andy's Chest," only to break suddenly at "I'm Sticking With You" — *I fucking love this song!* — which was so true, so perfect, that as far as he was concerned, as of this moment, it was their song now.

They'd both felt like shit from the comedown this morning, and he'd had that weird thing of knowing that he'd talked so much shit last night, knowing that the loved-up mutual adoration was as much chemicals as chemistry, the two of them still strangers to each other really, but still being…over this threshold. It wasn't just because they'd fooled around – that was just getting off – but their barriers dropped by the drugs, they'd woke naked with each other in a deeper way, and both of them strays who didn't know their own name let alone the other's.

8.

—Eeny, meeny, miny, moe. Catch a nipper by the toe. If he squeals let him go. Eeny, meeny, miny, moe. You are not…

– Maximulligan Mitchskip? says Flashjack.

– Yeah, real original, snarks Joey. We had a *mulligan* already, bright spark, from Hopper.

– Yeah, but a whole *minute* ago, says Bananastasia.

– *We had a mulligan already,* mocks Puckerscruff. Moany Prickaroni.

Still, the fresh-Fixed Scruffian weighs the name. He could be a Max or a Mitch for short, or even a Skip. But the full Maximulligan feels a little…grandiose.

– It ain't even like he's Irish, says Joey.

– Tasty as stew though.

Quip stands in the doorway to the kitchen, leaning on the frame, hands shoved in the pockets of his red windbreaker, a twinkle in his eye and a crink of smile, same look he had when he went in to take the Stamp: *Should've kept an E for this, got Fixed fucking flying, eh?* Same look he had when he came back out, black weavework of soul on his chest: *See that bit there? Yeah, the little spirally bit. That's where I was thinking of last night.*

A wink then and a wink now, from Quippersnap Rannigant, prince of pwnage.

He came out of it himself feeling the same but different. Like the story-starting or last night's drug communion, it's as if all the parts of himself he's kept locked inside forever have been brought out into the open, all armour stripped. So what he is…is just there now, in this Stamp he can study in the bathroom mirror. Only it's just a base for who he's to be.

Maybe he'd pick a real hero's name, he'd thought, something cunning, quick, a name to be worn in a grand adventure, fighting the Big Bad, whatever the fuck it was.

—Eeny, meeny, miny, moe. Catch a nipper by the toe. If he squeals let him go. Eeny, meeny, miny, moe. You are —
— Slickspit Hamshankery, Quip cuts in.

There's a sudden silence at the breach of Teh Roolz, eyes turning to Foxtrot, who apes outrage with hands on hips, a waggle of moustache — bad form, old boy, bad form — then loses it, corpsing — *Slickspit Hamshankery!* — then they all corpse, even Joey, even Puckerscruff who declares his sneaky-handed squeeze-filching nemesis *banged to rights, banged to bleeding rights*, but most of all the fresh-Fixed Scruffian himself.

Most of all Slickspit.

The Behold of the Eye

The Imagos of Their Appetence

—The Behold of the Eye, Flashjack's laternal grandsister (adopted), Pebbleskip had told him, is where the humans store the *imagos of their appetence* — which is to say, all the things they prize most highly, having had their breath taken away by the glimmering glamour of it. Like a particular painting or sculpture, a treasure chest of gold and jewels, or a briefcase full of thousand-whatever notes, or the dream house seen in a magazine, a stunning vista seen on their travels, even other humans. Whatever catches their eye, you see, she'd said, is caught *by* the eye, stored there in the Behold, all of it building up over a person's lifetime to their own private hoard of wonders. The humans say that beauty is in the eye of the beholder, you know, but as usual they've got it arse-about; what they should be saying is something else entirely.

— Beauty is in the Behold of the Eye, Pebbleskip had said. So that's where most of us faeries live these days.

Flashjack had hauled himself up beside her on the rim of the wine-glass he was skinnydipping in, shaken Rioja off his wings, and looked around at the crystal forest of the table-top he'd, just a few short hours ago, been born above in a moment of sheer whimsy, plinking into existence at the *clink* of a flippant toast to find himself a-flutter in a wild world of molten multicolour — mandalas wheeling on the walls and ceiling, edges of every straight line in the room streaming like snakes. He'd skittered between trailers of wildly gesticulating hands, gyred on updrafts of laughter, danced in flames of lighters held up to joints, and landed on the nose of a snow-leopard that was lounging in the shadows of a corner of vision. He'd found it a comfy place to watch one of the guests perform an amazing card trick with a Jack of Hearts, so he'd still been hunkered there, gawping like a loon at the whirl of the party, and making little flames shoot out of his fingertips (because he could), when Pebbleskip came fluttering down to dance in the air in front of him.

— Nice to get out once in a while, eh? she'd said. Hi, I'm Pebbleskip.

— I'm…Flashjack, he'd decided. What's *in a while*? Is it like *upon a time*? And out of what?

Her face had scrunched, her head tilted in curiosity.

— *Ah,* she'd said. You must be new.

Since then she'd been explaining.

The funscape had settled into solidity now, with the drunken, stoned and tripping human revellers all departed into the dawn, the host in her bed dead to the world, but through a blue sky window to the morning, sunlight slanted in to sparkle on the trees of wine-glasses and towers of tumblers all across the broad plateau of the breakfast bar. It painted the whole room with a warm clarity which Flashjack, being newborn, found easily as exciting as the acid-shimmered kaleidoscope of his birth. The mountains and cliffs of leather armchairs and sofa, bookcases and shelves, fireplace, fridge and counter were all very grand; the empty bottles had such a lush green glow to them inside; the beer-cans with the cigarette-butts were seductively spooky spaces, hollow and echoing; even the ashtrays piled high with roaches had a heady scent. As Pebbleskip had been explaining, Flashjack had been exploring. Now he dangled his legs over the edge of the wine-glass alongside her, surveying his domain.

— You mean they'd keep all this in their Behold? he said. Forever?

— Nah, probably not, said Pebbleskip. Mostly they'd think this place was a mess. The rugs are nice, and it's kind of cosy, but they'd have to be a quirky bugger to Beholden this as is. No, if this place was in the Behold it'd probably be a bit more…Ikea.

Flashjack nodded solemnly, not knowing what *Ikea* meant but assuming it meant something along the lines of *goldenish*; the sunlight, its brilliant source and bold effect, had rather captured his imagination.

—You'll see what I mean when you find your Beholder, said Pebbleskip, which you'll want to be doing toot sweet. I'd take you home with me, see, but two of us in the same Behold? Just wouldn't work, ends up in all sorts of squabbles over interior design; and the human, well, one faery in the Behold of the Eye, that just gives them a little twinkle of imagination, but more than one and it's like a bloody fireworks display. They get all unstable and *artistic*, blinded by the glamour of *everything*, real or imagined, concrete or abstract. They get confused between beauty and truth and meaning, you see, start thinking every butterfly-brained idea must be true; before you know it they've gone schizo on you and you're in a three-way firefight with all the angels and the demons, them and their bloody *ideologies*.

Pebbleskip sounded rather bitter. Best not to ask, thought Flashjack.

— I'm not saying it can't work sometimes, she said, but a lot of humans can't handle one faery in their Behold, never mind two. Mind you, if you find one that's got the scope…well, it can be a grand thing…for all the arguments about where to put the Grand Canyon.

She looked kind of sad at this, Flashjack thought.

— Anyway, I'm off. My Beholder's too fucked from the comedown just now to know I'm gone, but she'll miss me if I'm not there when she wakes up.

And with that Pebbleskip whirled in the air, and swooped to slip under the door, Flashjack darting after her, crying, *Wait!* as she zipped across the hallway and into the bedroom. He poked his head round the door to find her standing on the host of the party's closed eyelid.

— How do I find my Beholder? he said.

— Use your imagination, she said.

— But how will I know if it's the right human?

— They'll know you when they see you, she said.

And disappeared.

The Azure Sky and the Golden Sun

Using his imagination, because he wasn't terribly practised at it and couldn't think what else to do, simply took Flashjack back to his birthplace in the kitchen/living-room, where he sat down dejectedly with his back to the trunk of a bonsai tree on top of the fridge, gazing out of the window at the azure sky and the golden sun rising in it, at the backyard of grass and bushes and walled-in dustbins, the blocks of sandstone tenement ahead and to the left, all with their own windows facing out on the same backyard, some windows lit, some dark, but each with different curtains or blinds, flowerpots on a ledge here or there, and the odd occupant now and then visible at a window, making coffee, washing dishes, pottering, scratching, yawning. Using his imagination then, because he was a fast learner, had Flashjack quickly off his arse, his face pressed through the glass, realising the true potential of his situation.

There were a lot more rooms in this world than he'd previously considered.

Slipping through the window with a pop, he spiralled up into the air to find yet more tenements beyond the rooftops, roads and streets of them, high-rise tower-blocks in the distance, a park off to his right, a ridiculously grand edifice to the west which, a passing sparrow explained, was the university building, in the mock-Gothic style, and not nearly as aesthetically pleasing as the Alexander "Greek" Thomson church across the road from it. He snagged the sparrow's tail, clambered up onto its back, and let it carry him swooping and circling over the "West End" of the "city" (which was, he learned, called Glasgow), nodding as it sang the praises of its favourite Neoclassical architecture. The sparrow had a bit of a one-track mind though, and Flashjack wasn't getting much of an overall sense of the Big Picture, so with a *thank you, but I must be going* he somersaulted off the bird to land on a chimney, considered his options for a second then, rising on the hummingbird blur of his own wings, he hovered, picked a random direction, and set off at his highest speed.

An hour later he was back where he'd started, sitting on the chimney pot, prattling excitedly to a seagull about how cool the Blackpool Tower is.

—Ye want to be seeing the *Eiffel* Tower, mate, said the seagull. Now that's much more impressive.

— Which way is that?

Having been instructed in all manner of astral, magnetic, geographical and meteorological mechanisms for navigation, in a level of detail that raised suspicions in Flashjack that all birds were rather obsessively attached to their own pet subject and lacking in the social skills to know when to *shut the fuck up about it*, he set out once again, returning a few hours later with a very high opinion of Europe and all its splendours — including, yes, the Eiffel Tower.

— Better than Blackpool by a long shot, eh? said the seagull.

— What's Blackpool? said Flashjack.

It was at that point that Flashjack, after a certain amount of interrogation and explanation from the seagull, who had met a few faeries in his day, came to understand that it would be a good idea to find a human to get Beholden by ASAP.

— See, they do the remembering that yer not very good at yerself, said the seagull. Memory of a gnat, you faeries. If I'd known ye weren't Beholden yet, I wouldn't have sent ye off. Christ knows, yer lucky ye made it back.

— How so?

— Yer a creature of pure whimsy, mate. What d'ye think happens if there's no one keeping ye in mind? Ye'll forget yerself, and then where'll ye be? Nowhere, mate. Nothing. A scrap of cloud blown away in the wind.

Flashjack looked up at the azure sky and the golden sun, which he'd only just noticed (again) were really rather enchanting. He really didn't want to lose them so soon after discovering them, to have them slip away out of his own memory as something else took their place, or to have *himself* slip away from *them*, fading in a reverie to a self as pale as those sensations were rich.

— Go find yer Beholder, mate, said the seagull. Yer already getting melancholic, and that's the first sign of losing it.

Flashjack was about to ask how, when his now rather more active imagination suggested a possible plan; to get Beholden obviously he'd have to attract someone's attention, catch their eye so as to be caught by it. Being a faery, he reasoned, that shouldn't actually be too difficult. Over in the park, he'd noticed in passing, a whole grass slope of people were lazing in the afternoon sun, drinking wine, playing guitars or just lying on their backs, clearly the sort of wastrels who'd appreciate a bit of a show. So with a salute to the seagull, Flashjack was off like a bullet, over one roof, then another, a gate, a bridge, a duck pond, and then he was directly above the slope of sun-worshippers, where he stopped dead, whirling, hovering, spinning in the air, reflecting sunlight from his whole body which he'd mirrored to enhance the effect, so that any who looked at him and had the eyes to see might imagine he was some ball of mercury or magic floating in the sky above them. Or possibly a UFO.

He wasn't sure who he expected to Behold him, but he did have a quiet hope that they'd be someone of relish and experience, the Behold of their Eye full to bursting with the things they'd seen and been struck by. In fact, it was Tobias Raymond Hunter, aged nine months, currently being wheeled by his mother and escorted by his toddling older brother, who looked up from his pram with blurry, barely-focused vision and saw the shiny ball in the sky.

A Rather Strange Kind of Room

There was a *pop*, and Flashjack found himself in what he considered a rather strange kind of room. The Behold seemed to be the inside of a sphere, its wall and ceiling a single quilted curve of pink padding, which Flashjack, being a fiery type of faery, born of drink, drugs and debauchery, was not entirely sure he liked. Added to this, it was velvety-silky-smooth and warm as skin to the touch; in combination with the pink, it was like being in a room made of flesh, which Flashjack, frankly, found either a little creepy or a little kinky. He wasn't sure which, and he had no specific aversion to kinky as such, but the whole feel of the place...he just wasn't sure it was really him. Still, the three most striking features of the Behold very much *were*: above his head wheeled coloured forms, simple geometric shapes in basic shades, but radiant in hue, positively glowing; beneath his feet, layer upon layer of snow-white quilts, baby-blue blankets and golden furs formed a floor of luxuriously cosy bedding wide enough to fit a dozen of him; and in front of him was a great circular window, outside of which the sky was bluer than the bright triangle circling overhead, the sun more golden than the fur between his toes.

What with the breast/womb vibe, the primary-coloured mobile and the oh-so-cosy bedding, it didn't take Flashjack too long to figure out where he was. It wasn't quite what he had been hoping for, he had to admit, but there was a certain encompassing comfort to the place. He flopped backwards onto the bed, wondering just how far down into the cosiness he could burrow before hitting the bottom of the Behold. As an idle experiment, just out of curiosity, he imagined the mobile overhead changing direction, spinning widdershins instead of clockwise. It did.

— Okay, he said. I think this'll do nicely.

—No, no, no, said Flashjack, this just won't do.

It wasn't the sand or the water that was the problem per se so much as the fact that they were in entirely the wrong place. It was all very well for Tobias Raymond Hunter to love his sand-pit and his paddling pool, and for the bed to have changed shape to accommodate these wondrous objects in the Behold of his Eye, but the boy clearly had no sense of scale; they took up half the bloody room. And to have them both, well, *embedded* in the bed, that was just silly. At the moment the bed was cut into a thin hourglass by the sand-pit and the paddling pool; add to that the fact that more and more of the remaining space was being eaten up by Lego bricks, lettered blocks and other such toys, and Flashjack was now left with only the thin sliver between sand-pit and paddling pool to sleep on. He wasn't a big fan, he'd discovered, of waking up spitting sand or sneezing water because he'd rolled over in his sleep and been dumped in the drink or the dunes. No, it just wouldn't do.

He sat on top of a lettered block and studied the situation for a while, then set his imagination to work on it. When he was finished, the paddling pool covered the whole area of the floor that had once been bed. Within that though, the sand-pit was now a decent-sized island with the bright blue plastic edge of it holding back the water. In the centre of the island, the Lego bricks and lettered blocks were now a stilted platform, with blankets, quilts and furs forming his bed atop it, and a jetty reaching out over the sand and water, all the way to his great window out into the world.

— That's a damn sight better, said Flashjack.

—Da' si' be'r, said Tobias Raymond Hunter, giggling as Flashjack performed his *Dance of the Killer Butterfly* for the tenth time that day. He never tired of it, it seemed to Flashjack, but then neither did Flashjack, as long as the audience was appreciative. As Tobias Raymond Hunter patted the palms of his hands together in an approximation of a hand-clap, Flashjack gave an elegant bow with a flourish of hand, and started it all over again.

— Da' si' be'r! Da' si' be'r! Da' si' be'r! said Tobias Raymond Hunter.

His father, entirely unaware of Flashjack's presence and convinced that his son was referring in the infantile imperative to his own (*Da*) singing (*si*) of what was apparently Toby's favourite song, "Teddy Bears' Picnic" (*be'r*) was meanwhile launching into his own repeat performance with somewhat less enthusiasm. As much as he was growing to hate the song, he did put his heart into it, even using Toby's own teddy bear, Fuzzy, as a prop in the show, though Toby, for all his enthusiasm, seemed to pay little attention to it until halfway through the third chorus (Flashjack, by this time, having finished his eighteenth performance (his *Dance of the Killer Butterfly* being quite short) and decided to call it a day), whereupon the previously ignored Fuzzy became an item of some interest.

In the Behold of the Eye, Flashjack was guddling goldfish in the paddling pool when Fuzzy came dancing out of the forest of sunflowers that now obscured most of the pink fleshy walls.

The bear was one thing, but this was getting ridiculous. Flashjack knew what was to blame; it was that bloody bedtime story that Toby was obsessed with. Oh, it might seem all very innocent to his parents but, like Toby's brother, Josh, who he shared his bedroom with and who groaned loudly each time the rhyme began — *that's for babies!* — Flashjack was getting deeply tired of it. No one had ever told him (as far as he remembered) that the Behold of the Eye might turn into a bloody menagerie of fantastic animals, flions soaring through the air on their great eagle wings, manes billowing as they roared, little woolly meep getting underfoot everywhere you go, rhigers charging out of the trees at you when you least expect it, giraphelant stampedes…and the rabbull was the last straw. *The rabbull is quite funny, half bull and half bunny, with horns and big ears that go flop.* Funny. Right. *Because when it sees red, it'll lower its head, and go boingedy-boingedy-BOP!* Well, Flashjack had had quite enough bopping, thank you very much, and did not consider the rabbull funny in the slightest.

— We're going to have to do something about this, Fuzzy, he said, standing on the jetty looking back at his Lego-brick tropical jungle-hut, and rubbing the twin pricks on his arse-cheeks where he'd been bopped from behind. They're bloody overrunning us, he said.

— Fuzzy, said Fuzzy, whose vocabulary wasn't up to much.

Flashjack turned to look out the window of Toby's eye, at the azure sky and the golden sun, which were particularly new to him today. He wished he could get out there, get away from the zoo of the Behold even just for a few hours, but Toby, it seemed, was not as…open as he once was. Last time Flashjack had decided to pop through the window he'd found himself nursing a bopped nose. That's another problem with being a creature of pure whimsy, you see; when your Beholder grasps the difference between real and imaginary, as they're bound to do sooner or later, they decide that a faery must be one or the other, mostly the other. Flashjack gazed at the blue and gold.

— See that? he said. That's what we need. Room.

Not just *a* room, he thought. But *room*. *Space.* He looked down at the water below, sparkling with the blue of the sky even though the ceiling above, which it should have been reflecting, was pink, and he wondered if…with just a little tweak…if he could draw that blue sky out of it…it shouldn't be that hard for a faery…

And the Behold of the Eye was, after all, a rather strange kind of room.

In the Land of His Stories

Flashjack leapt down from the giraphelant's back and flicked his flionskin cloak back over one shoulder as he strode across the savannah to the cliff, then, dipping so his feathered headdress wouldn't catch on the lintel, entered the darkness of Fuzzy's cave.

— I've had an idea, mate, he said cheerily. I've had an *inspiration.*

— Fuzzy, said Fuzzy pathetically.

If Flashjack had thought about it he would have regretted his words; The poor bear had been getting tattier and glummer ever since his own *inspiration* had been lost (or so Toby's parents claimed; Flashjack suspected foul play on the part of Josh, sibling rivalry and such), and Toby's infantile attention slowly turned to other objects of desire. So *inspiration* was rather a button-pusher of a word for Fuzzy, who was fading week by week and now convinced that the process of being forgotten would eventually end with him disappearing entirely. If Flashjack had thought about it he might have tactfully rephrased his boast. Flashjack, however, partly because he was a faery and dismissed such fatalism with a faery's disregard for logic, and partly because he was a faery and had little sense of the impact of his words on others, simply breezed into the cave and hunkered down before his old friend, a glinting grin on his face.

— Fuzzy, me boy, he said, if you want to call me a genius right now, feel free to go ahead and do so, or if you want to wait until you hear my Plan, then that's just as good. Either way, I cross my heart and hope to die, stick a needle in my eye, but fuck me if I haven't found a solution to your problem.

— Fuzzy, said Fuzzy.

— Why, thank you, said Flashjack. Okay, come with me.

It had been a while since Fuzzy had visited the island, so when the good ship *Jolly Roger* docked at the new jetty and the monkey crew leapt off to moor her soundly, despite the three-day voyage, the general glumness of the bear, and the actual purpose of the visit, Flashjack blithely forgot the fact that they were actually there to *do something* in his keenness to show just how much improvement had been made. The old jetty now had a troll under it, the island now had its own lake — *with an island on it, with a castle, and a beanstalk going up to the clouds, and there's a castle there with a giant in it and everything!*

— Fuzzy, said Fuzzy impatiently.

— Okay, okay, said Flashjack and took him in to his stilted jungle-hut (which was now all but covered in vines, barely recognisable as Lego-bricks and lettered blocks), shifted the bicycle with stabilisers (which Toby's brother, Josh, refused to let him ride), sat him down on the pouffe (which Toby had seen at an aunt-and-uncle's house and thought a strange and wondrous thing, this chair with no back), took a seat on the ottoman himself (which Toby's parents had in their bedroom and which, being half backless-chair and half treasure chest, was even more wondrous than the pouffe), and began to explain his Plan.

Toby, Flashjack had realised, had become utterly enchanted with the fairy stories once read to him at bedtime, now devoured over and over again by Toby himself. He'd come to desire adventure, to yearn for it, such that the Behold

The Behold of the Eye

of the Eye was blossoming with new wonders every day. He wanted a dream-world to escape to, the place that Puss-in-Boots and Jack-the-Giant-Killer and the Three Billy Goats Gruff lived. These were the imagos of his appetence, so here they were in the Behold of the Eye. But something was missing in the land of his stories.

— He wants a Monster, said Flashjack. I've looked out of the window as he checks under the bed, looks in the closet, or opens his eyes in the dead of night and sees scary shapes in the patterns in the curtains. It frightens him, of course, so he can't admit he wants a Monster, but it thrills him too. You can't have a land of adventure without the giants and trolls and the Big Bad Wolf, but the ones he's Beholden, well, they're straight out of the cartoons. I just *know* he wants something more.

— Fuzzy?

— Well that's where you come in.

The sky overhead darkened with nightfall, the sun descending from the wheeling mobile of moon and stars and planets to sink below the horizon and let the shadows escape from beneath the canopy of trees and slink up and around them, shrouding the island till only the flickering glow of the great pyre of a night-light on the beach was left to light Flashjack and Fuzzy as they stood down by the water's edge.

Flashjack reached up into the darkness, up into the sky, and plucked a sliver of moonlight, kneaded it and rolled it out like Plasticene, then blew on it — *puff!* — to make it hard as bone. He did it again, and again, kept doing so until there was a pile of moon-bones there before him. He grabbed the silver of the surf and made a pair of scissors to cut Fuzzy open, then one by one he put the moon-bones in their place. Then he caught a corner of the night between thumb and forefingers and peeled away a layer of it which he snipped into shape and started sewing onto Fuzzy with a pine-needle and vine-thread, a second skin of darkness to go with his skeleton of moon-bones.

Flashjack was very proud when he sat back and looked at the Monster he had created.

A Perfectly Ordinary Kouros

The books arrived slowly at first. For a long time it was jungles with pygmies and dinosaurs, deserts with camels and wild stallions, forests with wolves, mountains with dragons, oceans with sea serpents. There was one burst of appetence where Flashjack woke up one day to find the blue-sky ceiling of the Behold just gone, inflated out to infinity, the planets and stars of the mobile suddenly multiplied and expanded, scattered out into the deep as whole new worlds of adventure, and spaceships travelling between them, waging inter-galactic battles that ended with stars exploding. He would fly off to explore them and get drawn into epic conflicts which always seemed to have Fuzzy behind them, or Darkshadow as he now preferred to be called (which Flashjack thought was a bit pretentious). He would find magical weapons, swords of light, helmets of invisibility, rayguns, jet-packs, some of the snazziest uniforms a faery could dream of, and with Good on his side he'd defeat Fuzzy and send him back to the darkness whence he came. After a while he began to find himself waking up already elsewhere and elsewhen, a life written around him, as an orphan generally, brought up in oblivion (but secretly a prince). This was a lot of fun, and for a long time Flashjack simply revelled in the fertility of his Beholder's appetence, the sheer range of his imagos. For a long time, whenever he woke up in his own bed he would leap out of it and run down the jetty to look out the window in the hope of catching a glimpse of whatever book Toby was reading now, some clue to his next grand adventure. For a long time it was simply the contents of the books that were Beholden by the boy. Then, slowly at first, the books themselves began to arrive.

It's a very nice bookcase, Flashjack thought to himself, but why a boy of his age should be Beholdening bookcases is frankly beyond me. I mean, a chair can be a throne, a table can hold a banquet, a wardrobe can be a doorway to another world, but a bookcase? A bookcase is a bookcase is a bookcase. It's not exactly bloody awe-inspiring.

He paced a short way down the jetty towards the island, then wheeled and paced back, stood with his hands on hips staring at the thing. It wasn't ugly with its dark polished wood, clean-lined and solid. It was even functional, he had to admit, because he could replicate a whole bundle of the buggers from this one, and he could really use something to store the mounds of books — leather-bound tomes, hardbacks with bright yellow dust-covers, cheap paperbacks with yellowed pages and gaudy covers — that were piling up everywhere these days, appearing in his bed, on the beach, in rooms in the castles, clearings in the forests, caves in the mountains; he'd found a whole planet of books on his last interstellar jaunt. But *functional* was not an aesthetic criterion that Flashjack, as a faery, had terribly high on his list of priorities; it was well below *shiny* and nowhere near *weird*.

It was, in his considered opinion, actually rather dull.

— It's safe, said a voice behind him.

The Behold of the Eye

Flashjack turned, but no one was there.

The statues began to appear not long after the Voice Incident. There had been statues appearing for years, of course, along with the busts and reliefs, even a whole colossus at one point — Toby had clearly gone through a romance with all things archaic as a side-effect of his absorption in the adventures of ancient myth — but where before the statues had just seemed another facet of the cultural background, set-dressing for the battles with minotaurs, chimaera, hydra and what-not, these were different. Flashjack didn't notice it with the first one; it seemed a perfectly ordinary *kouros* of the late Classical tradition, in the mode of Lysippos. He didn't notice it with the second one, which looked fairly similar but carried a certain resemblance in the facial features to statues of Antinous commissioned by the Emperor Hadrian, though he'd clearly been rendered here as he would have looked in his early adolescence. He didn't even notice it with the third one, which was quite clearly a young Alexander the Great. It was only with the fourth, the fifth, the sixth and the seventh that Flashjack, starting to wonder at Toby's...consistency of subject matter, took a quick flight out to his galleon built of bookcases, went down into the captain's quarters and, after a few hours cross-referencing the Beholden statues with the images in the books (from which, of course, in a previous period of idle perusal he had learned everything he knew about Lysippos, Antinous and Alexander (and if you're wondering how he managed to remember such things when he couldn't even remember the sun in the sky, well, Flashjack was by now a faery on the verge of maturity, beginning to reach a whole new level of inconsistency)) and realised the discrepancies.

On a factual level, he could find no traces of such statues actually existing out in the world. On a stylistic level, there were a number of deviations from the classic S-shape of the contrapposto pose, hips cocked one way, shoulders tilted the other. And on a blindingly obvious level, which had not occurred to Flashjack simply because he was a faery and had little concept of decorum, never mind prurience, the sculptors of the Classical period did not, on the whole, tend to give their statues erections.

— Our little boy is becoming a man, said Flashjack to himself, smiling because, as a faery, he also had little concept of heteronormativity.

—My power grows every day, old friend, said Fuzzy.

— Now's not the time for the Evil Villain routine, said Flashjack. I'm worried about Toby. Books and statues, statues and books. And now this.

They walked through the library that had appeared over the last few weeks, coalescing gradually, as shelves appeared, thin slivers in the air at first, then slowly thickening, spreading, joining, walls doing the same, until the whole place had just...crystallised around Flashjack's island home, sort of fusing with the structure that was already there, almost matching it, but...not quite. Flashjack's bed was on a mezzanine floor now (with the Children's and YA Section) which hadn't even existed before. Downstairs from this, in the centre of the structure and facing the entrance (flanked by twin flions), where his bed *should* have been, was a counter-cum-desk thing that ran in a square, four Flashjacks by four Flashjacks or so; with the computer and the card files and the date-stamp and the oven and the dishwasher and so on, clearly it was meant to fuse the functions of librarian's desk and kitchen area. Beyond this was the main library-cum-living-room (which mostly consisted of the SF/Fantasy Section). There were even male and female bathrooms, which Flashjack avoided; he quite enjoyed pissing where there was snow to piss in, but he'd tried the whole dump thing once and just wasn't impressed with the experience. And everywhere there were the bookshelves, everywhere except the Romance section, which was like a museum with all its statuary.

All in, the place wasn't much bigger than Flashjack's hut, so it wasn't a grand library; in fact, it reminded Flashjack quite strongly of the public library he often saw out of Toby's eye, the boy spending so much time there these days; it seemed that he had come to adore his literary sanctuary so much that it had become his dream home, usurping the more Romantic jungle-hut of Flashjack's preference. Now Flashjack was quite okay with his *own* reimaginings of Toby's imagos, but now that the tables were turned he was feeling rather put out. It just wasn't healthy, a teenage boy Beholdening a dream home full of books. And a haunted one at that.

— You don't get it, said Fuzzy. My power grows every day, old friend.

— Look, I'm just not in the mood to play Good versus Evil today, Fuzzy. I heard the Voice again this morning, over in the Romance section. *It's safe. It's safe.* That's all it keeps saying. There's something wrong with our Beholder.

— You don't understand, said Fuzzy. That's what I'm worried about. Whatever's happening to him is making me stronger, more vital. More intense. I'm his monster. And I feel like a fucking god some days.

Flashjack turned to look at Fuzzy, who had stopped asking to be called Darkshadow a while back, and would now simply laugh bitterly and say: *I have no name, Flashjack.* His skin made out of the night itself, he seemed a black hole of a being, an absence as much as a presence.

— And I have...urges, said Fuzzy. I want to burn this place to the ground, I want to smash those statues to dust, and I want to feast on that Voice, make it scream itself out of existence and into silence.

Fuzzy was getting rather over-dramatic lately, thought Flashjack.

The Ghost of an Imago

Most weekdays it rained corpses, faceless, gurgling blood from slit throats. Flashjack would sit in the library, listening to the pounding on the roof, or stand to look out the floor-length windows and watch the bodies battering the jetty, falling out of the sky like rag dolls of flesh, slamming the wood and bouncing, slumping, rolling. He'd watch them splash into the water, sink and bob back up to float there, face-down, blood spreading out like dark ink until the sea itself was red. The troll under the jetty, who never showed himself these days, would be a dark shape in the water after the showers of death, grabbing the bodies and dragging them down into the depths; Flashjack had no idea what he was doing with them, wasn't sure he wanted to know.

The lake on the island was on fire. The island on the lake was choked with poisonous thorns. The castle on the island was in ruins. At the top of the beanstalk which was now a tower of jagged deadwood, bleached to the colour of bone, the giant sat in his castle, eyes and lips sewn shut, and bound into his throne by chicken-wire and fish-hooks that cut and pierced his flesh. Flashjack had tried to free him, but every time he tried the wire grew back as fast as he could cut it. Flashjack wept at the giant's moans, which he knew, even though they were wordless, were begging Flashjack to kill him; he just couldn't do it.

The worst were those that Flashjack *could* kill, the torture victims who were crucified, nailed to stripped and splintered branches, bodies dangling in the air, all the way up and down the thorny tower of the dead beanstalk. He recognised the faces he had seen through the window of Toby's eye, laughing in crowds, he knew that these were imagos of tormentors tormented, imagos of vengeance, and when he'd tried cutting them down they simply grabbed for him with madness and murder in their eyes; but he couldn't suffer their suffering, not in the Behold of the Eye, which was meant to be a place of beauty, and so he put them out of their misery with his knife as they appeared, most weekdays, one or two of them at a time, just after the rain of corpses.

When the body of the Voice manifested, it was that of Toby himself, or of a not-quite-Toby. Where Toby was dark-haired, not-quite-Toby was fair. Where Toby was pale, not-quite-Toby was tanned. Where Toby was slight, not-quite-

Toby was slim. Where Toby wore jeans and a tee-shirt, trainers and a baseball jacket that just didn't look right on him, not-quite-Toby wore exactly the same clothes except that on him they looked totally right. Where Toby moved with the gangling awkwardness of a growth-spurted adolescent not yet in full control of all his limbs, not-quite-Toby rose from the chair in the library's living-room with the limber grace of an athlete, an animal. He strolled up to Flashjack, where he stood at the entrance, one hand reaching out to lay the book he had been reading down on the countertop of the librarian's desk, the other reaching out to stroke the purring gryphon guard at Flashjack's side, in a fluid move that ended with an offered handshake.

— It's safe, he said.

— Why is it safe? asked Flashjack, shaking his hand.

The ghost of an imago, the imago of a ghost of Toby looked up at him with a wry smile, a raised eyebrow. Something about the causal self-confidence was familiar to Flashjack — a hint of Toby's brother, Josh, maybe, or someone else he couldn't quite place.

— I'm not gay, said not-quite-Toby.

He laughed, patted Flashjack on the shoulder and turning, plucking his book back off the countertop, sauntered back to his chair, plumped down on it and put his feet up on the coffee-table.

— Hang on, said Flashjack, whose curiosity about the word Toby so furiously scrubbed from his school-bag had led him to some startling realisations. I mean, I've seen what Toby looks at when he's wanking, mate. You've only got to look at his —

It was then, as his hand raised to point and his head turned to look, that Flashjack noticed the statues in the Romance Section were all now draped in white sheets, and not-quite-Toby's smile was that of Josh when he'd bested his little brother easily in a sibling spat, of the tormentors after Flashjack had put his knife into their hearts, or of Toby, some days, when he just stood looking in the mirror for minutes at a time while corpses rained in the Behold of his Eye.

Fuzzy was smashing the statues with a crowbar that had been matted with blood and hair when it appeared in the Behold. With every statue that was smashed, the ghost of an imago, the imago of a ghost of Toby gave out a scream of blue murder and tried to curl himself into a tighter ball. With every statue that was smashed not-quite-Toby was less and less the easy, graceful, carefree straight boy that Toby wanted to be, more and more another version of the lad, another not-quite-Toby: one that was not just dark-haired but dark of eye and fingernail and tooth; one that was not just pale but corpse-white; one that was not just slight but skeletal; one that tore at his jeans and tee-shirt till they hung as rags; one that moved in twisted, warped, insectile articulations.

With every statue that was smashed, Flashjack just whispered, no.

— He's killing us, Fuzzy had snarled. He's killing *himself*. *They're* killing him. *He's* killing *them*. Don't you get it, Flashjack? Don't you fucking get it? Can't you see what's being Beholden here every fucking day?

He'd fought his way through a five-day hail of corpses that sank his ship, hauled himself up onto the jetty with the troll's broken, bone-armoured body slung over his shoulders, hurled it through the doors of the library and stormed in, caught the defending gryphons by the throat, one in each hand, snapped their necks. Flashjack had roared to the attack, swashbuckling and heroic, a sword of fire whirling over his head, and been batted out of the air with a backhand slap.

Fuzzy had grabbed the crowbar from the coffee table, where Flashjack had been studying it, worried, and strode into the Romance Section, ripped the sheet off the first statue. Not-quite-Toby had run at him in a frenzy of rage, horror, fear, despair, but he'd not reached Fuzzy before the crowbar swung, connected with the white marble and shattered it utterly.

Now Fuzzy swung the crowbar for the last time, shattered the last marble statue and, as the thin shards of stone flew in every direction, the last beautiful corpse of Toby's stone-bound desire slumped to the library floor amid the dust of its thin shell. Fuzzy grabbed the stillborn imago by the hair and hauled it up so Flashjack could see and recognise the face, one of Toby's tormentors but, oh, such a good-looking one. Fuzzy turned on the wretch of a not-quite-Toby, pointing the crowbar at this thing now cowered in a corner, hissing, spitting madness at the revelation of its untruth.

— This is what Toby wants to be, he snarled. Aren't you?

— Fuck you, fuck you, fuck you, fuck you!

— You're the imago made of his self-pity and self-loathing.

— Fuck you!

— And just what is it that you are? Inside, beneath the lie? What do you really want to be? Tell him! Say it!

The creature lunged, tears streaming down its face, clawed fingers out.

— I want to be *dead*!

And the shadow that was Toby's Monster and the most loyal of all his imagos swung the crowbar in a wide arc, hard and fast, and brought it down with a sickening crunch upon the skull of not-quite-Toby.

—You can't do this, Flashjack. I can't let you.

— Was your solution any fucking better? Was it? You thought if you just shattered the lies, made him face the truth, that would make it all peachy? That it wouldn't be the final fucking straw?

Around them the storm was raging through the Behold of the Eye, a fiery hail of planet-shards, stars falling from the heavens, smashing everything beneath it, burning everything it smashed, in an apocalypse of desire. The ruin of the library burned. The island itself burned. Every castle and kingdom, every city and savannah, forest and field, all the Beholden wonders of Toby's dreamscape burned. Only Flashjack and Fuzzy were able to stand against the scouring destruction, the one more fiery than the flame itself, the other darker than the blackest smoke, only them and the tiny broken piece of jetty that they stood on, Flashjack firing jets of ice-water into the sky like anti-aircraft fire, shattering the burning hail above them into sparks, and desperately trying, at the same time, to focus his concentration on the pile of bodies that he knelt over.

— I can do this, he said. I can give him something to hold onto, something to want.

His fingers worked furiously on the flesh and bone, twirling and tweaking, squeezing and stretching, two skeletons into one bone, muscle woven around muscle around muscle then stitched into place.

— He doesn't *want* to want, snarled Fuzzy. He *wants* to *not* want.

— I can make him want, said Flashjack.

At its core a heart that had once been not-quite-Toby, its body built of all the imagos of thwarted yearning, the boy would be beautiful when Flashjack was finished. He would be all Toby's desire-to-have and desire-to-be fused into one, and he would be irresistible, undeniable.

— I can't let you do that, said Fuzzy. He *wants* me not to let you do that.

Flashjack looked up at the crowbar in the shadow's hand, then up at the empty darkness where the face should be. Had there been eyes, Flashjack would have stared straight into them with a fire the equal of the holocaust around them.

— Does he? said Flashjack.

And as the shadow swung, a solid wall of ice smashed up through the wood between them, sparkling with the blue clarity of the sky but solid as a storm door, and though the shadow brought the crowbar down on it like a pick-axe, again and again and again, left a hairline crack and a smear of red blood, the wall did not break as Flashjack raised his finished creation up, cradling its head in his arms, and lowering his face to breathe himself into it with a kiss.

Flashjack huddled in his prison of glass, watching the flames ravage the Behold of the Eye, engulfing everything, even boiling the very waters of the seas, setting fire to the coral and seaweed and dead fish of their dry beds. Soon there was nothing to be seen but the fire or, once in a while, a dark shape striding through the inferno, stopping to raise its arms, turning, revelling in the desolation. Flashjack watched this for a long time — he wasn't sure how long — arms wrapped round his tucked knees, missing his wings and his innocence. His strange new body was a work of art, but he wasn't exactly using it for what it was meant; he should be out there in the Behold, being shameless in his enjoyment of it, offering Toby an imago of desire unbound. But it wasn't safe. It just wasn't.

He waited, expecting Fuzzy to come back and try again to smash his way into the sanctuary and cage Flashjack had made for himself, turning water into ice, ice into glass. Fuzzy, however, was too busy with his new position as king of hell. So he waited, expecting the flames to burn themselves out any day now, any day, reasoning that once the broken dreams which fuelled the inferno were all stripped away to nothing, then the very lack of anything to care about would kill it; the fire would consume itself.

The fires of hell burned on.

Flashjack huddled in his prison of glass, watching the boy outside batter his fists against it. He buried his face in his crossed forearms, but it didn't really help; he couldn't hear the screams, which comforted him a little when he curled up in a ball at night and tried to sleep, but even when he closed his eyes he could see this new generation of tormentors tormented, each arriving naked and afraid, to be broken, mutilated, maimed for days, weeks, months, and then their skin stripped off, sewn to moon-bone structures speared into their shoulders until, eventually, they rose from the carnage of themselves, spread wide their ragged leather wings and joined the ranks of the tormentors to set upon the next new arrival.

Occasionally, something pretty, something beautiful would appear but it didn't last long; everything else almost immediately smashed and soiled by the demons, ruined and then burned, only those few imagos which had appeared inside Flashjack's glass prison had been spared destruction. There was the last remnants of the jetty, of course, now reshaped into a little pallet bed of driftwood. On the floor was sand, soft and warm and golden, which had trickled down one day over his shoulder, as if through invisible fingers. There were a smooth pebble and a sea shell which Flashjack held now, one in each hand, wondering if in holding on to them, in being himself something to hold on to, he was only perpetuating the pain, if by letting the walls fall and walking out to let the demons tear apart the last vestiges of desire he could perhaps bring it all to an end. He couldn't do it.

Flashjack huddled in his prison of glass, his back turned to the horrors of the Behold, looking out the window of Toby's eye at the azure sky and golden sun. Then the vision shifted and there was a face, laughing but with warmth rather than cruelty, a friend mugging ridiculously, pushing his nose into a pig-snout with a finger. The boy's life was not bereft of happiness, kindness, joy; his world had autumn leaves, crisp winter snow, the buds of spring, and it had summer, hot and shimmering summer days like this when Flashjack would press his hands up to the glass and yearn to bring that sky and sun back into the cavernous waste of the Behold. Toby's friend mouthed something, listened to the response then laughed, went bug-eyed with his disbelief — *no fucking way, man* — and Flashjack wondered how his Beholder could be in a friend's good company, laughing and joking, and yet still so desolate of desire.

For the umpteenth time that afternoon, Flashjack lifted the little shard of mirror that had dropped into the sand in front of him a few mornings ago. He held it up as close to the glass as he could get it, angled it this way and that.

When you see someone with a twinkle in their eye, you must understand, often that twinkle is their faery flashing a little mirror to see if you too have a faery in your Behold, a little *how-do-you-do?* from one sprite to another. But sometimes what seems like a twinkle of whimsy might well be a glint of madness, the faery in the Behold of their Eye sending a desperate SOS in the hope that someone, anyone, will help.

For the umpteenth time that afternoon, there was no answer.

Flashjack woke with a start, and rubbed sleep from his face, ran his fingers through his hair. And felt the dampness of his fingers. And saw —

The Behold of the Eye was dark and empty, and he was wet from the drip-drip-drip of the ceiling of his prison of glass which had become a prison of ice and — as he clambered to his feet and reached out to touch the wall — now transformed again, losing its form completely and collapsing, in a rush of water, to soak into the sand beneath his feet and into the ash beyond. The window at his back, Flashjack peered into the gloom, but there was nothing, no fire, no demons, only darkness.

The Behold of the Eye

Yes, it's me, said the darkness, in a voice that Flashjack knew and that, for a second, frightened him, knowing as he did what Toby's Monster was capable of. Then he realised there was something different in its tone, something that was far more awful than the bitter, raging thing that had smashed the statues, far more terrible than the dark, despairing thing that had stood above him with a crowbar and with nothing where its eyes should have been. But he also knew, somehow, it wasn't a threat.

— You don't want to kill me, he said.

It doesn't matter any more. Nothing does.

The words sent a chill down Flashjack's spine.

— I don't understand.

The darkness said nothing, offered no explanation, but it seemed to coalesce a little, a vague shape, black upon black, that stood back a ways from Flashjack and off to one side, staring out the window. Slowly, Flashjack turned, not understanding what he was seeing at first, a cup of tea held in Toby's hands, the family dog sat in front of the armchair, looking up at him, people milling in the living-room — an aunt and uncle visiting, it seemed, and more — Toby's father in the kitchen at the phone, his mother getting up off the sofa to make more tea, wiping her eyes, his father dialling another number, and talking, then dialling another number, and talking, then dialling another number, and talking, and Toby was just watching him now, transfixed on him, though it seemed like he was saying the same thing over and over again, except now he wasn't saying it at all, just dropping the phone and burying his face in his hands, and Toby had turned to stare straight ahead at the TV set with the framed photograph on top, of Josh.

Then there were tears running down the window.

A Handful of Forevers

All through the funeral Flashjack worked. As the car drove them to the church, Toby looked out to one side, and suddenly there in the Behold was a shimmering image of the road the car was on, the spot they were passing, with Josh standing there, sun in his hair, hair in his eyes, about to step out but *not* stepping out, caught in an eternal moment. Flashjack grabbed the road and pinned one end to the window of Toby's eye, threw the other out into the ashen darkness as far as it would go, as far as Toby could want it to go, which was forever, and the fields unrolled from its verge as far as the eye could see, a moment transformed into eternity.

As the family sat in the church, oblivious of the minister's mute mouthings over the boy he'd never, as far as Flashjack was aware, had the slightest contact with, Flashjack took the frozen moment of a Josh-who-did-not-step and, grabbing every glint of a spark of a memory that appeared in the Behold, layered in the smiles and the strut and the style and the spats and the football trophies and the record collection and the David Bowie poster and all the vanity and cockiness and sheer shining brilliance that was Josh-before-he-stepped.

As the car pulled out of the driveway of the church and, out on the high street, an old man walking past came to a stop and took his hat from his head, then stood to attention with a sharp salute for the hearse of a total stranger, Flashjack grabbed the flood of unspoken gratitude, the tears of a Toby overwhelmed by the gesture, by wanting so much to respond, to say how much that simple silent respect said all that could or should be said in the face of death, and from the tears Flashjack made a sea, from the sea he made an azure sky, and into the sky, fashioned from the sunlight in the hair of the imago standing before him, Flashjack hurled a golden sun to light and warm Josh on his road into eternity.

As the coffin of polished mahogany slid slowly away through the red velvet curtain, Josh disappearing forever into the beyond of the crematorium, into the fire and the ash and the smoke, Flashjack grabbed the funeral pyre and the Viking longboat and the mausoleum and the torn lapels and the fistfuls of hair, the whole vast stupid spectacle of grief that Toby conjured in the Behold of his Eye, as if any monument or ritual could be sufficient, as if any monument or ritual could even begin to match the scale of his sorrow. And Flashjack turned the pyre into an autumn forest of yellow, red and orange leaves; he turned the longboat into a dragon that soared up into the sky, its sails now wings, to swoop and soar and turn and dive and bury itself deep in the earth, a vast reptilian power coiled within the land, *alive*; he turned the mausoleum into a palace, the palace into a city, the city into a hundred of them, each no larger than a grain of sand, a handful of forevers which he scattered out across the Behold to seed and grow; then, with the hair, he stitched the torn lapels together around his own body until he had a harlequin suit, not formed of elegant diamonds of black and white, but rather a rough thing of rags as rich a brown as the earth.

He turned to the imago of Josh-who-did-not-step, Josh-before-he-died, Josh-who-*did-not-die*, the Josh that Toby would now always and forever want so much and so unattainably with a desire that made all other desires seem as inconsequential as ash scattered to the wind; and Flashjack bowed, beckoning along the road with a twirl of his hand.

EPILOGUE

It should not be assumed that this ending, this new beginning was, for Toby, a moment of apotheosis which healed all wounds and banished all horrors. There were many bleak times in the years of Flashjack's journey with Josh into the wilds of the Behold, times when the old darkness would rise again in other forms, and fires would burn in the cities of the Behold. Although it was impossible for Toby to deny the crystal clarity of his yearning for an endless summer day of azure sky and golden sun and green fields in which his brother still lived, although from this imago whole fields of illusion sprang under Flashjack's dancing feet, filling the Behold of the Eye with new wonders, and although, somewhere along the long and winding road, it became clear that many of the imagos now popping into existence daily were clearly reflections of Toby's own appetence rather than grave goods for his lost brother (the shepherds fucking in the meadows were more than enough evidence of that, Flashjack thought), still, sometimes the wind would carry smoke and ash, and sometimes, when the storms rose, there would be a deep crimson tint to the clouds, a hint of blood and fire; and Flashjack would raise his eyes to the heavens, hoping not to see a falling corpse. It took Toby many years to learn to cherish life again.

But when he did, as he did, Flashjack was amazed at the vibrancy of the boy's reborn desire. It wasn't that the imagos it created were grand and exciting, wild worlds of adventure. If anything, many of them were so subtle that Flashjack nearly missed them: the swirl of grass in a field blown by the wind, the delicate streaks of stratocirrus in the sky; the way an orange streetlight on sandstone at night could give a building a rich solidity, like in some old master's oil painting. But all these imagos, Flashjack understood, spoke of an appetence that craved reality, that relished life, a passion for the fragile moments of beauty that might pass unnoticed if one were not, like Toby it seemed, all too aware of how ephemeral they were. So he knew that a change had taken place. It was only when Flashjack found the teddy bear lying in the field of long grass, however, that he truly realised how deep this change had been. The bear was smaller, and it didn't dance — didn't move at all — just a normal, everyday teddy bear, slightly tatty, but there was no mistaking this imago of an appetence out of lost childhood. There was no mistaking the bear, and there was no mistaking the darkness in his eyes, empty of rage now, empty of hate, not a darkness of lost hope but a darkness of quiet sorrow.

— I remember that, said Josh. It was his. Fuzzy.

His tiny hand reached out to pluck the bear from Flashjack's grasp.

— I'll take it back to him, the little boy said.

He turned and began running across the field, head no higher than the grass. Flashjack took a step after the child, smiling to himself as he thought of the Grand Quest he could make of this, but a voice, low and resonant in his ear, brought him to a halt.

Let him go, said the wind in the grass, the emptiness that was, perhaps, Flashjack thought, the real spirit of the Behold. *Let him go,* it said. *I'll look after him from here. He wants me to. Go home.*

Flashjack nodded, but he stood for a long while, watching the boy disappear into the grass, bear in hand, before he turned to leave.

It was years since he'd last stood looking out of the window of Toby's Eye, and with the healing of the boy's desire Flashjack was curious to see what new marvels he might find back where it had all begun. So what did he find there? Well, perhaps, in keeping with the most noticeable effect of that transformation, we should phrase it like this: What should he find there, but another faery! Why, there he was, sitting on the branch of an apple tree, sipping wine of the very richest red and smoking what can only be described as the Perfect Joint, rolled so straight and so smooth it seemed a veritable masterpiece. Batting his iridescent wings in the wind, picking dirt out from under his fingernails with his little kid-horns, or scratching and scruffling his green tousle of hair, he seemed quite at home.

— Who the fuck are you? said Flashjack. Where did you come from?

— A'right there, said the other faery. I'm Puckerscruff. I'm a faery. You're a lust-object imago, right? Not bad, not bad at all. Taste *and* imagination; I knew I'd picked the right Beholder. Fancy a toke?

— Wait a minute. *I'm* the bloody faery here, said Flashjack. This is my Behold. Go find your own sodding Behold.

— Pull the other one, mate. Where's your wings?

Flashjack's wings popped out on his back in a fit of pique as he crossed his arms. Puckerscruff looked surprised, then suspicious, then worried, then guilty.

— Look, mate, there wasn't a twinkle. I checked and there wasn't a twinkle. He was looking to Beholden someone, *itching* to, *bursting* to, and my hoary old tart was boring me towards self-lobotomy, so I was on the lookout for new digs, and this place seemed empty, see, so I thought, well, I can put on a little show just on the off-chance, while they're gazing into each other's eyes and doing the old tongue tango, right, and…and…hey, don't look at me like that. If he hadn't been *looking* for a faery, I wouldn't be here, would I? Seems to me like *someone* must have been neglecting his duties. Too busy making whoopee with the porn imagos, eh? Sorry, okay, okay, I take that back. I didn't mean it. It's just…please…don't make me go back. He's a fucking label queen, all fashion and no style, imagination of a seagull, does my fucking nut in. You and me, mate, you and me, we'll be a team, a twosome, a dynamic duo. I'll show you tricks you never dreamed of, mate.

All through this speech Flashjack had been gradually advancing on Puckerscruff who had been backing away, hands raised placatingly, but at this last sentence Flashjack stopped. Through the window, he could see, Toby was looking down over the sweep of his own chest and stomach towards the head bobbing up and down at his groin.

— What kind of tricks? said Flashjack.

So Puckerscruff showed him.

It should not be assumed that this ending, this new beginning was, for any of the parties involved, a moment of cathartic release in which sexual identity was affirmed and all insecurity banished. For Toby it was by no means the first time and it was by no means the last step. For Flashjack it was one of the most spectacular experiences he'd ever known, but not quite, he claimed rather tactlessly, as good as when he did it. For Puckerscruff it was merely one in a long line of sexual adventures, and while Flashjack was a definite looker, he was a barely competent lover, clearly in need, Puckerscruff thought, of some good solid training.

So the Behold of the Eye was not transformed in an instant to utopian bliss. The rains of shattered albums, storms of semi-molten mixing decks and exploding glitterballs that followed most of Toby's explorations of the gay scene were, as far as Flashjack was concerned, a complete pain. He felt — and would say so loudly and repeatedly — that if Toby wanted to get laid so bad but found the clubs such a bloody agonising ordeal then Toby should just go to the bloody park at night and look tasty in the trees. In truth, he was worried — though he did not say this at all — that Toby didn't do the *cruising* thing because he was, on some level, still uncomfortable with his sexuality. Puckerscruff on the other hand, who had been horrified by his old Beholder's lack of musical taste, and who now revelled in Toby's imago of an ideal record collection, would bounce through these storms, fists flying, punching and head-butting the debris as it rained down, singing "Anarchy in the UK" at the top of his lungs.

It also has to be said that Flashjack and Puckerscruff were, as his laternal grandsister (adopted), Pebbleskip, had once warned Flashjack, not always the most tranquil of couples, with the result that more than a few arguments ended with the Behold divided in two as *your half* and *my half*. And what with two faeries in the Behold of his Eye rather than one, as Pebbleskip had also once warned, Toby's passions did at times tend to the intense, the glint in his eye more a fireworks display than a twinkle; Flashjack and Puckerscruff could see it in the way he drank and smoked, and partied and painted…and always with gusto. But Pebbleskip's talk of glory and truth, angels and demons was long since forgotten, so it was something of a surprise when the invasion came, though not *too* much of a surprise given the hallucinogen Toby had dropped a few hours before and the fact that Flashjack and Puckerscruff were now having a rare old time outside, whirling and twirling as they performed Flashjack's updated, two-man *Dance of the Killer Butterfly* to Toby's great amusement, his idea of the boundary between real and imagined being rather relaxed right now. It was Puckerscruff who noticed the demons crawling out of a corner of the room, first one, then another, then more, very soon a whole host of them, and angels too.

— Yeah, right, he said. Not a chance, mate. You lot can just fuck off.

Then he and Flashjack began a variation of the *Dance of the Killer Butterfly*, this time aimed in the general direction of the angels and demons, with a little extra jazz hands. By the time it was over so was the invasion, the inventions of visionary rapture fluttering up into the air on their iridescent wings, every one of them reborn in a pirouette of pure whimsy.

— That's a damn sight better, said Toby.

Scruffian's Stamp

O.

Orphans, foundlings, latchkey kids. Urchins, changelings, live-by-wits. Rascals, scallywags, ruffians, scamps. Scoundrels, hellions, Scruffians STAMP!

From his seat on the bench, the Scruffian who didn't know he was a Scruffian yet, who didn't even quite know what a Scruffian was, watched the other kids in the park, half-wishing he was like them, with their homes and happy families — well, families, at least — and half-hoping he would never be like them, *never*. Soon they'd all be going home to their tea, though they probably called it dinner. He wasn't going home to neither, not ever, not likely.

Orphans, foundlings, latchkey kids. Urchins, changelings, live-by-wits. Rascals, scallywags, ruffians, scamps. Scoundrels, hellions, Scruffians STAMP!

They were playing hopscotch, boys and girls together, which was a bit strange cause hopscotch was really a girl's game, he'd always thought, and none of the boys looked like sissies. Not that looking like a sissy meant you was one, or that *not* looking like a sissy meant you *wasn't* one. The Scruffian, who wasn't *really* a Scruffian yet, just on his way to it, knew that.

He shivered in his thin red windbreaker, which wasn't anything in this kind of weather.

Orphans, foundlings, latchkey kids. Urchins, changelings, live-by-wits. Rascals,
scallywags, ruffians, scamps. Scoundrels, hellions, Scruffians STAMP!

With the last word the girl or boy playing hopscotch would come down hard
with both feet, and the rest would all stamp a foot. Made it all like some…war-
dance. Weird. And some of them was a bit old for hopscotch surely.

Orphans, foundlings, latchkey kids. Urchins, changelings, live-by-wits.

They all had such sharp looks on their thin faces too.

Rascals, scallywags, ruffians, scamps. Scoundrels, hellions, Scruffians STAMP!

And they was all looking at him on that last word.

1.

Orphan was the first Scruffian, they says. See, he had the sweetest voice
ever heard, did Orphan; so sweet it was, there's many as think he must have
come from Heaven. Well, he *was* found as a babe, abandoned on a mountainside.
Would have been left there too if it weren't for the fact that even his crying was
like music. The shepherd that found him, he was flat astounded, took the lad
home just so's he could sit there listening to him…bawling and bawling. Why,
that's bloody beautiful, the shepherd thought. And did fuck all to soothe him.

Weren't long before the lad started singing. And how! When he sang a sad
song, that's what made the willow tree weep, and when he sang a happy song,
why, even the stones would dance. So naturally the groanhuffs all wanted him
singing at their funerals and weddings. No matter how he felt. Sing us a sad
song, they'd say, even if he was happy. Or sing us a happy song, they'd say, even
if he was sad. And because the foundling didn't have no one as truly cared for
him, they'd just clip his ear if he says no.

You was in one of those foster homes before you run away, right? I've heard
what goes on in some of those places, from the telly, from the news. And I remember me own days in the workhouse. I'll tell you this: I don't know if it really
happened the way the stories tell it, but even if it didn't, it did, I'll bet. If you see
what I mean. Even if Orphan's story was just made-up to fill in what none of us
know, it's not a fucking lie the way that pixie dust and pirates bollocks is.

2.

Anyways, one day Orphan's singing at the wedding of a princess, a song
about how beautiful she is, how lucky any husband is to have her, and the danc-

ing of the stones, well, that carries his music right down to the Lord of the Dead, who comes up to investigate. Death, he takes one look at the princess and snatches her away to be his bride. The groanhuffs are right fucked off at that, and they blame Orphan, which is bloody typical, right? It were his singing about the bride's beauty, they says, what set Death's heart on having her.

So it's him, says they, as is going to have to bring her back, go down to Hell and charm the old bugger into letting her go. All he has to do is sing a song about how sorely she's missed. Oh, yeah, that's all. Just find the entrance to the underworld, cross the river that washes away all memory, find his way to the house of dust and ash, go through the seven gates where all you ever were is stripped from you by the guardian of Hell, and sing a song to melt the heart of Death himself.

Yeah, easy peasy, lemon squeezy, eh? Might as well send a nipper off to fight a fucking war. They did that, you know, still do, though not on the same scale, not since we nicked the Stamp. They don't have so many of us now, and there's no way to make more, not like it was in my day, with the Waiftaker General and all. And before then? Fuck, you ever heard of the Children's Crusade? Them was Scruffians mostly. A whole bleeding army of Scruffians sent to fight the Muslims. Most of em ended up as slaves, of course.

3.

But yeah, the groanhuffs realised their pickle: it wouldn't be much good if Orphan arrived there not remembering why he'd come, and without his song anyways. That's when the groanhuffs came up with the idea of the Scruffian's Stamp. If that river washes away all memory, why, they've got to write his memories on him in a way that won't wash off. If the guardian of the gates will strip him of everything he ever was, why, they needs to put his song in him in a way that can't be stripped off. They need to *stamp* it into him.

So off they goes to the local wise man, the one what knows writing and such malarkey. They didn't use pen and ink back then, mind; they used sticks and clay, of all things, scratched their words into mud. Still, they wasn't daft; they could print things like that. They'd take a rolling-pin of clay and stick more clay on it in the shape of letters, spell out their message. Then when it was hard, they'd roll it across other slabs of wet clay, print out that message as many times as they wanted. Stamped in the clay, like.

Scruffian's Stamp

Can you read? Not many of us Scruffians so good at it; not like anyone ever taught us. Only lessons we was ever given, most of us, was in how to shut up and do what we was told on pain of a right good thrashing. If anything they'd tell us we wasn't able to because we was born stupid, bad breeding and all, the scum of the earth. Some of us keeps learning, but…it don't stick. Just can't get our heads round all the squiggles. Not like you can with a Stamp. Soul writing's a different thing altogether.

4.

So. The wise man listens to the groanhuffs and their scheme. He looks at Orphan, right into his eyes, and tries to read his heart, his soul. Cause everyone has their story written in their eyes, if you look hard enough, all their memories, all they've ever been, till now. But the old man, he realises what's written in Orphan is more than he can put into words on any old lump of clay. Why, it'd take him as long as the boy'd lived just to read it, and by then there'd be the same again waiting to be read.

No, he realises, what they need is a stamp that does more than just write; they need to work the whole magic of writing in reverse too. By fuck, it occurs to him, what they need is a stamp that's soft as wet clay at the first pressing, so's it takes its shape from the story written into the boy already, and hard as stone at the second pressing, so's it writes the shape of that story into the boy's skin, his heart, his soul, forever and ever until the end of time. So's it Fixes him as he is.

Now I ain't going to tell all the stories I've heard about how the wise man made the Scruffian's Stamp, cause most of them ain't too pretty. There's a lot as say the clay it was made from was graveyard dirt made moist with the blood of babies, that it had ground bone for lime in it, and sand from Old Man Time's hourglass, and the ash of burnt cities, and all sorts. But the truth is, no bugger really knows how it was made, not even us Scruffians. Still, made it was. And with it, Orphan…he was *Fixed*.

5.

Being Fixed meant the same then as now, though the groanhuffs didn't twig to it straight off. Sure, they knew that Orphan being Fixed meant he could walk into Hell without fading away into a scrap of a shade. But they wasn't really thinking that he wouldn't ever grow up, just stay the way he was now for as long as he lived. They wasn't really thinking that the only way to hurt him permanent would be to fuck up the stamp on his heart, ruin it. No, they didn't really see the *potential* of hardy little bastards like us.

They knew it in my day, they did. Oh, we was perfect for factory work, they reckoned. Send us in to clean out all the nooks and crannies of the machines in the mills. You lose a hand or a foot, it don't matter; it'll grow back eventually…after a shortish forever of screaming agony. Or say you want some tyke to scramble up chimneys, someone you can lash their feet raw and they'll be right as rain in a few days. Someone *resilient*. Just pop down to the workhouse, take your pick, and drag him along to the Institute.

Oh, they don't gab about it, never did. Never wrote it down in the history books neither, except maybe between the lines. Like to pretend we don't even exist, they do, the groanhuffs that knows about Scruffians. Some of em don't, right enough. It was always a bit hush hush and how's yer father, you know? Only known about in *certain circles*; I suppose they thought the Quakers might get their knickers in a twist or summat. But I remember the bastard as bought me for a guinea. And how much more it cost for him to get me Fixed.

6.

It hurts like buggery when they put the Stamp on you. I won't lie; it hurts like…like when they cut a monkey open while it's still alive, just so's they can poke around inside and see how it ticks. Yeah, it's *exactly* like that, and that's not just some fancy, mate. I'd show you the scars if that old Scruffian resilience hadn't healed em. You'd see how neat the bastard cut, so careful not to slip a scalpel into the Stamp on me chest; cause as long as that was intact, the anatomy lessons could just go on forever.

They say Orphan went through something like that in Hell, hung up on a hook and cut open by Death. There's some as say that part's really just about what it's like to be Fixed. Maybe it is. But sod it, what's a dead cert is, he healed up pretty as a picture. And sure enough, he sang before Death. Sure enough, he melted Death's heart. Sure enough, Death let the princess go. And it was all for fuck all, because her beauty was given back at the gates but her *self* had been washed away completely in the river.

Not that the groanhuffs gave a toss about that. They had their princess back, and if she wasn't *really* back, not all of her, well, pretty and empty like a shell is how a lot of husbands like their wives, innit? That way they can fill her up with any old tosh they want. A woman's place is in the home. Stand by your man. All that bollocks. So they was happy as Larry and went right back to their wedding celebrations. Sing us a happy song, they said. Only Orphan wouldn't now. Or *couldn't*. Not after all of that.

7.

I'll never sing at no weddings again, says he, no matter what you do. They clipped his ear for saying no, but that weren't nothing to Orphan now. They slapped his hands and rapped his knuckles, but that weren't much either. They pinched him and punched him, but he didn't even bruise. They kicked him, whipped him, thrashed him, lashed him, but his broken bones mended quick as a flash, and his cuts closed up ungodly fast. They snapped his fingers and cracked his toes, gouged his eyes and cut off his nose. They tore him apart, limb from limb.

They left his body bloody and broken, his clothes ripped to rags, a right fucking state. But they never thought to scratch out the Stamp that had Fixed him forever, so even as the groanhuffs walked away feeling all smug, what was left of Orphan, which wasn't bloody much, lay on the ground healing. Slowly. Days it took before there was enough of him to crawl away to a hidey-hole, weeks before even that looked like an actual person, months before he was back to himself. A whole half a year it took in all, but in the end…

In the end, he was a Scruffian, the first of us all, and not nearly the last to suffer so, though none of us can say we've been *to Hell and back*, least not in any way but what they call metaphorical. In the end, he clambered out of his hidey-hole, and whiles he was dressed in rags, and filthy with the blood and mud he'd been trodden in, he was alive, and would be forever. Didn't have no choice in it and weren't sure how he felt about it, but, well…that's what the Scruffian's Stamp means, innit?

8.

For most of us, that is, them what was Fixed down the centuries by groan-huffs looking for littl'uns they can work not just to death but past it, stepping sideways, like. A pickpocket who can come back from having his hand chopped off. A drummer boy who can crawl out of any carnage so's all the brave Johnnys will feel bolder than buttons. Mill workers or chimney sweeps, like I said. And things you can't imagine, don't want to imagine. Long as the groanhuffs had their bloody hands on the Stamp, we was all just waifs to be Fixed. Used.

It wasn't like we could all stand up to em like Orphan. Just cause you heal, don't mean you don't hurt. And you heard the Rhyme, right? It's what brought you to us. *Orphans, foundlings, latchkey kids.* We were all of us Fixed when we was nobodies, nothings, bastards and bitches ground down by the groanhuffs, taught to know our place. Then Fixed that way for good. Took a long time before any of us figured to tinker with the Stamp, do a little nipping and snipping on the writing over our hearts. But time's one thing we've got, mate.

Might never have cottoned onto it meself, if it hadn't been for one little nick from the scalpel of the bastard who bought me, one little nick so tiny he didn't even spot it himself. But *I* did. And after a little tailoring…well, the good doctor had a bad end, nuff said. I was lucky, you know; didn't even have to gnaw off any appendages to escape me shackles, not like some. No, I just played the broken little blighter until my chance came, one *fine* day. Escaped into the streets and found my way here after some…adventures.

9.

I'll tell you all about em if you decide to…well…you know. There's a lot more stuff behind the rumours we spread, and a lot of those are misdirection anyways. Like we're not all kids, you know; you can be Fixed at any age, and not all of us are in the flower of youth like yours truly. And then there's them what's *really* messed with their Stamps, or had them messed with. They can be scary, mate. They can be *anything.* I'll even tell you the tale of how we stole the Stamp. If you stay, that is.

See, you have the choice we didn't. You wanna think about it though, you do, before you decide to throw your lot in with us. Cause it's not just about living in society's stitches, you know, the bits in between, the squats and secret places. It's about being Fixed. You'll be twiddling and tweaking your Stamp, no doubt, as we all do here, but age is a right bastard to fiddle with, so best be savvy of whether you want your Stamp…with sauce or without, if you catch my drift. Still, it's your choice. Scruffians don't knock nobody back.

Orphans, foundlings, latchkey kids. That's what we are, what we've always been, always will be; and fuck the groanhuffs who'd chain us up in the workhouse or the mills. *Urchins, changelings, live-by-wits.* Them buggers made us that way, right? So are we ashamed of surviving as thieves and beggars? Not bloody likely. *Rascals, scallywags, ruffians, scamps.* We got tribes in every city now; and outside certain circles most groanhuffs have forgotten we even exist. *Scoundrels, hellions, Scruffians STAMP!* And we *will* stamp one day, mate, *real hard.* So the question is… You wanna be a Scruffian or not?

An Alfabetcha of Scruffian Names

A IS FOR APPLE

A Scruffian *god* is Apple, and a fine feller he is too, the pipsqueak, named for his rosy cheeks and sweetness. Ain't no choirboy can sing as angelic as Apple, not even Orphan, cause it's him what invented singing in the first place, so's the world'd have rhyme and reason. And there's nine Scruffian girl gods what follows him about everywhere he goes — the Mouses we calls them, cause he learns em his songs, then they scurries round the world disguised as mouses, whispers em in our ears whiles we're asleep, a whole song speeded up into the tiniest squeak.

B IS FOR BANANASTASIA ROAMINHOPPER

Now, *she* says she's a Russian princess what had her family topped and had to go on the lam, all across Europe. Snuck her way onto a boat for London, right? But got snatched by the waiftakers on the docks. Sold to a brothel after they Fixed her, she was, so's all them fine gents could have the pleasure of popping her cherry each and every time, it growing back and all, each and every time. And we don't catch diseases, course. Don't none of us believe her about the princess part, right enough, even if she do talk funny.

C IS FOR CURSMIDGEON Q. TYKE

Him over there what's scowling like a rooked scofflaw playing horsey for a scrag. Yeah, don't be fooled by the pint-size of that scamp; that there *Q* stands for "Quicktemper" on account of he was Fixed furious. Took three of em to hold him still while they put the Stamp on him, and even then he bit a finger right off one of the Waiftaker General's stickmen, he did, spat it right in the bugger's face. Never heard no one who can swear like Tyke. Turns the air black *and* blue most times he opens his mush, he does.

D IS FOR DINGUSES

He's another Scruffian god, Apple's brother and as saucy as his twin is sweet. We calls him Dinguses cause he's always swiping any dingus, doohickey or thingamabob you leave lying. He invented dancing to go with his brother's songs, see, so he thinks nothing should sit in the same place for too long. Invented make-believe too, so's the world wouldn't have *too much* reason. Some folks calls him Baccy cause he smokes like a lum. Drinks like a fish too. Ain't much he *don't* do, actually. There's girls what follows him too, a right bunch of hellions.

E IS FOR EARWIGGER CHATTERMONKEY HIDENSNEAK

Can't keep a secret and fuck me if anyone can keep a secret from *him*. He's our eyes and ears on the streets — and sewers, tube tunnels, rooftops too. Don't know how he does it, but back in the day, if the Waiftaker General had a shit in a Spitalfields stickman's lodge, Earwigger could tell you how squishy it were, how long it took, and who licked his arse clean afterwards. And don't think cause there ain't no Institute no more, he ain't needed. There's been Scruffians disappearing, and the Law don't know nothing about it, Earwigger says. He's investigating.

F IS FOR FOXTROT WAINSCOT HOTTENTOT III

That'll be the one with the fake moustache and the monocle. He's the boss round here, oldest of the lot of us, even if he don't look more'n a nipper. Smart with it too, that scamp. You might think that 'tache and monocle is a daft disguise, but close your eyes, right? Right, now try and tell us the colour of his peepers or how many freckles on his nose. See? All's any groanhuff is gonna remember is the 'tache and monocle on some boy what looks around ten. Ain't so daft now, is he? Fox's a cunning little stunt.

G IS FOR GOBFABBLER SAINT HALOYSIUS DUNKLING, ESQUIRE.

That's me. But you can calls me Gob for short, cause that's what everyone else does. I'm the fabbler of this here crib so it ain't hard to see where I gets the name, right? *Fabbler?* Well, mostly fabbles is fibs what we babble to fob off groanhuffs, but there's the tales what we tells between us too, so's to teach new Scruffians how it is. Every crib has to have a fabbler for that, like meself. Rest of me name's a long story what I'll tell you sometime, just not right now when we're trying to learn you letters.

H IS FOR HALFJACK SCARAMANDER

She ain't been Scruffian long, actually. Says that's why she's always cutting herself, cause she's still amazed at it healing up so sharpish, but I dunno. She's fiery and all, happy to take on groanhuffs as look like giants beside her — which is why we calls her Halfjack, see? — but I ain't sure. I wonders if she ain't had some nasty notions Fixed into her, hurts crying out to be made flesh, you know? Not like we had the happiest of upbringings, is it, not any of us? She wants to be taking that razor to her Stamp, says me.

I IS FOR ICKSQUICK SCRAGGERTY

I ain't sure you really wants to know how Icksquick gots his name, but I'll tell yer anyways. See, he's from my day, only he managed to escape the workhouse. Waiftaker General and his stickmen nabbed him in the sewers they did, living off rats and all sorts, and having gotten himself a taste for it. If it wriggles, squiggles or jiggles, like as not Icksquick will stick it in his mush to see how it tastes. Says he's a *connoisseur of queer cuisine*, he does. Rest of us says he's bonkers when there's spag bol on the table, eh?

J IS FOR JACK SCALLYWAG

Scallywag Jack, the Scruffian Knight! Only that weren't really his name, cause he didn't have one. He were the greatest Scruffian ever; it's him what started the Liberating. And there's hunners of other tales to tell of him. Don't know where he is now though; he Gone Offsky before even Foxtrot was Stamped. Puckerscruff says our Flashjack is him, on account of his Stamp's so hacked and slashed he don't even remember being Fixed, but Puckerscruff's all sweet on Flashjack, so that's just his fancy. Nah, someday Jack'll come back, I says, from whatever grand adventuring he's off on now.

K IS FOR KATZENJAMMER ALLEYTAT

It were Katz who first noticed the disappearances, on account of her spending so much time in the backstreet bivouacs. Scallywags is prone to wandering, see, likes to put their lanky limbs to use, and scofflaws is moody cunts — thinks they knows better than everyone, just cause they was Fixed almost as groanhuffs. Anyways, they're always *needing some space* and fucking off from their cribs for days on end to get it. Only Katz says she ain't seen some of the usual suspects for weeks and they ain't showed up back at their cribs. Foxtrot, he's right fussed about it.

L IS FOR LIGHTFINGER LARKER

There's some as say a certain Charlie Dickens character was based on Larker for his skills in petty pilfering and pickpocketing. Mostly those *some* is Larker himself, right enough, and he ain't never worn no top hat long as I knowed him, so I reckon he's full of it. He *is* good at the thieving though. So you stick by him when yer out as he'll learn you proper in how to survive as a Scruffian. Fact, if there's summat you need, best ask him, as he'll likely nick it for you — just for the fun of doing it, like.

M IS FOR MUGWUMP BUMFLUFFERY

That's the scallywag over there, yeah, the one whose 'tache is real...as far as you can actually call that a 'tache. Bane of his life, it is. He was Fixed in the eighties, see, when he were desperately trying to look all butch. Leather-boy hat and all. Anyway, all's he could ever grow was that wispy bumfluff what he now hates. He shaves it off all the time, but it grows back in a few hours cause he were Fixed that way and he ain't figured out how to tweak his Stamp to get rid of it yet.

N IS FOR NUFFINMUCH O'ANYFINK

He were the boss of bosses back in Foxtrot's day, as Fox tells it, the King of all Scruffians, before he Gone Offsky like Jack. Said it weren't proper Scruffian to be in charge, and he couldn't be arsed with it no more. He were a right royal too, king of the tinkers by way of his da, who were killed when Nuff were taken. So his word were law, leastways near to law as Scruffians has. That's how come, when an argument ain't got nothing can challenge it, we says, Nuff said. Cause whatever Nuff decided, that were it.

O IS FOR ORPHAN

The first ever Scruffian. Some says the Stamp was made so's he could be Fixed, so's he could stroll into Hell and sing to Death, make him give up this princess what he'd taken away. Though there's others as say Orphan's just a tale, that the Stamp existed before him, or that it weren't used to make Scruffians until Jack Scallywag got Fixed. Me, I likes the story of Orphan. Except for the bit where he gets Scrubbed by Baccy's girls. That don't seem right to me. Scruffians might hornswoggle other Scruffians, but we don't Scrub each other, not *ever*.

P IS FOR PUCKERSCRUFF RAGAMUFF

That's him with the green hair and the metal spikes sticking out his wrists. Yeah, they's sort of a…distributed tribe — urchins we calls em, them what's into that stuff. Mostly rough trade. And there's hellions too, like Flashjack, who takes their tweakings even further. The groanhuffs? Well, mostly the urchins' spikes is in hidden places — elbows and heels and suchlike — but the ones what have em on the wrists, they just has leather straps they buckle on. The spikes poke through, but they looks as if they're on the straps, see? Comes in useful if a mark gets nasty.

Q IS FOR QUIZBY MACCHUILLICAN

Most famous Scruffian in the world and ain't no groanhuff even heard of him. How come? He only went and wrote his monicker all over London — in the short form, that is — and got it in the bloody dictionary. Imagine it, all them groanhuffs walking around, seeing the word *quiz* everywhere, and not even figuring it for the obvious Scruffian name it is. What does it mean? says they. And it were such a puzzle to them, they ends up using it as the measure of all puzzles. That's a real quiz, says they. Give him a right big head.

R IS FOR RAKE JAKE SCALLION

Not all what's grown up is groanhuffs, but not all what's Fixed is Scruffians. There's a few adults as was Fixed in various Institute schemes to create super-soldiers or such shite. Mostly they's bad news, but them what's Scruffian inside is called Rakes. Rake Jake Scallion ain't told us his whole tale but I knows it's a sad'un, summat to do with him loving the Waiftaker General's girl. And she ain't around no more, of course, but he's Fixed as deep in love as the day he met her. Won't touch his Stamp neither, says his broken heart's her memorial.

S IS FOR SQUIRLET NICELY

You want summat hidden, she's the one to hide it for you. Fact, she's about the one Scruffian as can keep something secret from Earwigger and not have her stuff nicked by Larker cause he don't have a clue where it is. Reckon her stuff's even safe from Dinguses himself! I been joshing as how we ought to be asking *her* about the disappearances. *Where you hidden all em scallywags and scofflaws, Squirlet?* Foxtrot, he don't even crack a smile at that though, which is how I knows it's serious. They can't all have Gone Offsky, he says. Tain't kosher.

T IS FOR TOLLIVER WHISTLER

He's mates with Upsadaisy and Firepot. Him and Firepot's a bit of an item actually, though you wouldn't guess from the way she punches him. Yeah, he's a spiv if ever there were one, Fixed in the sixties when it was all sharp suits and scooters, and him too podgy to play fop in his Mod clobber. First thing he done after was take a cut-throat razor to his Stamp, carve off the weight. Looks right slinky now and he knows it, but he ain't an arse about it. They's like that, them what ain't *always* looked so dandy.

U IS FOR UPSADAISY FAGSPUFFER

Looks like a scrag, but I reckons she *has* to be a scallywag—growth stunted by the smoking, yeah? — cause only a scallywag could be that gangle-legged when it comes to the war-dance. Yeah, the Rhyme we was chanting in the swing park; it ain't just for hopscotch. *Scoundrels, hellions, Scruffians STAMP!* You ever seen them Maoris doing that whatchamacallit...haka? You want to see a score of Scruffians with dustbin lids for shields and iron railings for spears, all thumping chests, clanging weapons and stamping feet in time to the Rhyme. Except Daisy ain't ever in time.

V IS FOR VERMINTRUDE TOERAG

Vermin for short, and her and Icksquick make a right pair, cause she's as happy in the filth as he is. I swear they's competing as to who don't wash for longest. It's funny, cause she *hates* wearing a dress, but she do clean up the best of us all — face like a cherub under the grime, and knows how to talk proper too — so Fox sends her out as *Trudy* whenever we needs someone to play innocent, infiltrate the groanhuffs. She's out right now, actually, playing lost little girl to the pigs. Just in case the stickmen *is* back.

W IS FOR WAG

Ain't much of a name, but dogs ain't ones for fancy names, is they? You try and call em by a long name, they'll just get bored halfways through and wander off, or sit down on the ground and start licking their balls, like. It's only them poncy pedigrees what's named Archduke Humperdinkle Fifi MacTavish-Golightly and stuff; and they ain't real dogs anyways. Nah, three letters is enough for any dog, and Wag here likes his name fine, dontcha, Wag? See? Fixed? Don't matter. *All* dogs is Scruffians, Fixed or not. Fact is, tain't a crib without a dog.

X IS FOR X

Cause that been the name of a whole lot of Scruffians down the years, leastways on all the official paperwork what they had to put a mark on as says they was happy to be slaves, thank you kindly, fine sir. Or *indentured*, or *under contracts of service*, or whatever fancy words and labels groanhuffs likes to use for it. Like we hadn't *really* been bought from the workhouse or the Institute or the fucking rag'n'bone man. See, that's why reading's important, why I has to learn you it, even if it don't stick. So's you can learn *me* later.

Y IS FOR YAPPER WHELPWRANGLER

He's the one what's playing with Wag now. We calls him that because he speaks dog. Says it ain't too hard to learn on account of it's mostly *gimme* and *shift it* and *squirrels!* but then he's a hellion what's tweaked himself a bit weird; growls in his sleep, he does. Even got old Whelp eating out of his hand, and Whelp's fearsome. He's a proper Fixed dog is Whelp – long story. Yapper says he's in a right flap these days though, yowling on about a smell he knows from way back. Only ain't no word for it in dog.

Z IS FOR ZIGZAG PADDYRAG

You probably heard the groanhuff version of the song. *This old man, he had one. He played knick-knack on his drum.* Well, the right words is, *smacked Zigzag on his bum.* Then it's *with his shoe* for two, *on his knee* for three, *off the door* for four, and *half-alive* for five. Cause it's about a Scruffian dodging an owner come rolling home drunk. *Give the dog a bone?* Old men ain't so nippy as us, see? They's liable to trip. Down stairs, like. And *broke-necked bastards* in dog is *food*. Heh. Yapper? What's *waiftaker* in dog?

Jack Scallywag

Ace Jack, King Jack, Queen Jack, Fool.
Poor widow's son got beans for a bull.
How many beans did the Scruffian get?
One, two, three, four, you are het!

IN WHICH OUR HERO IS INTRODUCED

Once upon a time, there was a poor widow's son who lived out in the forest with his mum. He didn't have nothing to his name — *couldn't* have nothing to his name on account of he didn't have a name. See, his mum were so awful sad at her husband's death, all's she ever called him from the day he was born was Poor Dear. You want fed *again*, she'd say, Poor Dear? How'd you get the busted lip *today*, she'd say, Poor Dear. The other boys calls you a bastard, do they, she'd say, Poor Dear? You don't say?

Mostly though, what the other boys called him—what everyone in the village called him — was Parish Fool. Cause his mum didn't have no money to dress him in aught but a suit of rags, stitched up from scraps of handmedowns and castoffs what had been worn to nothing and chucked away. A right motley, it was, in every sodding shade under the sun. Every shade what's been faded and filthed to a shade of dirt and dust, that is. So they calls him the Parish Fool for it, shouts, Where's yer bells? and, Tell us a joke? Fucking cunts.

But we don't call him Poor Dear or Parish Fool, us Scruffians. Don't call him any of those names the groanhuffs use in their stories about him neither. Cause what do groanhuffs know? All's they've done is heard our tales and passed em along in a game of Chinese Whispers, getting em all mixed up, like. Peer-a-Door and Pierce-a-Veil, they calls him! Dozy twats. Still, we gots to call him summat. Hero needs a name, don't he? So we Scruffians calls him Jack, cause that were a word for any Scruffian-to-be in those days.

Anyways, one day, Jack's out poaching rabbits in the wild woods when these knights ride up, all grand on their gallopers, armour gleaming in the sunlight. Jack, he ain't been schooled, so he don't rightly know what an angel is, but he's seen pictures and carvings in the church, right? Fine looking fellers with breastplates and helmets, swords and shields, you know? So Jack, he falls to his knees, thinking it's Judgement Day itself, praying for mercy. Course, the knights all have a right good laugh at that. No, says they, we're knights, lad, noble-born but mortal as you.

In which our hero aspires to greatness

Huh? You hush yourself, scrag. Yeah, course I'm leaving bits out. These is fresh Fixed scamps, and they ain't in need of hearing things what they won't understand. So let's not confuse em with details about where the knights was headed and how's they'd decided to have some fun on the way. Besides, it messes up the story if you starts bringing in crusades and pogroms and Jack's mum getting — whassat? A pogrom? Well…it's sort of…a monster they had in them days. Yeah, a bit like a dragon. *See? Just lemme tell it simple, like, eh?* Right then…

Jack, he ogles these mortals. If knights look so grand, says he, by buggery, he'll be a knight himself. The nobs near split their sides, them being nobs and all. Parish Fool, says they, there's squires and serfs, and you're no squire. Bollocks to you, says Jack. Off into town he skips. I'm gonna be a knight, says he. Parish Fool, says everyone, there's knights and knaves, and you're no knight. Fuck you, says Jack. Off to his mum he skips. I'm gonna be a knight, says he. Poor dear, says she, there's paladins and peasants, and — Whatever, says Jack.

No, Jack won't have nobody tell him what he can't ever be, even if he weren't born with a silver spoon in one end and an Harley Street hooter up the other. He ain't secretly a prince, ain't got no sword what was his father's. And he ain't gonna make much of a knight without a sword and such. But Jack ain't bovvered. Come morning he sneaks out, whiles his mum's snoring off last night's gin, with a pot for an helmet, a stick for sword, and his trusty old slingshot. Bollocks to them all, he thinks. I'll show em.

Now, being a Scruffian at heart, even if he ain't Fixed yet, Jack ain't the most responsible type, so thieving a horse does strike him as an obvious option. But being a Scruffian at heart, he ain't the most reputable type neither, so it also strikes him as all the groanhuffs in the town would likely finger him straight off. And he's been near enough hanged for an apple, never mind an horse. So, no, he reckons, he'll have to get it legit, like. But it ain't like his dear drunk mum'll miss the old bull in the meadow, eh?

In which our hero sets out on his adventuring

So, off he skips, takes the bull by the horns, as they say—or by the ring in its nose, strictly speaking — and leads it off to market to trade for a horse. No surprise, really, that he don't make the best bargain, cause us Scruffians ain't much when it comes to monetary matters, is we? Ducking and diving, yes. Wheeling and dealing, no. Anyways, what our Jack ends up with is a piebald foal as starved as himself, scrawny as a scallywag and skittish to boot. Calls it Beanstalk, he does, cause it's so skinny-legged and splotch-coated.

Now, don't be getting ahead of us, littl'un. Weren't *that* beanstalk, and it ain't *that* story. No, there's no giants and no goose what lays golden eggs in this tale. There's monsters what's *like* giants and a treasure what's even *more* valuable than that there goose, but this here tale ain't about castles in the clouds, scamps. No, it's about the kind of castle us Scruffians knows only too well, like Buck House and Westminster, Newgate and that Bad Place what we sprung you from. We calls it the Institute. And this here story's sort of about the *first* Institute.

So Jack climbs up onto his Beanstalk and off he sets to become a knight. And some sight he is to all who sees him, scallywag Jack on his scallywag horse, a stick for a sword and a pot for a helmet, no shield or armour, just his clothes all ragged, stitched-together patches as higgledy-piggledy as the pattern on his pony. And Beanstalk's prancing canter like a dance, more foxtrot than horse trot, left and right, to and fro, quick, quick, slow, slow. Why, any as saw him would laugh their arse off as he clop-clipped past.

Now, there's a few fine tales to be told of all the high-jinks Jack got up to even before he got Fixed like you and me. Cause he was *just like* we was, not so long ago. And all of us here is *still* just like him; ain't no real difference between a Scruffian and a Scruffian-to-be, and don't you forget it. If us Scruffians stick together, don't mean we look down on what we was. Like Jack didn't do nothing before he was Fixed! But them tales is for other days, and this one's for tonight.

IN WHICH OUR HERO HAS HIS FIRST TUSSLE

So. Weren't long before Jack happens upon a strange sight: a fancy pavilion in a field, a knight in red armour outside on his horse, and this old geezer stood guard at the doorway. And a right racket of sobbing and snuffling coming from inside. Oh, for a champion to save me from the red knight! comes a cry. Oh, for a hero to rescue me from marriage to a monster! Up gallops Jack as directly as Beanstalk has a notion to — which ain't that directly, in truth. Hey ho, Jack calls to the knight. Where'd you get the armour?

Begone, varlet! says the red knight. Back to your master! Bid him send no lackey if he'd champion this maiden. Cause that's the sort of fancy wank nobs come out with when they ain't bleeding listened to what's been said. Jack, he just shrugs. Don't have no master, he says. Now the red knight, he turns his head, looks Jack up and down, all snooty-like, cause your everyday commoner not having a master…that's an idea as don't sit too well with him, not fucking well at all. You're a serf, says he. You're a twat, says Jack.

You challenge me? snarls the red knight. Do I get your armour if I win? says Jack. Impudence! roars the knight. Straightforward question, says Jack, but if you're going to be a twat about it, come ahead. And without another word — though with a fair amount of angry spluttering — the red knight rears up his steed, brings it round, and comes galloping full tilt at Jack, lance at the ready. You're going down, mister, says Jack as he squares the pot on his head and points his stick at the red knight. And I'm having those shiny togs, I am.

Course, no sooner has Jack said this than—thump!—he's on his arse in the mud, watching Beanstalk gallop for the hills, his horse being smarter about this jousting malarkey than Jack. Bollocks, says Jack as the knight bears down on him. Bollocks, he says again as he looks from his short stick to the knight's long lance. But as the knight comes charging, lance lowered to skewer the lad, up Jack scrambles to his feet now, stone in his slingshot. He aims, he fires, and — thwack! — he drops the bugger dead, straight through the visor, square between the eyes.

In which our hero passes on the fair maiden

Of course, even as Jack's strapping on his shiny new kit, and feeling well chuffed with himself, out comes the fair maiden what he's just inadvertently championed. Oh, you've won my heart, says the damsel. And a lovely heart it is too, says Jack, filching a brooch from her dress as she presses his palm to it. You shall have my daughter's hand in marriage, says the old geezer. And a lovely hand it is too, says Jack, snaffling a ring from her finger as he kisses it. Well, he's a Scruffian-to-be, ain't he? Marriage is for groanhuffs.

No, says Jack, I wouldn't make you happy, love. I'm not the marrying type, not husband material, too young to settle down, too wild and wayward, foot-loose and fancy-free. A gay bachelor, as they say. Confirmed, even, by reliable sources. See, it's just, well, maidens is all very well and all — and you're the fairest of the fair when it comes to maidens, if you ask me, cross my heart — but that's the thing, that heart, it's set on being a knight, you see, got a dragon to slay and everything, and…I swore to avenge me dear old mum!

And with that—*what? No, I don't see as how we ought to be explaining the Queen Jack part here. It ain't as if these scamps need to know about the birds and the bees. All right, the birds and the butterflies, whatever. Remember, these littl'uns is still the age they look; they'll get savvy to that soon enough with mollies like you mincing around. So you knew at their age; look, we only just sprung em from the Waiftaker General, and they barely understands what Scruffians is, and that's what matters. Just lemme tell em enough to be going on.*

Where was we? Right. And with that, Jack hops up on the red knight's horse and scarpers sharpish. Off he goes in his armour, with a proper sword and shield and everything now, looking for all the world like a real knight. And you know what? That meant he *was*. Oh, the groanhuffs might say some king has to knight you Sir Whatever, but that's bollocks. If them nobs didn't get their old man's handmedowns, likely they'd just killed other nobs and took their stuff like Jack did. Most the king ever done was point em at who to kill.

Jack Scallywag

So Jack went off feeling grand as a king. He rode for days and weeks and months, had some more adventures and all, what we won't go into, cause they ain't no matter. But one day he finds himself riding through a strange forest. All the trees was bare, like it was winter, but instead of snow it was ash as coated em all, thick as the muck on a Wandsworth sewer-rat. He came to a village called Shtetl, only it'd been burned to the ground, and all's was left was womenfolk weeping about the dragon what done it.

It came flying in from the north, says they, and it ate up all the men and carried off all the children. It set fire to everything with its terrible breath, and off it went on its way south. And all their clothes was torn like his, Jack noticed, but when he asked as why they didn't mend em, they says it was on account of the little boys and girls that had been ripped away from them, as a reminder. And Jack, he felt right sorry for them, but there weren't nothing he could do, so he rode on.

He didn't feel like so much of a king now in his armour. Fact, he felt so glum as he barely rode for a few hours but it seemed like days and weeks and months. And now he finds himself riding through strange fields. All the earth was barren, like it was winter, but instead of rain it was blood as made the ground mud, deep as the filth of a Whitechapel midden. He came to a camp of travellers, only all the caravans had been smashed, and all's was left was womenfolk weeping about the dragon what done it.

It came flying in from the north, says they, and it ate up all the men and carried off all the children. It smashed everything to bits with its terrible claws, and off it went on its way south. And all their faces was grimed in ash, Jack noticed, but when he asked as why they didn't wash em, they says it were only if the little boys and girls returned, then they'd clean their faces with their tears of joy. And Jack, he felt right sorry for them, but there weren't nothing he could do, so he rode on.

And so it was Jack finds himself not feeling like a king at all now as he rides on for what seems like forever and ever. And now he finds himself riding up to a strange fortress. On an island in the middle of a lake it sits, an island that's naught but dead rock and a lake that's stagnant and stinking, vile as the stench of an Hackney abattoir or a Tottenham tannery. But what's this Jack spies out on the lake? A little wooden rowing boat it is, with a hooded man sat in it, fishing no less!

I wouldn't eat no fish out of this lake, shouts Jack. Nor would I, says this hooded feller as he rows over to Jack. I ain't out to catch fish for eating, says he. It's just, I stay in that castle, in the middle of this wasteland, and it ain't much fun at all, so I come out here now and then, to fish as I once did as a young man, on the shores of a foreign sea, in a far-off land I once called home. For there's not much else as eases my sorrow and my pain.

Now as the man comes closer, Jack spots a queer thing. Why, if the bottom of the boat ain't sopping wet and glistening thick with blood. The feller catches the pale fright on Jack's face and holds up a gloved hand. Don't worry, my good knight, says he. The blood is only the mark of that sorrow and pain, of a wound as was got in the folly of youth, and will never heal now for all as I'll never die of it. The wound will bleed forever, but the blood is only blood. You've nothing to fear from it.

Fair enough, says Jack. Then I feel right sorry for you, as that looks a right sore wound. The hooded feller thanked Jack for his kind thoughts. My good knight, says he, if you're tired from your travels, well, my castle has many rooms. Let me offer you a warm meal and a bed for the night. A company of your brethren is already here, and following the same road as you; you can dine and rest with them tonight, and join their journey in the morn. Ride round to the south and you'll find a drawbridge to the island.

IN WHICH OUR HERO FINDS HIGH SOCIETY LESS THAN CHARMING

And so, as the hooded man rowed back to the island, Jack rode south around the shore of the poisoned lake, until he came to the drawbridge. As the hooded man's servants came out to take the boat's mooring-rope, they came out also to take the reins of Jack's steed. As the hooded man clambered out of his boat, Jack clambered down from his horse. And as the hooded man hobbled slowly, as if every step were painful, over the dead rock of the island and into the castle, so Childe Jack came merrily strolling, strolling into Chapel Perilous.

Right enough, it was as the man had said. Inside, the castle was playing hostelry to a whole host of knights, in tunics of all colours and all heraldry. There were knights wearing white, black, gold, silver, blue, green, all the colours of every circus poster ever printed. There were knights wearing lions, eagles, stags, boars, unicorns, dragons, all the animals in every bestiary ever drawn. Jack hadn't the faintest notion why so many knights would all be travelling on the same road as him. Found it right puzzling, so he did. Unfortunately, he didn't have no time to ask.

See, as soon as he was in the door, well, all the castle servants they started to help him off with his armour, to make him comfy like all the rest of the knights, only unlike all the rest of the knights Jack didn't have no coloured tunic with no heraldry, neither a beast as you'd find in farmyard nor fancy. All's Jack had was that patchwork suit of rags what he still wore under his armour. So when all the other knights saw this, oh, how they laughed. A knight of naught, they jeered. A jester dressed as jouster!

Well now, Jack, he was all for taking them all on, right then and there, cause it weren't the first time he'd faced foolish odds; besides, they couldn't do much worse to him than had been done already, and by nobs such as them no less. But just as he was about to take a pop at the nearest twat of a toff, out comes the hooded man. If you wish my blessing, says he, my bread and my bed, you'll treat this fool as your peer, for he's your equal in my eyes. What shuts them up right proper.

In which our hero discovers the reality of monsters

So, seeing as there's a few hours to spare before it's time for grub, Jack stashes his kit in the room what's set aside for him and goes for a little gander round the castle, giving the place a quick shufty, like, just to see if any of the knights have got some trinkets of treasure they might not miss. He's listening at doors to check if there's anyone inside, peeking through keyholes and cracks. But blimey if mostly what he finds ain't trinkets but tittle-tattle, not treasure but talk of it, of gold and glory, fame and fortune.

It's off to war they are, you see, to conquer the far-away Holy Land, where they're aiming to win all the riches and renown a knight could ever dream of. As Jack goes from room to room, he patches it together from the scraps of what he hears. Oh, they'll be bringing back all the jewels of all the Jews in Jerusalem, they says, all the precious artefacts of all the Arab princes in all the palaces of Antioch. Not to mention the lands the Pope and the Emperor will give em all when they get back, of course.

But there's more. Some of em, they gets to talking about what they've won already on the way. This one's bragging about a village of Jews they raided, how they found golden candlesticks and all sorts there, though not as much coin as they'd hoped. That one's bragging about a camp of gypsies they raided, how they found nothing much there at all, but at least they got rid of the vermin. And both is bragging, natch, of how they took all the children to work on their own lands, cause everyone knows how Jews and gypsies steal children, eh?

See, that's just like what happened to you, scamps. Some of you might have heard the tales before you was nabbed, eh? Of how the Waiftaker General preys on the poor and miserable, them what can't defend themselves cause they ain't got nothing to defend with. Some of you might have heard the fucking lies spread by gobshite groanhuffs, of how it's tother way about, how it's Jews and gypsies as steal kids, but that weren't never true, *never*. These nippers was stole, they'll say, but that's just so's they can whip you away and make you work their lands.

In which our hero is mostly interested in the food

Now, being a Scruffian at heart, even if he ain't Fixed yet, for all that Jack fancies this gold and glory malarkey — cause it sounds like a right adventure and he ain't got nothing against a little thieving — Jack don't think much of this knighthood shite no more. Why, these knights is the fucking dragon, he thinks, eating men, burning houses, smashing caravans, stealing children. And since he's just a scallywag himself — lanky-limbed and with balls and voice both dropped, but still with plenty growing to do — the thought of em stealing children for slaves is worst of all.

He don't have no time to reckon how a scallywag knight might slay this sort of dragon though, as just then there's the clang of an almighty gong, calling em all to grub in the great hall. And all the knights are pouring out of their rooms, all greedy for their free nosh and dragging Jack along with them. Still, as he takes his seat, Jack looks around at the faces of all these nobs, and he thinks to himself, You're going down, mister. He don't say nothing though; grub's up and an empty stomach always comes first, don't it?

Now, by fuck if it isn't the finest feast our Jack has ever had. There's roast beef and roast chicken and roast every meat you can think of. There's bangers and mash, dumplings and gravy, pies and pease pudding, muffins and marmalade. Oh, it's a feast even finer than what we had tonight, scamps, in celebration of your liberation, of *our* liberation, and in remembrance of all Scruffians still enslaved. But just as this story's what matters most tonight, that feast were only the start of it. Cause when they're all done stuffing themselves the hooded man stands, he does.

And then it begins. And in comes men in aprons with trouser-legs rolled up, altar boys in cassocks with incense in censers, maidens in white robes with baskets of flowers, old men in sackcloth with oil lamps and staffs, women in scarlet and purple on cows. And there's pages with red velvet cushions with crowns on them, bells on them, old leather books and red candles and swords on them. There's a bleeding lance and everything. And finally, one littl'un, a scamp no bigger than you there, comes in with a cushion as ain't got *nothing* on it, *nothing*.

In which our hero sticks his big foot in it, don't he?

Leastways, it *looks* like nothing to Jack. Cause back in them days, so they says, the Stamp didn't always look like it does now, didn't *always* look like anything. That's right, the thing they pressed on you in the Institute, the thing they Fixed you with, made you Scruffians. Yeah, it does hurt, don't it? But don't you worry; ain't no one going to do that to you again, not ever. Wouldn't work a second time anyways. Point is, you all saw it as it looks now, how groanhuffs have all *agreed* on it looking, but back in them days...

Back in them days, there was some as saw it as it looks now, but there was some as saw it different. So some of the knights in that room, they looked at that cushion and they saw a cup, whiles others saw a bowl. Some saw a boulder as big as a scofflaw's bonce, whiles others saw a pebble as puny as a scamp's pinky finger. Some saw a man's head, its eyes staring back at them, whiles others saw a hand with flames aflicker on its fingertips. Only Jack looks at it and says, There ain't nothing there!

Well, this causes a right uproar in the hall. Why, this is the holiest of holies, says the knights. This is eternal life itself, they say. This is the Kingdom and the Power and the Glory, forever and ever and ever amen! See, if nobs is only knights cause they nabbed their armour off a dead man, they does have ceremonies and secrets so's to make themselves feel important. And Jack, he'd just fingered himself as not being a bona fide member of the Secret Order of Arsewipes. This scruffy ruffian don't belong, they shouts. He don't belong, this…*scruffian!*

They seized hold of Jack then, snarling and roaring, What shall we do with him? What shall we do? Leave him be, shouts the hooded man, but this time they wasn't listening. Some fisher of men you are, snarls they. Your catch is worthless, a sprat of a jack! Let's gut him and grill him or chuck him back! But fie, says one, there's a war to be won, and this little fish, this poor widow's son, there are more in the sea. We could take, as a fee, just a few of these foes to serve under our thumbs.

In which our hero becomes a Scruffian proper

Well now, Jack, he didn't have a clue what the fuck this nob was on about. Tell the truth, most of the other nobs didn't neither, but they knew enough as he could explain it to them. Jack, he stayed just as scared and confused as you scamps must've been, I imagine, when the Waiftaker General and his stickmen took you from your homes and hovels, from the streets of the slums, wherever you was before, and carted you off to the Institute. All's Jack knew was they was gonna do something to him, and to more if it worked.

All's Jack knew was it meant them holding him so tight he couldn't escape, though he fought like a hellion, kicking and biting. All's he knew was it meant them ripping open his suit of rags to bare his chest, though he screamed and shouted for them not to. All's he knew was it meant them taking this *thing* what he could see now — and there's some as say how Jack saw it in that moment is how the Stamp's looked ever since — and pressing it to his heart, once, twice. All's he knew was it hurt so, so much.

And after it was done, after the Fixing, it hurt some more, cause that's when the testing begun. You remember em cutting you on the hand after you was Fixed, scamps? Well, that's what that was, a testing, to make sure they'd Fixed you proper, that you went right back to the way you was, the way you'll always be from now on, less you gets Scrubbed. Course, the Stamp always works, so they don't really need to do the testing. But it's *tradition*, innit? And see, they tested Jack too, only they done him more thorough. Lots more thorough.

See, that thing they used on you, that thing we calls the Stamp—though there's lots of different names for it — it makes you stay the same forever and ever. It's like painting over a drawing made in chalk so's it can't be wiped away and something new drawn in its place. Them nobs was all crazy, calling it eternal life itself because of that, and that's mostly true. You can stab us or burn us, even starve us or smother us, but unless someone carves up that strange mark it give you on the chest, you don't die. Never.

In which our hero escapes a fate worse than death

That's a good question, scamp. That's exactly what Jack asked himself as he huddled in the dungeon that they threw him in, wondering at how such terrible wounds as they'd given him healed so fast, wondering at how such mortal wounds as they'd given him healed *at all*, wondering *why* they'd done this to him. He didn't have no certain answers, but he'd an inkling as how the *more* they was planning to do this to was all the children them nobs had taken away to work their fields. Cause a slave who can't starve is a cheap slave, see?

There was more to it, he reckoned, the way those nobs was talking, but he couldn't figure it then, he was so miserable, wishing it'd all go away. But the funny thing is it *did* start to go away, that misery. He was going back to how he was Fixed, see, and Jack was Fixed fighting, defiant. I can see by the anger burning in your eyes as some of you was Fixed like Jack. But those of you Fixed in fear, don't you fret; I was Fixed like you and I ain't feared now, am I? We has tricks.

Anyways, there's Jack sitting in the dungeon, trying to plot himself a plan for escaping the lair of this awful dragon with knight's shields for its scales, the castle of this terrible giant of the high and mighty nobility, this *monster* what has far more than a hundred hands and a hundred heads. And what does he hear whiles he's sitting there but footsteps, the hobble of someone moving slowly and unsteadily, as if every step's painful. Jack don't say nothing, just waits, as they get closer. There's a clatter, a creak, a clunk of a key in a lock.

Jack still don't do nothing as he listens to those same footsteps moving away. He's suspicious as fuck now, is Jack. He ain't trusting nobody no more, and rightly so. But after a while he gets up and he tries the door, and it swings open. The corridor is empty, no guards or nothing, so he sneaks his way down it, quiet as a cat. The stairs is empty too. Why, there's not a soul in sight all the way from the dungeon up through the great hall itself and out to the drawbridge. Where his horse and armour's waiting.

IN WHICH OUR HERO ADJUSTS TO HIS NEW CIRCUMSTANCES

He rides away from that place like the clappers, does Jack. He rides as fast as his horse will carry him, cause he's a Scruffian now, and the first thing every Scruffian learns is simple: if you don't like it, leg it. Don't stop and think yourself in knots as to whether it's as bad as it looks. Don't get daft ideas about fighting when the odds ain't in your favour. If you don't like it, leg it. You take that lesson to heart, scamps, cause if the Waiftaker General catches a Scruffian what's escaped, that Scruffian's for a Scrubbing.

Now there's a whole yard of yarns as long as the tallest scofflaw's arm of all the adventures had by Jack the Scruffian Knight. Oh, they's much happier tales than this one, and some of em'll have you howling and hooting at his highjinks. There's many a nob got his comeuppance at our hero's hand from that day on. Even the groanhuffs knows some of those tales in near enough their proper telling, though they calls him Jack the Giant-Killer without knowing just what kind of giants is meant. But this here tale ain't quite done yet.

See, after a while, Jack's inkling of the nobs' plans become a bit more than inkling. He'd go from town to town, sometimes in his patchwork armour, nabbed from all the nobs he'd seen to, sometimes in his patchwork suit, stitched together now from all the scraps he'd sliced from bright tunics as a trophy. He'd hear tales in these towns, gobshite groanhuffs blaming Jews and gypsies for stealing children. And worse, tales of strangers who'd come to town talking noble tosh. A Crusade, says they, with children as its vanguard, for who'd raise a sword against an innocent child?

Sometimes he'd get there early enough, and he'd sneak the children away, hide em in a cave while the waiftakers were about, bring em back when they'd gone. But all too often he'd arrive too late, with all too many children already gone to be Fixed, willingly too. So, one day, Jack set off to return to the Chapel Perilous, to where it had all begun. He rode through the waste land, the forest of ash and field of blood, to the poisoned lake, where the hooded man still fished. And Jack roared his defiant challenge. And the Fisher King wept.

In which our hero hears a tale grim as his own

That Fisher King had been a preacher once, see, in a faraway land, a long time before. He'd stood up for waifs and strays, folks like you scamps. He'd gotten followers, though they weren't half as smart as he was and didn't *listen* properly, heard his sermons and thought of swords and shekels. Still, he went on, telling folks as how paupers and prossies weren't actually the scum of the earth, until the nobs of then nailed him to a cross, stuck a spear in his side and left him to die, for sedition. Except his followers Fixed him.

See, they thought they was clever, thought the Stamp wouldn't just *Fix* him like you Fixes a Scruffian but *fix* him like you fixes a torn trouser-leg, thought all his wounds'd heal up and he'd be right as rain. Only that ain't how the Stamp works, is it? No, it just Fixed him exactly as he were, wounds and all. And they'd waited till he seemed dead to sneak him down from the cross. So, awfulest of all, they Fixed him how he felt in the depths of his soul when he really thought he was a goner...*abandoned.*

That were the worst of it. That Fisher King, he weren't a bad man. It weren't his idea to Fix all the children and send em off to be chopped up on the front line, to put the fear of God into the Muslims when these scamps, scrags and scallywags all starts clambering back up to their feet, marching on. It weren't his idea, once they was all Fixed and on the boats, that one as just sold em for slaves could make a fortune without fighting at all. He tried to stop em, even. Really. But he were...broken.

As broken as he was Fixed, Fixed in a way what was broken, for all's he had the Stamp in his castle, he didn't have no control over it. All's he had was servants and ceremonies, and his word of what'd happen if the Stamp was used wrong. All's he had was the wisdom he'd got from his sorrow and pain, and all of that wasted cause he couldn't do nothing himself and his followers didn't listen. And them nobs weren't going to listen to no cripple. When they come and took the Stamp all's he could do was watch.

In which our hero sets out on the real adventure

You're not wrong there, scamp. It *is* a horrible story, but it's pretty much the truth of it, as best we know, told as we tells it to scamps on all such nights, when they just been sprung and they needs to know what we sprung em from.

Cause it ain't like *they* told you fuck all, is it? When they snatched you off the streets or when they had you in the cages? When they brung you out of em for the Fixing or chucked you back in em, to huddle there shivering, waiting to be bought and sold?

It *is* a horrible story, but you got to understand that it's a *beginning* story, see? It's a story of the first Institute for your first night *free* of it, a story of how Jack become a Scruffian but weren't *never* a slave, how he had a whole life of adventures even before he was a Scruffian, and being a Scruffian didn't change him one bit. No, he stayed exactly as he was, a rogue in rags. It weren't an ending; he didn't stop being Jack. Why, he went on to be one of the greatest Scruffians as ever lived.

He couldn't stop the Children's Crusade, see, cause the nobs had taken the Stamp from Chapel Perilous, spirited it away into hiding, under lock and key, guarding it with their lives ever since, using it to this day on the likes of you and me, fixing to make us slaves to toil in their fields or factories. He couldn't stop em stealing children from the poor and unfortunate, making Scruffian after Scruffian after Scruffian. But it were Jack as began the struggle, riding out of Chapel Perilous that day, bent on liberating every last Scruffian — scamp, scrag, scallywag or scofflaw.

Those of you what was Fixed as Jack, I see that gleam of defiance in your eyes. And those of you what was Fixed as me, so frightened you even messed yourself, maybe? Still feeling that way too, ashamed even, thinking it's your fault? Well, we has tricks, I says, right? And it was Jack as discovered em, putting a little nick in his Stamp for every Scruffian he saved. Changes the Stamp see, like stitching a whole new bright coloured patch into a suit of rags. We can patch you up, scamps. You won't never fear them fuckers again.

The Disappearance of James H‑‑‑

The New Boy

There is a new boy at the school. He sits at the desk where Brown once sat and carved his name in the wood with a pocket-knife's point, and was caned for it; but he is not Brown. He is green. His eyes flash emerald and jade, the colour of gemstones and jungles, foreign seas and forest serpents. He sits where Brown used to sit but the teacher does not notice, nor order him to read from Homer, snap his name as he gazes out the window. As he turns to look at me, languid, smiling in his sly silence.

A Fob Watch

We watch the fifth formers standing in the cloisters, all tall enough to wear tailcoats, dandies in their top hats, thin cigars in their mouths. I have studied their stance, perfected the slouch — with both knees bent a little and one shoulder slightly higher than the other, one hand jammed into a pocket. But I still need my fob watch to strike that pose, to be *fetching it out to check the time*, not simply, self-assuredly louche. So Scottish in my reserve.

— Why do you want to be like them? he says.

— I do not want to be like Brown.

He takes off the starched collar and the bum-freezer jacket, unbuttons his shirt. In his white breeches and shirt open to the waist but still tucked in, he looks like some prince kidnapped by pirates to serve as cabinboy, or some pauper taken in by a kind doctor, scrubbed clean to wear a lost son's clothes. Half-dressed he seems half-costumed. An actor changing between scenes. His nightshirt lies on the bed, long flowing white as if he is to play Juliet. But it is my cheeks that are blushed and virginal. He removes the shirt. The breeches. His undershorts.

Never Never

—Shall I play the pipes for you, James? he asks. Shall I play a hornpipe that'll make you jig?

The others lie asleep in their dormitory beds while I sit on the edge of mine, watching him in the moonlight, the way it throws the shadow of his cock's-comb shock of hair on the wall behind him, spikes on either side like horns. In the shadow his peter rises to his jutting chin, cocky with his cocked head, cocked hip. I want…

— Come with me, he says quietly.

— I can't, I say.

— Come with me.

— Never, I say. Never never.

A Roasting

—What happened to Brown? he asks.

I look at the empty bed where Brown lay sobbing from the pain and humiliation after Flashman was done.

— Flashman gave him a roasting, I say.

I picture them holding Brown to the roaring fire, turning him, laughing. But that is not how it happened, not how it happened to me. I picture them stripping him, spit-roasting him between them, fingers twisted in his hair, holding his head down, fingernails digging into his hips. That is what the fifth form do here, why Flashman left in disgrace.

— How savage, he says. How truly beastly.

A Crocodile Tear

He lies on top of the bed, on top of the empty nightshirt, knees curled up to his chin, arms wrapped around them. His eyes glint green even in the moonlight. He does not sleep, does not close his eyes and sleep, only bats his lashes slowly closed and open again, once, twice. It seems a considered, reptilian action, as inscrutable as the tear that trickles down his cheek. A crocodile tear.

His shadow rises on the wall behind him, pads across the floor to my bed. I pull the covers back, and the darkness climbs in to my embrace.

Morning Will Not Find Us

—Let me help you sleep, the shadow says. It is only when you sleep that we can disappear into your dreams.

His shadow curls to fit my form. I feel its breath on the back of my neck, its arms wrapped round my ribs, one hand over my heart, the other sliding down into black, curly hair. I feel safe with his shadow as my cloak, pressed into me so close, so tight, it seems within rather than around me.

— But in the morning… I say.

— Morning will not find us here, it says. We must go looking for it.

Lush Green Vines

We sail on oceans uncharted, gliding through the night by constellations we invent. We hunt the morning, the rising sun, but for him it is the morning of yesterday, I think, of youth, for me the morning of tomorrow…*tomorrow*. We hunt it as something we desire and fear. The dawn we find is a beach of azure sky above, golden sand beneath us, flesh hard between us, edged by lush green vines and veins. I kiss —

— I'm not like that, he says. I'm not a…

Fairy?

— Every time you say that, I whisper, a little part of you will die.

Lions and Tigers and Bears

Adventurers on this island, we explore its reaches and its recesses. We glimpse beasts in the forest, in ourselves — the pride of lions, the camouflage of hidden tigers, and the vicious, swinging hook of a bear claw — but he laughs at them all. I strut in the frock coat and tricorn hat his shadow has become for me. He crows like a cockerel in the green rags of my lust, legs spread wide, hands on his hips, up on a rock. A statue on a pedestal. He darts from my grasp, teasing.

I brood. Will he play games with me forever?

The Lost Boys

—Come with me, I say.

My hand reaches out for him, to wipe the tear that is always on his cheek but which only I ever see, to grasp the smooth skin of his shoulder with gentle strength. To hold him so he knows that we are both lost, with each other. To possess, to do unspeakable things to his flesh.

— Never, he screams. Never never.

His blade flashes a wide, panicked arc through air, through skin and bone. I fall to my knees, clutching a bloody stump.

It is the hook in my heart however which hurts the most.

The Island of the Pirate Gods

Black leather boots a-smoke with powder-burns from the big gun of my beloved *Pride of Kentigern*, I hurtle through the rain, a human cannonball, balloon-sleeves of my pink silk shirt frilling in the wind as, arms a-flap like a panicked duck, I do my best to come out of the head-over-heels tumble, screaming a prayer out to the pirate gods in the hope that I won't hit the foremast of the *Determination* with a head only as thick as iron in the sense of witlessness and obstinacy.

— Fuuuuuuuuuuuuuck!, I scream.

It's not a prayer as any man of the cloth would be proud of, I grant you, but to my renegade deities, Matelotage and Mutiny, it's the sentiment that matters, not the subtlety; and bless them if they don't look out for their beloved son.

As I reach the zenith of my trajectory, I straighten out face-forward, find myself in an arc that should take me nicely past the *Determination*'s foremast and towards the rather softer target of the main topgallant. Or at least towards where the main topgallant would be if the bloody bastards weren't furling it for the storm.

My prayer becomes a chant as I hurtle through the air.

— Fuck fuck fuckety fuck fuck fuckety fu —

¿Qué? Sat on the railing of the crow's nest, I notice, dangling his legs as casual as can be, a peachy young lad in stripy top and knee-length breeches is stirring the contents of a china tea-cup with one finger. I could swear the saucy bugger winks at me, before I blink and he's gone.

An almighty crack of lightning shatters my curiosity as it shatters the air, forks blasting all three masts of the ship simultaneously, shattering the mainmast and bringing the tip of it down in a mess of splintering timber, burning canvas and whiplashing ropes. My trajectory suddenly acquires a lateral dimension as the twisting topple of mast and rigging nabs me neat as a ball in a lacrosse racket. I catch glimpses as I swing down, sailors on deck, waves crashing over the port side, jibs flapping loose from the foremast where the *Pride of Kentigern's* cannon have blown the bowsprit to bits. Serves you sodding right, I think, as the arc of the tangle brings me round, upside-down and facing back the way I came at the burning wreck of my beautiful brig, almost swallowed now by the tempestuous ocean.

They sank my favourite ship, the bastards.

—One little cannonball, I yell down my outrage as more ropes give and I swing back over the deck, where Black Joey staggers through the carnage, hauling sailors to their feet, hacking ropes, pointing this way and that. He stops suddenly, looks up directly at me, pulling off his black leather tricorn and shaking rain from his eyes and his dreadlocks. Gaze as black as his skin and his skirted coat, even from here I can see the hatred in his deadlights.

— It was only meant to be a warning shot, I shout.

There's fury on his face as he pulls his flintlock out, tries to hold aim on me against the yaw and pitch of his ship. Bollocks. And I can't even reach me own twin pistols, caught in the rigging as I am like Saint Ahab on the whale. The boat lurches wildly to starboard and I hear the whine of his shot; then we lurch to port, and Black Joey reels, turns to curse the pilot.

— Hold her steady, you scabrous…what the…?

Up on the poop deck, the saucy sprite from the crow's nest is whirling the wheel this way and that with gay abandon. Actually, it's the fact that he's doing so with his monkey-tail that's truly queer. Again, though, there's not much time for curiosity as the boat jolts hard as a horse-hoof in the head. There's a scream of splintering wood — a reef, I reckon — and then a lightning crack hits what's left of the mainmast, courses down to the deck (tingling my tongue with a nutty taste), and sends a searching spear right down into the hold. Big hairy bollocks, I think, as the powder magazine of the *Determination* blows the whole ship apart.

Articles and Arcana

—What does the Book say? whispers Twinklenose.

  — Is these betrayers? hisses Dustbunny.

  — Perfidious brothers? glitters Tiffin.

  — Pompous dukes? whooshes Buttersick.

  — Misguided kings? thumps Tatters.

  — We haven't done a king in ages!

  — Or a duke.

  — Feh! Dukes are *duuuuullllllll*.

  — I like dukes. They get really cross when you —

  — Hush up! I say. I'm trying to read.

The other sprites continue with their chitter of chat, so I roar — fierce as a lion, if I do say so myself — shaking the leaves and fronds of the trees, and sending the pesterers skitter-scatter off through the branches. Hunkered on my perch, looking down on the bedraggled pair unconscious on the beach below, their hands still wrapped around each others' throats, I empty my teacup with a slurp, note the arrowed heart-shape in the leaves before I toss the teacup over my shoulder for Dustbunny to catch, and turn back to the Book.

Not that the Book is much use, most of the pages being stuck together or rotted to unreadability by its time however many fathoms deep. And I was never much of a one for letters anyway, in truth. No matter how hard His Nibs tried to teach me, I'd rather make up my own sounds for the pretty symbols. I mean, *Q*, for instance — that's the drooly gurgle of a mouth open, tongue out to one side, right? *D* is a yawn. *Y* is the hiss of a snake's tongue flicking. It's *obvious*. Not that His Nibs ever saw it that way

  — My tricksy sprite, thine ear shall cuffèd be, he'd say, if thou dost not attention pay to me.

  — *P*, I'd say in response, *P* being a big fat raspberry blown with a sullen glare.

So what with the water-damage and my literacy issues, the Book's oracular powers aren't always much cop. But the others do expect.

  — It says they're mortal enemies, I proclaim highly, damned by Davy Jones to hunt each other across the high seas until the end of time!

Which gets a few appreciative *ooooohs*.

The pink-faced one with the yellow hair and the human cannonball act groans and stirs, so I tuck the Book under my arm, pick a coconut — not *too* big — and drop it on his head. Can't have him waking up and wandering off when we haven't even started to plan his Redemption.

It's been a while since we had a good Redemption, you know. Since His Nibs buggered off back to Italy, all we've had is a couple of dukes, the odd king and a whole bunch of merchants. Do you know how hard it is to Redeem a merchant? Wreck their ship and they're more worried about their precious cargoes than getting home. Offer them a banquet and they complain about the vintage of the wine. Give them the harpy act and they want to catch you, cage you, take you home to impress the hoity-toity. Show them cloud-capped towers and gorgeous palaces…all they want to know is, *How much did the builders charge?* I tell you, try and make someone have a change of heart when they don't have one; it's not easy.

Still…it gives us something to do. After the squillionth time you've heard Tiffin murder "Juno Sings Her Blessings On You" in front of an audience of monkeys, even a tobacco-ship on the horizon is a blessing.

—I found something! I found something!

Buttersick bounces through the canopy towards me in a series of tumbles and flutters somewhere between a squirrel and a butterfly, catching branches with his tail, catching air with his wings. He lands on a branch just over my head and rolls down to hang like a bat by his feet, gloating imp-grin in my face. He flaps a scrap of parchment in one hand, rather raggedy-looking to my mind, babbling about how he found it on the beach amongst the driftwood *and the drownded, and what does it say, what does it say?* The others flip and flit nearer until I'm surrounded by a score of popping eyes and perky ears.

I take the parchment from Buttersick and turn it a few times, furrowing my brows till it resolves into a series of yawns, raspberries, squeaks and giggles and whatnot. As I read it out, translating into human-talk in my head, my audience nods vigourously…where they're not picking their noses, scratching their arses or elbow-fencing.

— It's a set of rules, I say…

— What are *rules*? says Mugwump.

-…for who gets what when a ship gets caught, I say. And how hostages are not to be moles…moles' teeth.

— You mean *molested*? Buttersick says. That would make more sense.

— They're by some Greek guy, I carry on. Artikles.

— *Articles!* says Buttersick. They're *pirates.*

All heads turn to the unconscious pair below. The black-skinned one is stirring now — he sees the other and gives a growl — so I pinch Buttersick's toes and redirect him with a little shove as he falls past, to land square on the man's head, noggin to noggin.

— Smart-arse, I say.

Then I pull the Book out from under my arm and open it at *P* for *Pirate*. Or *P* for *Plan*. Or *P* for *Prospero*-went-away-and-left-us-here-and-it-seemed-great-at-the-time-but-now-there's-fuck-all-to-do-on-this-island-and-I'm-*booooooored*. Anyhoo…

J…K…L…M…

Aha!

Matelotage and Mutiny (Part I)

—Arrrr, says he, fixing me with his deadlights. The story of Matelotage and Mutiny is it yer after? The story of the Pirate Gods?

He leans in close, breath stinking of rum and rot, grins at my keen nod.

— See now, he says, they was mortals once, lovers, so the story goes, two ensigns on a merchant ship of His Majesty's Royal Navy, who swore an oath to be together forever. Loved each other so much, they did, they shared their rum rations, their goods, the very shirts on their backs, even put their wages together and bought themselves a pair of flintlocks, one for each of them and each engraved with his lover's name, worn loaded tucked into the belt at the front where it isn't smart-like, savvy? On account of the potential for accidents.

I glance down at the twin-flintlocks tucked into me own belt. He has a point, I'm sure, but then POTENTIAL FOR ACCIDENTS is on me calling card, right under FLASH JACK CARTER, FREELANCE PRIVATEER. He winks and carries on:

— *If I ever as much as look at another,* says one — he says, waving a hand — *man or woman, let me balls be blown off.* And, *Why sure, if that ever happens,* says the other, *I'll be doing the same, cause if my balls don't keep ye faithful, they're no use to me anyways.*

He slugs back some grog, points the tankard at me.

— They laughed about it, he says, oh yes, but they meant it true as the North Star, mind. They meant it.

—Only this was the Royal Navy, he says, savvy, and the British they don't smile upon two sailors getting too…familiar, like. Oh, sure, it happens like as not, now and then, on those long voyages where the only female company is the sea, the ship, and the Captain's Daughter. But it's not approved of, officially.

I nod, knowing that form of unfraternal officialdom all too well, and the Captain's Daughter's too. She's the only girl I ever got truly intimate with, mate, and I can't say we was suited. But I try not to dwell on her not-so-delicate touch.

— Now the rest of the crew, he says, as they came to see how these two were sweethearts, they just said: Well, each to their own, matey. And doesn't it sort of warm yer cockles, anyways? Aren't these lads just like two pieces of rope tied together, a little work of matelotage made by an idle sailor to pass the time at sea? And what's the harm in that? So after a whiles it came to be that others on board found themselves…inspired…thinking similar thoughts about a mate of theirs, and blimey if they didn't decide they wanted to *tie the knot* too, so to speak. Which is how, of course, the marriage of man and man came to be known as matelotage, and a grand tradition it is too.

—But the captain of that ship, he was a cruel man with a leathery Bible in place of his heart, and when he got wind of this queer love aboard his ship, well, one day he bursts in on our lusty lads and interruptus their coitus, he does. They try to explain theirselves, to say that they're bound together in true love but, O, he just glowers dark as the deep at them. *If that's the way ye want it,* says he, *well, so be it.*

I lean forward in my chair till the pistols press into me waist, keen as a cock in a Tortuga brothel.

— So he has the lads trussed up together — still naked, by the by — and keel-hauled, dragged under the ship's hull, to have their skin ripped to ribbons by the barnacles.

The old salt slugs back more rum, lays down the tankard.

— And that should be where the story ends, he says, by all that's *righteous* and *decent* and *godfearing.* But 'tis not. For if 'twas, why then, 'twould be the story of Matelotage and Murder, not the story of Matelotage and Mutiny.

Plots and Pageants

—All right. I was wrong before. They're not enemies. They're lovers, thrown to the cruel sea by an even crueller captain, doomed to —

— They don't *loooook* like lovers.

— They're in a loving embrace.

— Looks more like they're trying to strangle each —

— The Book says they're lovers, so that's what they are.

— But does it actually *say* they're lovers?

— Well, not *literally*. But you have to read between the lines.

— But there's no words between the lines. If there were words *between* the lines, then they'd actually *be* lines, wouldn't they?

— You're not looking closely enough. See here? No, right *here*.

— I still don't see — Ow!

—Right, then. Since they're *lovers* we have to separate them. We have to give them Trials and Tribulations, a Terrible Ordeal and a Tearful Reunion and —

— And a pageant at the end?

— Ooh, yes, let's have a pageant!

— We could all dress up as goddesses, and sing blessings on them!

— *Bounteous* blessings!

— I could be Juno. I do an *excellent* Juno.

— An excrement Juno, more like.

— *His Nibs* used to like it.

— *His Nibs* was tone-deaf. He…

…

— What?

—As. I. Was. Saying. A Tearful Reunion and a Happy Ever After.

— And a —

— And *maybe* a pageant. But first we have to separate them. Twinklenose, Buttersick, Handshandy, you take the one with the hat up to Pointy Point and do the old twiddly flute music in the woods thing, lead him back down here via the bears.

— Won't that be a bit…dangerous?

— It's not a Tribulation if it's not dangerous.

— But what if one of the bears tries to eat us?

— The bears won't try to eat you.

— They ate Honeyarse.

— He shouldn't have mooned them.

—Mugwump, Tatters, you go set out a banquet in the Otherwise-Boring Clearing. Suckling pig, roast chicken, fruit-baskets, lots of grog, the usual.

— Should I make little swans from the napkins?

— Let's not. I nearly lost my tail last time.

— But swans are pretty.

— Geese with grandiose delusions, they are, and a badger's temper.

— She was just protecting her cygnets.

— No swan napkins. Right? Good, go on, then. Scoot.

— Ariel?

— What?

— Are you *sure* they're lovers, thrown to the cruel sea by an even crueller captain? The black one seemed awful angry at the other.

— Well, maybe they had a tiff.

DEADLIGHTS AND DREADLOCKS

Black Joey opens his eyes to find himself staring up at the blue sky and the noonday sun, with solid ground under his back and soft grass between his fingers. Gulls wheel overhead, but the sound of the ocean is too distant, quiet enough he could swear he hears whispers and hisses over it — then a sudden rustle of brush that brings him bolt upright and looking over his shoulder, hand reaching for his sword as he scrambles to his feet. But the underbrush of the tree line settles and, peer as he might, he can see no shapes shift in the shadows. Curious.

He scans the full length of the trees that edge the clearing, north to south, turns to take the full compass-spin of his surroundings — and steps back in vertiginous alarm. He recovers his composure, shuffles forward for a tentative glance over the edge. Something queer is afoot. He has vague memories of a beach, of that cur Carter, but it's no more than a snatch of a blur; he can be sure that someone's playing games with him, though.

A man doesn't get washed ashore on the edge of a cliff with a hundred-foot drop down to the sea, no matter how high the bloody tempest's waves.

He crouches down to pick up his tricorn hat from the grass. His sword still in its scabbard, his frock coat still on his back, boots on his feet, his hat left at his side, he finds it hard to fathom the purpose of whoever brought him here, but Black Joey's not one to worry over such trifles. He has his own purpose to worry about, and the stories of this isle involve all manner of strangeness anyway: some say it gives you all you desire, others that it gives you all you fear; some say it's an island of savage demons, others that it's an island of innocent spirits. These are the tales of white men, of course, Christians and cowards. Black Joey's all too familiar with the fears and desires they project on anything that's…other.

In the pocket of his frock coat, Joey finds the spyglass still intact, puts it to his eye and scours the forest as it rolls up into the hills, looking for some sign of the object of his quest. He almost misses the crumbling dome – the overgrown remnants of what looks a little like a Spanish Colonial church but more fussy, more decorative – but *almost* is the watchword; his deadlights keen as a crow's in the nest, he spots it even with the stone nigh drowned in vines. Looks derelict. That's a little disconcerting, true, but perhaps the new master of the island has less taste for pompous grandeur. By all accounts, the Good King of this isle is a much simpler soul than its previous sovereign. So with only a little grin of grim satisfaction, and a shake of his dreadlocks before he sets the tricorn on his head, Black Joey sets out through the jungle towards Prospero's Cell, towards a treasure more precious than anything that scurvy dog, Flash Jack, can dream of, wherever he may be, aye, even now, no doubt, fixing his eyes on the same sight but with the glint of gold or glory blinding them, as dedicated to his greed as Joey is to his own goal: freedom.

GUNPOWDER AND GROG

—Cry, Haul! Aye! A-diddle-aye-dee!

The map is dried out nicely now and it's not too water-damaged, so I'm in good spirits as I roll it up and tuck it back into its case, then crouch to pour the sea and sand out of me sodden boots, in time with the dainty lyrics of me favourite shanty, "Matelotage and Mutiny":

– But a cold and angry captain with a Bible for his heart, *Cry, Haul! Aye! A-diddle-aye-dee!*

I wring me pink silk shirt out and flap it a few times at arms length, hook it on a twig.

– Knew naught of what his crewmen did beneath the shining stars. *Cry, Haul! Aye! A-diddle-aye-dee!*

Breeches draped delicately over a branch.

– Until one night, he saw a sight that stripped his anger bare. *Cry, Haul! Aye! A-diddle-aye-dee!*

I shake like a dog in me scarlet doublet, still damp as all else and hardly what a parson would consider modest, considering it's the only thing I'm wearing now – but then modesty never was me strong point, in any sense of the word.

– 'Twas Tom with Jack upon his back, his legs up in the air!

I take a pinch of snuff from where the pouch lies open beside the fire, wrinkle me nose with the peppery sting.

—Cry, Haul! sings a choir-boy chorus. *Aye! A-tiddle-ee-aye-tee-tee!*

— It's *diddle-aye-dee*, I call, ye scurvy — then do a double-take on the treetops where the voice came from. And sneeze.

— Bless you, the voice calls down, sing-song and sweet like.

I dive and roll for me pistols, come out on one knee, both flintlocks pointed at the source. Seems a polite enough sprite, but I've heard tell of the terrors of the Island of the Pirate Gods, and I'm not keen to be coming back from here like Barbary Bill Burroughs…Father William as he is now. Not bloody likely, mate. I'll be redeemed by the rope and naught else, thank 'ee kindly.

— Now who in the buggery was that? I say. Friend or foe?

There's a rustle in the branches, a glimpse of glittering feathers blue-green as a peacock's tail. A flutish sound twiddles off to the left and I spin — a glint of giggling grin and eyes — pull the trigger. *Click.* Arse and bollocks, I think, and start fanning the gun-barrel with the tail of me doublet…like that'll dry the damp powder sure as hanging. The voice sings from the right now.

— Thy lover lies drowned on the watr'y rock. No more, no more, shall he kiss thy —

BOOM!

—Bloody sodding buggering sodden powder-purse, I curse, flapping my burnt hand. *'Tis watertight,* says he. *Guaranteed to six fathoms deep.* My arse!

I bend down to pick up the pistol where the misfire made me drop it, muttering to meself about a dark, dark fate awaiting Gibson the Gunsmith when next I berth in Tortuga.

— …and a pox…with pustules…and a red-hot poker for his…

The toot of the flute sounds a little ways back in the trees, followed by more laughter, and I gather meself with a scowl and a growl. Right then, ye bugger, I think. I'll not be made a fool of by some tree-hopping powder monkey as dresses like a whoring parrot. Still hunkered down, I reload old Mutiny, and slink forward into the trees, deadlights scouring the thickage for this tricksy taunter, following the song as it retreats into the forest until…by the pirate gods, but I find meself in a clearing amidst the strangest sight.

A feast fit for a score of kings in practice for the Most Corpulent King Contest lies laid out on a banquet table afore me, chicken and pork and beef and lamb and —

— Grog! I say.

I slap the pistols down on the table.

— I think I've come to re-assess our relationship, I call out to my peachy pest. 'Tis clear yer a…well…a *thing* of good heart and grand hospitality.

I salute the canopy with a pork chop.

Now they say the dreaded Blackbeard ties fuses in his hair. Well, by the fiery shock on me noggin, there's those as say I *am* a fuse, and a lit one at that. They call me the Scarlet Buccaneer, the Peach Mutineer, the Pink Privateer. By the pirate gods, I'm Flash Jack Carter, the original gay blade, and there's nothing I'm afraid of on land or sea (excepting lemurs, that is — little incident in Madagascar, involved a gypsy love-curse and a colony of ring-tails, but that's another story and ye don't want to know, mate, trust me).

So me point is, when, with me in the middle of stuffing me chops with chops, the harpy comes a-screeching down out of the thick of the tree-tops, I'll be insisting as it was entirely intentional, me falling over backwards, regardless of what anyone says. And *there was no shrieky-hand-flapping*, I tell ye, *none*. I will admit, however, to a little haste in grabbing for me pistol, Mutiny, to put a shot square in the heart of the feathery fiend swooping down upon me. I realise I might not have applied due care and attention when, instead of dropping out of the air with a thud and a twitch, the bloody thing comes to a dead stop and gets this queer look on its face as it flaps there, just looking me up and down, long and lingering enough for me to scramble to me feet. Then it starts coming at me twice as fast. I look at the name graved on the grip of the pistol in me hand.

— Bollocks, I say. Wrong bloody gun.

Matelotage and Mutiny (Part II)

The old salt shakes his head in that *'tis a terrible tale* sorta way.

— 'Tis a terrible tale, he says. But the long and the short of it is that one of the lads died that day and the other one lived, but no one could tell which was which when they brung them back aboard, on account of them both being in such a shredded state. And the one what lived, when they asked him what his name was, well, he just fixes his deadlights on the captain and laughs, tells him how he made a deal with Davy Jones, to swap his own soul for his lover's, dead in the sea where neither God nor Devil has dominion. The one died in the flesh, ye see, but his soul lived on in the other; and the other — well, his flesh survived, but his soul went down to Davy Jones's Locker, tied up tight in the corpse of his lover. Truly bound they are now, *forever*, half-living, half-dead and all mixed up in each other, so as their old names mean nothing.

—Well, the captain he gets a fear in him and decides its best to hang this madman, so they hoist our lad from the yardarm. Oh, but he doesn't die, our lad, for his lover's soul's bound tighter into his flesh than ever any man's *own* soul could be; it can never be sundered from his flesh. So he just hangs there calling strangled curses down upon the captain. Day after day, he hangs there, night after night, and damned if, after three days of this, the crew didn't rise up against that captain. For so many of them by then were matelotaged to each other that there was more salt on that ship shared between the saucy sailors than there is in the sea herself. A ship of love it was — a ship of fools, you might say — but either way it was a ship of lusty seamen that would brook no more of such brutality. So in the dead of night, the jack tars gathered and they cut our lad down from his rope. They gave him his flintlock and that of his lover, the twin flintlocks that they'd had each other's name engraved on.

 — *We'll follow you where'er ye lead,* they says to him, *for 'tis love we'll fight for from now on, not God or King.*

—Then, with one pistol in his left hand and one pistol in his right, he leads them down to the captain's quarters, and he kicks the door right open. The captain, he can't believe it. *What's this?* says he. O, but looking into our lads' eyes, he finds no answer but lost love and a thirst for revenge. He begs for his life as they drag him up to walk the plank. He begs for mercy, crying out in the names of those two lads so terribly punished. But those names hold no sway no more, so our man just pushes him out onto the plank.

 — *We're neither of us those lads,* says he. *Not any longer. If ye want to call us something,* says he, *if ye want to know whose death you're dying for and who it is that brings the vengeance down upon ye…read the names of us on these flintlocks.*

And as the moonlight glinted on the pistols in his hand, all those who were close enough to see, they saw that even the very names inscribed upon the pistols had changed.

 — *If it's names ye want, says he, ye can tell Davy Jones that it's the murder of my sweet Matelotage ye're paying for, and that the man who sent ye to him goes now by the name of Mutiny.*

He leans back in his chair.

 — That be the story of the Pirate Gods, the story of Matelotage and Mutiny, aye, the Pirate God of Love and the Pirate God of Death. There be more to it than that — there be the tale of Mutiny's long search for his lost love, of Matelotage's adventures in Hell, of how they came to be together again, raised the wreck of the *Argo*, and gathered a crew of all the heathen deities of yore – but that's for another night, me matey. What I'll leave ye with is this: From that day hence those pistols have turned up in many hands, for there's many who have given themselves over to Matelotage and Mutiny, to be their mortal champion. They say that nothing can stand against such a man, for the one gun – that marked Mutiny – deals instant death, but the other – the one marked Matelotage – deals instant love, like the very darts of Eros. And who, I ask ye, who can stand up to love?

He downs his rum and scrapes his chair back, pulls himself to his feet and staggers off towards the barkeep, calling for more grog. I put my tankard down on the table and reach for the smooth cold handles of the twin flintlocks tucked into my buckler, finger the gravings on the grips, carved deep as the scars on me chest.

Maybe one man, I think.

Slaves and Sanctuaries

The dainty air of the tune has been growing more shrill now, more insistent, for the last half-hour, following him off to his left like it's trying to draw him off his path, but Black Joey ignores it and hacks his way on through the foliage. Every so often the tune stops, replaced by mutters – *I'm doing my bloody best – well, you try, wormtail – I don't care if he heard me.* Joey pays no mind to the frustrated tricksters. It takes him a good couple of hours to cut his path but eventually he's there, standing before the overgrown ruin, the now-pathetic palace of the magician duke, Prospero, master of spirits, master of men. The Good King must have moved his base, Joey tries to tell himself, but the dereliction of shanty-town civilisation around tells another tale, one he doesn't want to hear. It's one he has to face though, he knows, so he walks through the abandoned settlement now being swallowed by the jungle, past the wooden board of a sign scrawled with the name of *Sanctuary*, to the rotten doors of the ruin at its heart.

The thing of darkness sitting in the shadowed throne is half mummy, half skeleton, flesh weathered to a thin leather stretched across the bone, naked but for the tattered remnants of a cloak which drape the corpse like royal robes, a pattern of white stars on dark blue still vaguely discernible here and there. For an orb and sceptre of sorts, each claw of a hand clutches a thick wooden stick, three feet long or so and splintered at the top; looking closer, Joey matches the angles, sees that these are two halves of a broken staff. He walks up to the cadaver and gently touches his fingertips to what's left of the nappy white hair and the bush of beard which gives this legend of a man dignity even in death. He looks down at the shrivelled genitals, turns to gaze around the hall all scrawled with chalk veves, choked with foliage.

King Caliban the Good, thinks Joey, who was no man's but his own in the end.

A black king in the West Indies, they'd said, a child saved from slavery in Algiers by his Yoruban witch-doctor mother, spirited away to an enchanted island in the Caribbean only to be captured and bound into servitude while just a boy by the white man who murdered his mother. Accused of attempted rape — oh, but it's always rape, of course — by the white man's spoiled daughter. But freed, finally, to live in peace on this forgotten island, now *his* island. A kingdom for us all, a kingdom called Sanctuary, they'd said, the other marooners, those slaves like Joey brought to the Americas to haul the gold of rich men into galleons, taught their tongues so they could take their orders. Those slaves who, like Joey, had slipped their shackles and found what freedom they could on the high seas.

Black Joey isn't one for hope, but he named his ship the *Determination* for a stubbornness as powerful as hope. He's no dreamer, so he came here willing to face whatever truth lay behind the legends. But even so a man's will, his resolve, can be a little like a hope or a dream…breakable by cruel reality. Standing there before the dead king of rebellious slaves, though, Black Joey's resolve is only strengthened.

So he kneels before the corpse of Caliban and kisses its feet. Then he turns, and with his sword begins to hack at the foliage and rotten wood of panelling and furniture. He goes out into the town and returns with more wood and kindling. Then he gathers the Good King's body in his arms and carries it gently to the pyre he's built, prises the broken staff from its rigor-mortis grasp and wraps tatters of starry cloth around one end of each length, to make of Prospero's staff, Caliban's sceptres, twin torches which he sparks to light with flint and just a little powder, fizzling into fire as bright as any magic. He lights the pyre and stands back, watching as the flames rise, swallowing the body where it rests, the signpost of Sanctuary for its pillow. He looks at the sigils inscribed on his blazing torches for a second, wonders what power rested within this wood when unbroken, then he tosses them on the pyre and he turns, walks out of the ruin of a little palace, smoke and ash billowing out behind him as the broken halves of Prospero's staff are reunited in the flames.

So the king is dead, the kingdom in ruins. That just means there's work to be done.

MAPS AND METAMORPHOSES

I button the breeches and tuck in me shirt, flip the doublet back on with a swish. One boot. The other. I buckle my belt, jam Matelotage and Mutiny into place. I'm not sure whether the imp's eyes are wider at me dressed up in all me finery than they were at the naked flesh.

— Are you a pirate? he says with more than a little awe.

— Now that's an unkind way of phrasing it, I say. I'm more — stop that!

I bat his hand from my doublet's tail and he skitters back, all abashed.

— I'm sorry, he says. It's just...your coat is pretty.

— Many thanks. I'm rather fond of it meself.

— Your hair is pretty too. It's orangey. I like oranges. Does it taste like oranges. Can I try?

I halt him with a hand on his forehead only to find the mad little moppet grab my wrist and pull it down to start an intense study of my fingers, fondling them like he's never seen a knuckle before. That's the drawback with the gun of Matelotage, ye know; used carelessly it can start more trouble than the other's ever ended. Oh, it's grand if yer shooting someone in the back while their dead-lights are on the bosun, say, a peachy little diversion, but if it's yerself is the first thing they see...well, as a hypothetical example, when they're seven foot tall and known as Scurvy Shug, 'tis best to be avoided. My besotted sprite pulls my pinky towards his mouth, tongue out, and I flap him away.

— For pity's sake, I say. Will ye give me peace?

— I'll give you *bliss*, he says. I'll give you flowers and...quinces and a puppy dog and...[he scrunches his face in a queerish peer]...*explosions*. You like explosions; I can tell.

He's a canny lad — and uncanny, for that matter — I have to give him that; but I'm thinking it might be a good idea to get my arse off this island sharpish, before the *See How Much I Love You?* phase moves into the *How Can You Not Love Me?* stage with its attendant desperate measures.

— I'll give you anything you want, he says. *Anything.*

I pull the map case out of me pocket and set about unscrewing the cap, sharpish.

—Now, look, lad, I say. No offence to ye intended, and it's not like I'm averse to a bit of the old Purser's Pleasure, but I just can't be having a relationship with anything what has a tail.

He looks crestfallen, but I just turn to hold the map up, take me bearings with the compass once more.

— Not again, I mutter distractedly.

He scurries to keep up as I stalk through the bush. Now that he's dropped the harpy glamour, he's a winsome sprite, I have to admit. The wings are rather fetching, sure, and even with the horns and green hair, the golden flower behind his ear makes him a picture of…salacious innocence. I can't say as I'm not tempted, but it's the tail, ye see, the tail…I mean, three months living on leaves and insects, with the Lemur Queen and her — no! I shake the cruel memories from me noggin.

— It just won't work, I say.

— Wait! he says. If it's just the tail…

He bends over to reach between his legs, brings his tail through — and I mean the root of it, the shifty nipper, right round to the front of him — then with a bit of tugging and twiddling he reshapes it into…well, something else entirely.

— That's quite impressive, I say.

— I'm very versatile, says he.

—So which of the gods are you, anyway? I say as he stands there, hands on hips, all cocky and looking more attractive by the second. Yer too young for Dionysus, I'd wager. Pan, is it, with the horns and all? Though the wings…

— Pan? he giggles. No, he's two islands to the left, just after sunrise.

I cock my head like a curious dog.

— You'll get it in a few hundred years, he says. Call me Ariel.

— Flash Jack Carter. Ariel, eh? Curious. I've never heard of ye.

— No reason you should have, he shrugs.

— I know all the Pirate Gods, mate, old and new. I'm learned.

— What makes you think I'm a god?

— Well, this *is* the Island of the Pirate Gods, I say, isn't it?

He doesn't say anything, except with his eyebrows — a sort of *you're not entirely sane, are you?* look that has me waving the proof in his face.

— Look, I've got a map, I say. Cost me twenty bloody guineas. See, it says this is the Island of the Pirate Gods. Right here. The place where Mutiny was reunited with his lost love, Matelotage, where they built their pirate kingdom out of Spanish gold, a glorious haven for all the heathen gods of yore, those renegade deities accursed by a cold Christian tyrant with no true love of the blood and sweat and tears, aye, the salt of the sea that's in us all and that makes a life worth…living.

He looks at me, then at the map, then at me again.

— You've been diddled, he says.

—So you're not a pirate? he says, scuttling to keep up as I stride back down onto the beach, cursing all the way.

— I told ye, that's a slur on me good character. I prefer to see meself more as a freelance privateer.

— That's… Don't you need Letters of Marque to be a privateer?

I pull open me shirt to show the gravings on me chest, the lattice of scars etched by a captain whose opinion of Matelotage and Mutiny wasn't quite as progressive as mine, ye might say.

— There ye go, I say, signed by the Captain's Daughter herself…the lash, that is, lad.

— Isn't it normally…

— Done on the back? Bastard who did this was cruel as Blackbeard himself, wanted to see my face, he said, as he whipped the buggering devilry out of me. Thirty-nine lashes and a bucket of sea-water to wash away the blood. I swore that day I'd have the ship, cargo and crew, and send that pious blackguard's soul down to Davy Jones, if the Old Man of the Sea would only give me the means to do it. And bless him if he didn't do just that.

I let the shirt fall closed, tap me pistols. Found them in me bunk that night, I did, a gift from the pirate gods, so me crew mates were all a-whispering, who'd clearly chosen me as champion. I shot that captain with the gun of love, matey, had him weeping for me like a fallen maiden right up until I put a shot from the gun of death square in his broken heart. It didn't heal the scars though.

— Aye, I say. Written with the Cat O' Nine Tails, by a self-proclaimed Hand of God, and all the Letters of Marque I need to plunder the ships of any nation bar the one I serve.

— And what nation is that?

— The People's Independent Republic of Arse, Cock and Yo-ho-bloody-ho, I say. *PIRACY!*

— You *are* a pirate!

— Damn right I am! I'm Flash Jack Carter, the Darling of the Deep, the Blessed of the Briny, Sodomite Scourge of the Seven Seas and…

I trail off, sniff the air, turn to look inland.

— Is that smoke? I say.

Enter Buttersick, pursued by bear. He crashes out of the bushes, leaping, flying, running, out onto the sand, his stripy tail upright in terror, scorched like the rest of him and trailing smoke, wings flapping faster than a fury with the taste of blood upon her lips. I'll say this for Jack: he reacts fast, if not with the most rational of responses.

— Burning lemurs of bloody Madagascar! he shouts, in a pitch that some might call unmanly but which I just think of as him showing his more sensitive side. I try to reassure my darling.

— It's just —

But Jack already has his pistol out and cocked, the now back-flapping Buttersick dead in his sight, waving his hands before his face in what I recognise as utter panic but which Jack, I realise, sees only as rabid lunacy. The burning bear that follows hard on the sprite's heels, framing this winged, tailed terror with flame, and the full host of my faery brethren that *then* burst from the tree-line like a flock of flying fiends…they probably don't help matters.

— F-f-f-f-f-f-f-f-f-, stutters Buttersick, and I have a horrible feeling I can see what's coming.

— **FIRE!** he shrieks.

And Jack, naturally enough, does.

—No, no, it's all right. They're friends.

I grab Jack's arm as he pours powder in the pistol, bat his hands as he bats mine — *get off!* — I snatch the shot out of his fingers only to have him stamp on my toes and reload while I'm hopping. He whirls on the faery host now alighted all around us on the beach, arms waving frantically and dancing like they've bursting bladders as every single one of them chatters their own individual warning in a cacophony of squeals.

— Burning!

— Fire!

— Smoke!

— Demons!

— Dooooooom!

Jack spins from faery to faery and I leap for his back, clamp on like a limpet. He just keeps twirling with me half over his shoulder, grabbing at his gun arm.

— Avast! Get back! Begone! he shouts. Bloody sod off!

— **SHUT UP!** I bellow in my best leonine roar, loud enough to shake the trees and bring a sudden silence to the situation.

—If yer going to be doing that again, would ye have the good grace to bloody well warn me? says Jack.

Finger wiggling in his ear, the wince still on his face, at least he's not going to go off half-cocked again, I reckon, though I do worry about our future together if he can't get on with my family (it's just jealousy, I tell myself; he doesn't want to share me). Still, for all the sidelong glances and occasional hand-flaps at any sprite who gets too close, after the brief period of expletives and persuasion — and more expletives, and more persuasion, this time aimed at the good ear so it doesn't just result in a loud *What?* — I've managed to get him to grips with the notion that they aren't, in fact, a host of vengeance-seeking furies, fiends from Hell…or, to use his words, *some sort flying lemur demon thingies.*

— Ditch the tails, I whisper an aside to Dustbunny. Pass the word. No, I don't know *why*, but he doesn't like them. Don't ask.

Dustbunny looks dubious but skitters off to do what he's told. I'm just turning back to carry on with the soothing of my soulmate when a whimpery mumble comes from beneath the dead bear lying face-down on the beach where Jack dropped it with his shot.

— Can you get me out from under here, says Buttersick. It's still burning, you know. And rather heavy.

—It was the other one, says Buttersick. He's trying to kill us all.

He's a sorry sight, rather crispy round the edges and still smouldering a little, but us sprites are resilient, so I'm sure he'll be fine.

— You should have seen him set fire to His Nibs's old palace, he says. He's a maniac, a mentalist, a madman.

I nod solemnly.

— Driven to the very edge of reason by the loss of his love, I say, turning my gaze on Jack as he stands there so noble, staring out to sea, scanning the horizon for a ship to rescue us. Of course, I carry on, it's understandable, and a terrible shame, a Tragedy even. Why, it'll doubtless end in suicide for the poor man, a grand soliloquy, then a leap from Pointy Point.

If I have to push him over myself, I think. He's not bloody well getting my Jack back. Finders keepers.

— Ariel, says Buttersick, I'm *really* not sure they're lovers.

— How could they not be? I say. Just *look* at him. What's not to love?

Oh, my Jack, I think. You're so noble with your hand shading your eyes, so graceful as you jump up and down, as if in doing so you might see just that little further beyond the far horizon. He turns, shakes his head, and comes stomping towards us.

— Bloody ship sunk. Sodding map's a fuckin forgery. And now I'm trapped on an island with a bunch of...*things*.

— But we've got each other, Jack, I say.

— *And* the island's bloody burning! Whose idea was that? Banquets and harpies and burning bloody bears...yer all cracked!

— I was just saying, says Buttersick. It wasn't us started the fire. It was —

— Me, says the dark shape emerging from the forest, from the flickering shadows and the furling smoke, stepping forward till his face is lit in the flames of a burning bear.

— Black Joey, says Jack.

— Flash Jack, says Joey.

Then that shadow of a man is leaping through the flames, his frock coat billowing around him as his blade whips loose and high.

REVENGES AND REDEMPTIONS

The crossed pistols catch the sword blade and Black Joey feels the boot in his chest that flips him as the two roll back and over. He lands on his back on the sand but rolls on, out into a crouch and a twirl to see Carter twist onto his front, take aim. He leaps and swings to hack the pistol barrel aside, circles the blade on the follow-through to bring it down on the man's skull, but Carter rolls, whips himself back to his feet, brings the gun in his left hand up again, too close now for a swing. Joey spins like a dancer inside his reach, brings the guard of his sword down on the bastard's fist, then punches him with it full in the face. Carter staggers back, dropping the pistol, but now brings its twin to bear with a curse — only to lose aim as he twists out of the way of Joey's lunge, grabs his arm with his free hand and lets Joey's momentum pull them both to the ground. Sand in his eyes, Joey feels the teeth sink into his knuckles and he roars, slamming his left forearm into the dog's face even as he feels the sword fall from his grasp. A pistol-butt smacks his forehead and he grabs the wrist and twists with all his force.

Then it's just the two of them, spinning savage in the sand, all fists and knees, elbows and teeth. He feels a foot in his stomach that sends him flying back through the air, cracks his head on something hard as he lands, grabs for the rock and finds a pistol instead. He's wiping sand out of his eyes, rolling to his feet, but Carter is already up, running and diving, rolling.

Then it's the two of them there, both on one knee, both with a pistol in their hand pointed at the other's heart.

— I told you they weren't lovers, says one of the queer little creatures stood in a circle around them. Another of them, now holding Joey's sword, casually jabs him in the foot with its point.

Carter has a queer look on his face, a slight tilt to his gaze, a flick of eyes, as if he'd *really* like to check whether his pistol is loaded. Black Joey snarls.

— Typical Flash Jack, he says. Can't even remember if yer own pistol has a shot in it, eh?

Carter grins.

— Ah, now. No, that's not it at all. Thing is, well, ye do know whose pistols it is I carry? That these pretty little things we're pointing at each other aren't yer run-of-the-mill flintlocks, but the guns of —

— Matelotage and Mutiny, says Joey, the Pirate Gods. So I've heard.

— Well then, ye also know that this situation is a bit more complex than us threatening to blow each other's brains out, mate. Ye might want to be thinking it through a little.

Black Joey thinks it through a little. Suddenly he's aware of a slight tilt to his own gaze, a flick of eyes, as he'd *really* like to check just what the name is on the pistol in his hand.

— See now, says Carter, there's really just two potential scenarios here, with both of us being famed for our impeccable aim and all, and unlikely to miss at this range. Either it's Mutiny in my hand and Matelotage in yours, in which case you end up quite dead; or it's Matelotage in my hand and Mutiny in yours, in which case, yes, I'm well and truly buggered, I'll admit, but you'll be sobbing like a girly over my corpse, having just murdered yer true love.

— And won't you be weeping just the same, Flash Jack, if it's a shot from Matelotage in *your* heart, and me dead?

— Ah, but I'm a very fickle lover, Joey. And I'm known to recover quickly from me failed relationships. It's the drinking, ye see. But a man like you who's never known true love, Joey, and of a more temperate nature — it's inconsolable ye'll be. Inconsolable.

Black Joey shakes his head.

— I'll get over it, he says.

—Hurt my Jack and I'll chop your bloody head off! You won't get over that.

Black Joey clocks the queer little creature with his sword, now waving it clumsily in his general direction. There's a certain pluck to his pout.

— Faeries for your crew and all now, Jack? I know yer light on yer feet, but that's taking it to extremes.

Carter shrugs.

— He's loyal, he says. And a little bit besotted.

— Besotted? Black Joey laughs. With the glorious Flash Jack Carter. Has he any idea why I might want to kill you? Have you told your little admirer here of all your noble deeds and acts of valour? Introduce us, do.

Carter coughs.

— So I was involved in the taking of a few slave ships, Joey. Everyone was doing it at the time. And if ye look at it in a certain light, well, didn't we liberate you from a future on the plantations?

— No, you kept us in chains, in the hold, filthy and starving.

— Ah, but we introduced you to the *notion* of piracy, which was a sort of spiritual liberation, was it not? Made you the man you are today.

— You introduced me to the notion that there's no hope of rescue, no honour amongst your kind, only a greed for plunder, whether it's monies to line your purse or men to auction off on the market-blocks of Kingston.

— It was Barbary Bill's idea, says Carter. I was only First Mate, at the time. I swear on me heart, I didn't have a say in it.

— But you had a *hand* in it. You sold me. From the same sort of greed as brought you here, no doubt, to raid King Caliban's Sanctuary.

And the strangest look comes over the face of Flash Jack Carter as he raises his left hand, palm out in a gesture of surrender, it seems, gives a sad shake of his head.

— I came here looking for the Pirate Gods, Joey, cause it was never about the gold, not for me. It was always about the...freedom. I came here looking for me destiny. I never thought it would be this.

And he lowers his pistol.

And Black Joey fires his.

Carter rolls backward and Joey turns to deal with the sprite now running screaming at him, sword swinging wildly, but the yell from Carter stops the creature dead, whips Joey's head back round.

— The sword!

Carter's on his knees, blood streaming from his left hand, other outstretched towards the faery, who in an instant is spinning to hurl the sword through the air and into its grasp. Joey has no idea what the damnfool is up to but he's having none of it, on his feet and raging towards the man, the pistol turned as a club in his hand.

— Just die!

Then Carter has his bloody hand down on the ground, and the sword is swinging up and down like a butcher's cleaver, hacking clean through flesh and bone to sever it from the limb. And even as he screams, Carter drops the sword, grabs for the pistol of Matelotage, and swings it up, and fires, the shot thumping into Joey's shoulder, spinning him round to…the vision of his redemption, the winged wonder that he knows, he *knows*, he will never let a cruel need for revenge bring him to hurt.

He hears Carter's cries but he doesn't listen, just gazes in awe as the sublime spirit leaps past him, grabs the spent pistol.

— What are ye doing, my dear? he says.

He sees the flintlock being reloaded by the faery, but it doesn't quite make sense to him. Who could be needing shot in a world so full of joy as this, so full of such wondrous things as his beloved. O, but 'tis Matelotage they're loading, the gun of love, so it must be that Carter is to free this sprite before he dies, dart him with a love for Joey as deep as Joey's is for him, because how could he let the dainty spirit suffer mourning, how could anyone let the spirit suffer so?

Carter takes the gun in his good hand, pale and grim as the poison of Joey's shot seeps through his veins, his very body in mutiny against his soul. Joey sees him close his eyes, puts the barrel to his own breast and pull the trigger.

Paxes and Plunder

Standing on the edge of Pointy Point, his frock coat billowing with a peachy flourish in the wind, Black Joey lowers the spyglass from his eye and slides it away as he turns. Far off on the horizon, even without the glass, the distant shapes are clearly turning in the direction of the island, hardly surprising given the size of the signal fire, the seven-day beacon of black smoke that must have been visible for leagues.

— Five ships, says Joey, Spanish galleons by the looks of them and sailing low in the water, loaded with gold, like as not. Not that you care about gold, eh, Jack?

Sod the gold, I think. That's a sodding fleet for us, and money and men to build a pirate nation on this isle the like of which has never been seen, to make it a true island of the Pirate Gods, or a new island of Sanctuary, or simply an island of Redemptions, if that's what we all decide.

— Five ships, I say. That's three for me, and two for you.

— *Two* for you and *three* for me, says Joey.

Ariel coughs into his hand — *excuse me, hello.*

— Two each and one for the…*Technicolor Buccaneer* here, I say. Whatever the sodding hell that means.

— Agreed, says Joey.

— Agreed, says Ariel. And it's in the Book.

As we head down the path to the beach, I raise the stump where my left hand used to be, study the smooth pink skin, poke it with curiosity. More bloody scars, I think…but in truth I did deserve it, for there's only so far that roguishness is charming, and there comes a point even in piracy when a man knows that he's due a reckoning. I'm still a little worried, at times, as to whether Joey has truly forgiven me, the shot of love wiping all bitterness from his heart, or whether it's just that he knows to hurt me would be to hurt his dainty Ariel. Maybe it's all just a tenuous pax that could fall apart with one wrong word. And again, maybe I deserve that worry for me past sins; maybe it's as much about me making reparations as it is about forgiveness. A penitent heart is all very well, but it's Matelotage and Mutiny will help Joey rebuild Caliban's Kingdom, not contrition. I stroke the skin of the stump, this permanent reminder that destiny can sometimes be history coming back to bite you on the arse. Still, only a week, and while it's not healed, it's a damn sight better than it should be — one of the perks of having a magic sprite for your doting nurse, I guess.

I pull my snuff pouch from my waist, tip a little fairy dust onto the wrist and take a snort. That's another perk. And it really does help with the pain, ye know.

—CRY, HAUL! AYE! A-DIDDLE-AYE-DEE!

—Now you're sure this spell will hold till we get to the fleet, I call across the waves. We're not going to get halfway there and just plop down into the drink?

Ariel looks over at me like a puppy I've just kicked.

— You don't trust me. You don't have faith in me. *Joey* has faith in me. *He's* not worried.

In the lead…well…imaginary boat, Joey holds his sword in his right hand, Mutiny in his left, peering forward at the distant galleons, and seeming to float in the air like the faery crew behind him, heaving on their…well…imaginary oars. Just like Ariel and meself, at the prow of our own imaginary boats, with our own crew.

— *Cry, Haul! Aye! A-diddle-aye-dee!*

— Pumpkin, pumpkin, I say, quick to salve the flighty faery's sulk. Of course I have faith. It's just my…amazement at the veritable wonders you perform. Stupendous feats! Astounding enchantments! Incredible acts of illusionism to fool even the sea herself. By the Pirate Gods, my astonishment is as boundless as the briny blue.

— *Cry, Haul! Aye! A-diddle-aye-dee!*

— You *do* love me!

— Hush now, I hiss. Ye know that Joey must never find out or he'd surely do for me in a jealous fit of pique, rage even. Besides, look ahead at our plunder.

Afore us, a rowing boat of Spaniards all fine and dandy in their best uniforms, rifles high, is heading towards shore to investigate that beacon, hunt for us poor shipwrecked souls. Shrouded in glamour, we move in to intercept them, a pirate crew of salty sprites who, absent the tails, I have to say, aren't shaping up too badly — a little unfocused perhaps, but nothing a good shanty can't fix.

— *Cry, Haul! Aye! A-diddle-aye-dee!*

The Spaniards hear us now, turn this way and that, in panic at these invisible voices of the deep bearing down upon them from all around and nowhere to be seen. The officer in charge gives the order to turn round, back to the ship, and with that moment of the choice to retreat always being the best point to hit a man in his lack of balls, I give the shout to Ariel to lift the glamour, unveil these three boatloads of lusty imps, led by the infamous Flash Jack, the notorious Black Joey, and the hitherto-unheard-of Swishy Ariel, and we send the screaming heebie-jeebies right into their souls.

Grin of a scabrous dog on me face as I stand to leap across, I glance down at me reflection in the water. A handsome chap I am, ye know, with hair so fiery and eyes blue as the sea, as handsome now as when I staggered down to the surf, the shot of Matelotage in me heart, to open me deadlights to that same watery image. 'Twas love at first sight. I had to do it, ye see. Only sure cure for the one gun is the other, love conquering all and such-like, and I wasn't going to let meself be caught up in a buggering menage-à-trois. Besides, I always was a bit vain.

I will admit, though, to some strange temptations that have been confusing me these last few days, maybe on account of when I opened my eyes, the two of them were standing over me, the images of their faces peering back from the lapping water, one on either side. I'm sure it's only a passing fancy though. Better be or this could get bloody complicated.

I raise my gun and pick a target.

— For Matelotage and Mutiny! I roar.

— For Good King Caliban! bellows Joey.
— For the sheer bloody fun of it! shouts Ariel.
And we leap.

The Angel of Gamblers

—You know, said Guy Fox, rifling the cards…contrary to popular perception, there are no gamblers in Hell. Not one.

He sat back in the squeak of leather armchair, waiting to see if anyone would bite. Nobody did; we all knew, of course, that if we only gave him time he'd surely start on one of his outrageous stories.

There were five of us still in the game: Guy Fox; myself; Fast Puck; Joey Narcosis; and Jack Flash, whose deal it was, but who was busy with the craftsmanship of skinning up right now. Plush as a Mayfair casino — White Russians served with coffee beans sprinkled on top — CLUB SODA blends the luxury of a gentlemen's club with the squalor of a cannabis café: a den of exquisite iniquity. For quite some time now it has been the home to our regular Thursday-night card game: a friendly affair of alcohol, hashish and Texas Hold 'Em, where, more often than not, the players — dissidents, decadents and deviants to a man — are higher than the stakes.

It was Joey Narcosis who finally cracked. One eyebrow arched, he looked at Fox and asked him:

— Okay. Why are there no gamblers in Hell?

Fox grinned, his pencil moustache and black flop of hair giving him the look, for all the world, of a public schoolboy turned rake and scoundrel — which is, indeed, not too far from the truth. Fox has as many passports as he has stories, and none in his real name. He began to deal the cards for Jack, starting with himself, twice round the table.

— Well. Have you ever heard of the Angel of Gamblers? he said.

— I take it he's a fallen angel, said Jack Flash, looking up momentarily as he licked first here, then there, to seal two papers end-to-end but overlapping, a third folded around, gummed down to reinforce the back.

— In a way, yes, said Fox. In a way, no. You see, there are three types of angels. It's not just the rebels and the loyalists, you know. There's a third host, neither of Heaven nor of Hell… The ones who simply would not fight.

— The Nephilim, I said. Being something of a connoisseur of arcane and apocryphal Bible stories, I often find myself amazed at the obscurity of my own knowledge. Fox, of course, knows just the sort of story that will pique my interest.

—The Nephilim, indeed, he said. The Watchers. While the rebels fell—were cast from God's grace down into the very depths of Hell — a few who remained neutral also suffered exile, doomed to walk the earth until the Day of Judgement. These angels of the Earth, they say, being neither wholly good nor truly evil, sympathise most with those like them: the prostitutes, petty thieves and junkies…

At this, he looked directly at Joey Narcosis, well-known worshipper of opiate oblivion.

— The suicidal and the homosexual…

He glanced from Jack Flash to Fast Puck.

— Those who, if you take the Bible's word as law, are damned to fiery perdition for sins that, in this day and age, seem minor misdemeanours. So they watch over us like gods of old. Our patron sinners.

Joey, Puck and Fox had picked up their cards. Jack's hands were full with his black hunk of resin and his Zippo as he heated and crumbled the hash into the papers. I gathered up the two cards on the table in front of me to find that I had Kojaks, a pair of jacks, clubs and hearts. Not a bad hand to start with. Not bad at all.

—Anyway, said Fox. There is, of course an angel of gamblers.

— And how exactly do you know that? asked Joey, always the sceptic during one of Fox's tales.

— Why, I met him, naturally. Twice, in fact.

Jack had the tobacco in now and was sealing the joint closed with a tentative and tender touch, an almost beatific look of grace upon his face. He slid a tiny, rolled-up piece of card in one end as the roach, leaned back in his chair, picked up his cards and sparked up the joint. I studied Joey with his stone-cold poker face; Fox, laid-back and garrulous, as easy with a three and seven unsuited as with a pair of aces. Fox gazed back, smiled.

— It was on a riverboat on the Mississippi down by New Orleans, he said, the first time. I was playing in a high-stakes game with some of the most gentlemanly gamblers of the Southern States, men whose manicured perfection was no mere vanity, but... Well, I myself, while sometimes unkempt by nights of drunkenness and debauchery, am quite convinced a man's good character is marked by his impeccable attire. I'm sure there's many who would disagree with me.

The Blinds

—I'll say, said Puck, wearing the same skatepunk combats and baggy tee-shirt that he had been living in, and probably sleeping in, on a floor, for the last two weeks. Fast Puck, in direct opposition to Guy Fox, considers scruffiness a sort of assertion of social, political and, yes, spiritual autonomy. It's probably why the two get on so well. Jack wore his drummer-boy jacket and tartan trews as usual, Joey his black biker jacket and jeans: Rotten and Ramone. These weekly poker nights can be a little bit like costume parties sometimes, with these four.

— What are we on for blinds? asked Puck, blinking.

The blink was no sign of his luck, unfortunately. If Puck has tells they change with every hand. Blinking, twitching his nose or placing chips on top of cards, cards on top of chips, settling back, leaning forward in his chair, scratching his chin or playing with his hair, he fidgets like some schoolboy junkie with ants in his pants and bugs under his skin.

— I was dealing for Jack, said Fox. So I'm the small blind, Hal's the big blind. [He put a ten chip on the table.] Twenty for you, Hal.

I laid down my four fives. In Texas Hold 'Em, just to get the ball rolling, two small compulsory bets are made first, by the player to the dealer's left, who puts in the small blind, and the next player after him who has to double it. It's only then the betting really starts.

— Anyway, Fox carried on, when I saw him walk up to the table, I thought it was the devil himself come to play Five Card Draw for my soul. Those who have never seen an angel seem to think that they look much like us, that they could wander among us quite unrecognised, perhaps performing acts of random charity and kindness for young orphans and suchlike. The pernicious influence of the entertainment industry, I say.

— No. If they had ever seen an angel they would not be so foolish. An angel is a thing of terrible beauty; even those without the Glory on them have eyes that pierce you to the very soul and a voice that rumbles through your bones and echoes in your head like a thousand rivers thundering in an immense cascade, over the brink and down into the great abyss.

—He wore a suit so white it hurt to look at, a white necktie studded with a little tiepin made of ivory. And when he smiled the glint of teeth was such as would light up a room. It's strange: no matter how I tried to scrutinise his face, I couldn't hold against that stony gaze, couldn't focus for more than a brief moment on those icy, brilliant eyes. So I found my vision inexorably drawn to that little ivory tiepin, because that ivory was dull and yellow in comparison, not ageless but aged, a thing of this world, not of…whatever is beyond. It was the only thing about him that seemed wholly corporeal.

— Maybe this is where their idea of anonymity comes from. As I say, I don't think that any angel could walk through this world unnoticed. They might walk through it unrecognised, however; after all, what man would dare to stare an angel down? Who in their folly could look long enough to sear those features in their memory, knowing that an image of such beauty and terror in their minds would surely drive them mad?

— And before you interject, Jack, that was rhetorical.

Jack took a deep toke, blew it out in involutions of slow smoke and, passing the joint counter-clockwise round the table to Joey, shrugged as if to say, *What, me?* If anyone would take an angel's glory as a direct challenge to his anarchist ideals it's Jack — and madness, for him, being merely a vocational hazard, he'd probably set out to remedy the situation, with Molotovs against a flaming sword.

— Yes, said Fox. Jack here might well consider it a challenge to face down one of the "minions of the tyrant deity." I, however, am a different sort of chap: less forthright, less…impetuous. Which is why, right then and there, as this visage of majesty sat down in the chair across the table from me, I decided that if this indeed were Satan come to claim his own, then I would treat him with the courtesy which even the most dashed bounder deserves. Civility and etiquette, gentlemen, are all important.

Joey Narcosis passed the joint to his right, to Fast Puck.

— In a world of laws passed down from On High, good form is the most rebellious notion ever conceived, I've always thought. Whose bet is it?

— Puck, said Joey.

FOLD

—Fold, said Puck. Like origami.

— Puck folds faster than an admin flunkey stuffing envelopes, I said.

— We must bend like a reed in the wind, said Puck.

— Was it queens or cowboys this time? Jack asked.

Puck smiled. No one, of course, has ever quite believed Puck's claim that he ignores his cards, follows the Tao in his decisions, playing poker so loose that it's Zen. Perhaps that's not surprising, given Fox's claim to never bluff, and Joey's insistence that his Straight beats Jack's Flush any time we're stoned enough he might just get away with it.

— So, Puck said to Fox. The devil sits down at your poker table.

— Joey? You in? said Guy.

His sudden interest in the game smacked of a ploy to tease us with his tale, heighten suspense.

— I'm in. Just thinking.

Joey fiddled with his stack of chips, his hand poised with two twenty chips in it.

— Raising before the flop? I asked.

He might have killer cards, might simply be considering a bluff; either way I had a sense that he was testing the water. Who'd reach for their chips to see a raise? Who wouldn't? With a pair of hooks, I wasn't giving anything away.

—So the devil sits down at my poker table, Fox said. Or so I thought. Did I mention that the little ivory tiepin was in the shape of a goat's head, which rather lent itself to the whole devil hypothesis? Anyway, I had been staring at the thing for quite a while when he finally introduced himself — although it wasn't much of an introduction, I must say.

— *Forgive me, sir,* he said. *If I could tell you my name, I would, but alas that would be perilous for me and even more so for yourself. I am, as you are no doubt aware, a being of celestial origin, a creature of the shimmering æther, formed from the breath of God. Being created from a word, the Word indeed, we angels are quite...attached to our names. To give our names to someone is to give our selves. I must apologise, therefore, and ask for your indulgence.*

— Ah, Christ, said Joey. So he talked like you as well. How long's this story going to take?

I felt a tap on my arm: Puck offering me the joint. I accepted it with a thumbs-up of thanks, took a draw.

—Now his manner was sincere, believe me, and I am no stranger to the cultivated villains of this world, those with tongues as silver as their hearts are black. I know a scoundrel when I see one. This man — this angel, rather — was quite genuine, and I sensed from him a profound sorrow in his soul, as if he wanted nothing more than to tell me his name, as if it was a source of deep and brooding melancholy in him that he could not give...a loyalty that might be betrayed.

— A sad thing, don't you think, never being able to give that of yourself, never to hear it murmured by the dreamer lying in your bed beside you?

— But, as so many legends of Arabia tell us, any man may bind an angel if he only knows that angel's name. Solomon himself was said to be the master of both kherubim and djinn. One can only imagine what destruction might be wrought by someone with an angel at their beck and call. How quickly they'd become drunk with the power, blinded by the glory...

— And, my friends, this is exactly what he offered me. Ah, thank you.

I'd taken a couple of tokes on the joint by this time, and had passed it to Fox. I noticed that, sometime during Fox's anecdote, Joey had laid a twenty chip on the table and sat back, saying nothing, cards facedown in front of him. He had decided not to raise, and he had decided to not-raise with as little fuss as possible.

— Jack to go, he said, innocently casual, as if surprised that Jack had not already acted, as if to say, *What are we waiting for?*

— I'm in, said Jack, and dropped a twenty chip on the table in front of him with habitual confidence, the kind that comes so easy to a punk convinced that it's audacity, not love, which conquers all. Jack is notorious for being as reckless playing poker as in the rest of his life: a crazy kid with holes in his shoes, an empty stomach and a shiny new guitar he'll never learn to play. Tonight his stack of chips was looking the shortest of all.

— You know you might regret that, Jack, said Fox, inscrutable as a statue of the Buddha.

— Crash and burn, old man, said Jack. Crash and burn.

RAISE

—My call? said Fox.

He looked at his cards, thinking it over.

— Guy's call, said Puck, out of this hand but not out of the game. He would be watching from the sidelines, watching the action, watching us, and hoping to spot our tells.

— What'll it be, Guy? he said. In or out?

Fox added a twenty chip to the ten on the table.

— I'm in, and I raise it ten.

— Before the flop, I said. Is it possible the Fox has something wonderful?

— Maybe we all have something wonderful, said Fox. [For a moment, I thought I detected just a hint of sadness in his smile, then it was gone.] But I do have a terribly good hand, I must admit.

— Oh, and the Fox never bluffs, I said.

— Never. I may overstate the case occasionally, but never a bluff.

— Maybe he's got an angel working for him, eh, Fox? said Joey Narcosis.

— If only I had, said Fox. If only I had. Which way is this joint going?

— Jack, I said.

Jack looked up from his cards like a startled meerkat. Check.

— The joint, you spacer, said Joey.

— Oh. Cool.

— It's me to go, I said. How strong did you make that?

Jack shrugged naïvely. Strong enough.

—So, did you find out his name or didn't you? asked Puck.

Fox smiled.

— Now that would ruin the story. You see, that was the nature of his challenge. He challenged me to a game of poker, and the stakes were to be high for both of us, almost the highest stakes I've ever played for… Almost, I say. If I won, you see, he would give me his name and thus the power to call him, to bind him, to bend him to my will.

— And if you lost?

— If I lost, however, my soul was forfeit to him. Ten to stay in, Hal.

— Ten, I said, and put the chips down in front of me.

— I'm in, said Joey, laying down another two fives.

— So, said Fox. The game was Five Card Stud, the stakes my soul, his name. How could I refuse a challenge of such startling audacity?

— Quite easily, said Joey. Jack? Another ten to see the flop.

Jack looked long and hard at his cards.

— I mean, said Joey. The devil wants to play you for your soul. That's only going to end bad.

— Ah, but I only *thought* he was the devil, said Fox.

—So play I did, said Fox. I took his wager, shook his hand on it, and we began. And what a game it was. We agreed to use ten thousand dollars worth of chips each and to play until one or the other of us had them all. The casino gladly provided us with these tokens for the length of the game — most amenable of them, but then I was known as something of a high roller: someone to be accommodated, you understand.

— By this time, of course, a crowd of quite some size had gathered round us, intrigued by our unearthly compact, drawn to a spectacle the like of which they'd never seen; and these railbirds watched us intently for the first few hours, leaving the roulette wheel and the casino's other lucrative games of chance, to my knowledge, quite deserted.

— I bet the management were happy about that, said Joey.

Fox shrugged.

— Perhaps it was the ethereal solemnity of the angel's voice that persuaded the house to suffer this steep loss of their usual revenue. Perhaps they too were enthralled by the idea of such a game, enthralled by the possibility of my damnation. I do not know…

He paused to beckon the waiter for another round of drinks, and the man nodded, started gathering glasses, tonging ice into them.

— The game was close. We played for twelve hours straight, from dusk till dawn, the chips going back and forth between us, back and forth.

— After a while it became clear to me he was the better player. I became convinced, indeed, that he was toying with me, letting me win a hand here or there only to take my winnings back from me in the next one. It was as if this was his way of truly winning my soul: piece by piece, gradually stripping me of my confidence in myself, my faith in my own skill, in luck, in anything. By the time those twelve long hours were over I was a broken man, a man bereft of hope, and sitting on the table in front of me was only a single hundred dollar chip. I knew then that I had lost. I knew that I was lost.

He reached into his pocket for his silver cigarette case, clicked it open to take out a cigarette. He snapped the case shut, tapped the cigarette on it.

THE FLOP

—He beat me, ironically, with the Dead Man's Hand: two pair, Aces and Eights, all clubs and spades, as Wild Bill Hickok had when he was shot dead at the poker table. Anyway, as he took that last chip, he took something else. I felt it leave me but cannot describe it. Joy? Hope? Faith? Spirit? All I can say is that I was suddenly...hollow inside. I no longer had a soul.

— You are the devil, I said, and I found I could now stare directly into those piercing eyes. Where could they stab me now? What was there left inside me now but emptiness? And in those eyes I saw...a weariness; a look that told me he'd seen a hundred, no, a thousand men lose their souls by their own pride. How many men have you done this to? I asked him, though I didn't even have the heart to be angry.

— *You are the last,* he said. As the casino gathered up the chips, he stood up, walked towards the door. He stopped, silhouetted in the thin, first light of dawn, adding something which struck me with its strangeness. *I have enough now,* he said. And then he left.

—Okay, said Jack, putting down his extra ten. Let's see the flop.

Fox passed the cards to Jack, since it was, after all, his deal, and Jack dealt out the Flop.

For those who may not know the rules of Texas Hold 'Em, in this variant of poker five cards are played face-up on the table. Each player uses these community cards, with one or both of the two they're dealt, to make the best hand of five cards they can. The first three shared cards are dealt in what is called the Flop. A round of betting follows, then a fourth card, the Turn Card. Another round of betting leads us to the fifth, the so-called River Card.

In this case, the Flop was Ace of Spades, Queen of Diamonds, Ace of Diamonds: a dangerous board, if ever I'd seen one. Good for me, since I now had two pairs: Aces on the board, Jacks in the hole. Better for anyone who had a second Queen or a third Ace. Aces and Queens would beat me, as would Three of a Kind. There was even a chance of a Diamond Flush — five cards of the same suit, that is. I was worried.

—You're saying you lost your soul to the devil in a poker game? said Joey Narcosis, sardonic as ever. That has to be the best one yet.

— You weren't listening, said Fox, with a pained expression. I said I only *thought* he was the devil. As it turned out, I was quite wrong. Is it me to bet?

— You were the last to raise, I said. Your bet. Get on with the story.

Fox laughed.

— Very well. I only found out later that he was in fact the Angel of Gamblers, and why exactly he wanted my soul. My soul…I mentioned that I met him twice, that my soul was almost the highest stake I'd ever played for. Well, let me tell you about the second time I played the angel. I check, by the way.

Fox having passed up the chance to raise the betting, it was my turn to decide. I placed ten on the table, a small feeler bet that wouldn't commit me to the pot, but with which I could try to read what other people had from the way they responded. Joey responded almost immediately.

— See your ten and raise another twenty. Jack?

Jack, having smoked the last of his joint, was now in the middle of rolling another. He looked up like a squirrel with a nut, wary of passing humans.

— I check, he said.

— Reraise brings the bet to thirty, Jack, said Puck. You can't check.

— You have to put in thirty or fold, I said.

Jack looked at his hand for all the world as if he had forgotten what his cards were, then gazed at the Flop intently.

— Pair of Aces on board, together with a Shirley Bassey, said Puck.

— *Shirley Bassey?* I said.

— Queen of Diamonds.

— You're making that up, I said. The Queen of Diamonds is not known as a Shirley Bassey.

— Anyone got any roach material? asked Jack. I passed him an old underground ticket.

— *Diamonds Are Forever?* said Fast Puck. Oh, come on. Sparkly, sequin-wearing diva. Queen of Diamonds.

— Makes perfect sense to me, said Fox.

— Thank you.

— Can we get on with the bloody game, said Joey. Are you in or out, Jack?

Jack put the roach in his joint and his money on the table.

— I'm in. I want to see if the Fox can finish his story and still win this hand.

—Of course I can, said Fox. You can't beat the Fox.

   — The Angel of Gamblers did, said Joey.

   — Only once, said Fox. And after that I was unbeatable. He laid his cards down on the table and began to count his chips.

   — That was the strange thing. Once I'd lost my soul I never lost another game. I was unbeatable. After all, how do you read a man without a soul? How can you tell what someone's thinking when they have no heart, no hope, no fear, when there is nothing there to read? I only played the game because it was…the only thing I had left.

   — Oh, but I knew exactly what they had. Without my soul, it was as if a blindfold had been taken from my eyes. I saw how people thought and acted, driven by their hope, their fear, their faith and foolishness. I'd sit back and gaze at my opponents and I'd know exactly what they had. Every glance towards their cards, each nervous tic, each itch they scratched, each time they bit their bottom lip or reached for a glass of water. I knew, because I recognised the…absence of it in myself.

—I played in games across the world, for higher and higher stakes. I won every time. I became rich, and though the money meant nothing to me I kept on playing. By the time I met the Angel of Gamblers again, I had amassed a veritable fortune. I'm in.

   He put thirty down in front of him.

   — Now, I say that I was unbeatable, but I was not the only one. In my travels I was to come across many men such as myself. I recognised the same emptiness in their eyes, the quietness in their manner, the hollowness in their voices. These men I would not play, for if I had we might have played for an eternity, each of us as perfect a player as the other. There seemed little point. But I would take them to one side and we would share our stories and, yes, each of them had met the angel in white, the angel with the little goat's-head tiepin, and each of them had lost their soul. Slowly I learned from them that this angel was not the devil, as I had thought. At least, to some of them he had denied it.

—No. Some of them had asked him, accused him, drawn a little fragment of his story from him here and there, and gradually I began to put it all together. Bet stands at sixty. Twenty to see the next card, Hal, he reminded me.

   I knew that it was wrong. Something told me that I was getting in over my head, but Aces and Jacks was a good hand and I felt sure that Joey Narcosis was bluffing, that Jack Flash's recklessness was to my advantage, and as for Guy Fox…I was not sure, but he had only seen the bet, not raised it. Perhaps his hand didn't look as good after the Flop as before it.

— So you're unbeatable, eh, Fox? I said. You were cleaned out by Joey last week.

— One might lose on purpose every once in a while, he said. In order to be sociable.

I put my extra twenty on the table to cover Joey's reraise, and Jack dealt the next card, the King of Spades.

— Anyway, I learned, said Fox, that he was not a rebel angel, but rather one of those seduced by the…worldly delights humanity has to offer. The Bible tells us that there were sons of God who married with the daughters of men, angels who turned their love from God to Man…or rather, Woman. And, why not? The pleasures of the flesh are sweet.

—Mmm, flesh, said Puck.

— Anyway, this angel claimed that he was one of these, the Nephilim I mentioned earlier. It seems that he had reasoned that if the devil could win men's souls with double-dealing and deceit, well, so could another angel, an independent player, so to speak. Was he trying to win enough souls to buy his way back into Heaven? Or did he intend to sell them on to Satan for a seat of power in Hell? That was the mystery. That was the one thing that no one knew. He had been travelling the world for years, for decades, centuries perhaps, gathering the souls of gamblers. But none of us knew why.

— It's obvious, said Joey. What else would he want with them but leverage?

— Sometimes you worry me, Joey, I said.

— Is that all you think a soul is good for, old chap? said Fox. Power?

— What else would you want them for? said Joey.

— I bet they'd be pretty, said Puck. You could store them in jars on a shelf, or just fill a room with them. I bet they'd shimmer.

— Smoke 'em, said Jack. A truly spiritual high.

— You are all, said Fox, extremely disturbed individuals.

All-In

—But why? said Fox. It was one year later when I got the answer. I was in the Mammon's Temple Casino in Las Vegas, when he walked in from the neon night of that latter-day Babylon. Out of the corner of my eye I saw the crowd give way, knew it was him before I even looked, by now so well attuned to the unspoken moods of those around me that it seemed to many I possessed some extra-sensory ability. He strode through the crowd of the casino as his brethren must have walked through Sodom, sinners parting to make a path for him, turning their heads to follow him with hungry eyes, the glory of an angel more seductive even than the glamour of celebrity.

— The weak, it seems, are drawn to angels like moths to flame, drawn to the shining, bright destruction, mistaking power for perfection, beauty for truth. An angel seems the answer to our every secret need. I wonder if this is where the angels' true power comes from: the strength of our foolish, mortal desire for them.

— This time, for some reason I could not fathom, he wore sunglasses that masked his impiteous gaze…

—Is that a word? asked Puck.

— What? I said.

— *Impiteous?*

I shrugged, and took a deep draw on the joint Fox had just passed over to me, smokers' etiquette demanding that, since the last joint had travelled widdershins, this one should go clockwise around the table.

— *Without pity?* I suggested. Whose turn is it, anyway?

— Joey's, said Puck.

Joey picked his cards up, looked at them.

Fox picked his cigarette up from the ashtray where he'd placed it when the joint came his way, took a drag and blew it upwards, bottom lip jutting out slightly. It's a little habit of his I've noticed: the habit of a smoker who for once realises other people don't appreciate smoke in their faces. Civility and etiquette, indeed.

— Anyway, he said. He came straight across the room towards me, looking neither left nor right. I'd spent much of the night frittering away my money at the craps table before sitting down to win it back at poker, and was now, at the moment he had entered, in the process of gathering my winnings from a game just finished.

— *What would you risk,* he said, *if you might win your soul back?*

—I looked at my winnings, mentally added them to the sums I had in sundry bank accounts around the world. I calculated the net worth of everything I owned, liquid cash and assets, any credit I could lay my hands on, even the value of the clothes that I was wearing. Without hesitating, I named a sum that would make most men pale. Indeed, the cashier standing at my shoulder nearly fainted, poor chap; I saw him steady himself with a hand upon the table. But the money meant nothing to me.

— I said I would risk everything I own if I thought that I could win.

— *Would you sell your soul so cheap?* he said.

— I told him I thought that I already had...in a sense. He smiled and shook his head.

— *Money is not enough,* he said. *What have you got that measures up to one man's soul?*

— What did I have? My fortune? My luck? My life?

— Let me guess, said Joey Narcosis. Your first-born child?

— No, nothing so old-hat as that, said Fox. This was the Angel of Gamblers, not Rumpelstiltskin. Actually, there was nothing I could think of that I had to offer. Nothing.

—Joey? I said, blowing out a billow of smoke and watching Joey study Jack's pitiful stack.

— How much have you got left there, Jack? said Joey. As if he had to ask. A chip count when a player has four five chips on the table in front of them is just making a point...rudely. But then even a friendly poker game brings out the shark in some people.

— Twenty, said Jack.

I knew Joey wouldn't hold back, seeing a chance to put our reckless friend out of the game.

— I'll check, said Joey.

I passed the joint to Puck, surprised and suspicious. Was he bluffing?

— All-in for twenty, said Jack.

With all of his chips in the pot now, Jack had to win this hand or he was out. But he could sit back and relax. In Texas Hold 'Em, one player cannot force another out by raising the stakes higher than they can afford. The other can just "go all-in," and any subsequent betting takes place as side-bets between those who still have chips.

— Back to Guy, said Puck. Fox was studying his cards. So, Guy. What did you play for, if you had already lost your soul?

RERAISE

—As it turned out, there was something I had that he desired. Or, at least, there were a lot of little somethings. You see, angels are ethereal things, beings of spirit. We creatures of the mundane plane value our souls above all else, but to him the flesh was infinitely more…exciting. That's what the Angel of Gamblers wanted as the stake against my soul: my flesh.

— So he wanted you for his love-puppy? said Puck.

Fox laughed. Liberated from the betting, Jack was busy building yet another joint now. Puck played Cat's Cradle with a piece of string. Joey simply watched.

— Oh no. He wanted something far more intimate than that. He wanted the memory of a bee-sting in childhood, the feel of wet sand washing between toes as you walk down a beach, the taste of home-made lemonade. And more than that: he wanted my friends, my family…my mortality itself. He wanted to know what it was like to live as we do, from the cradle to the grave, not as some spirit thing, unbound by time but all too bound by their own insubstantial nature.

— What is a soul without a skin to walk in?

—We pray so fervently for our little lives to be extended just another year, another day, another second, Lord; but think about it. To an angel seduced by the thrill of chance and fortune, an angel of gamblers, isn't humanity defined by that…excruciating moment upon which everything depends, the turn of a card, the roll of a die, the whirring of a gun chamber loaded with a single bullet? Isn't humanity defined by the quickening of the heart, the sweat on your palms, the rush of adrenaline, the pupils widening to drink a sight in deep? And the moment when all that stops and everything is still, lucid?

— He would gamble with me, he said, for the chance to live my death. And in return, I had the chance to win back something of the faith, the hope…the dreams that had been absent from my life for a whole year. Believe me, my friends, if you have ever spent a year without a soul, you too would have leapt at such a tiny but tender morsel of spirit. What is a suit of skin without a soul to walk in it? A tattered coat upon a stick, unless…

Soul clap its hands and sing, I thought. And louder sing for every tatter in its mortal dress. Yeats in his later years, ageing and afraid of death, and understanding life.

— I'll see the twenty, and…

We waited as he seemed to consider whether or not to raise and, if so, by how much, picking up a handful of chips, passing them from one hand to the other. By now the atmosphere in the room was as thick with hash smoke as it was with tension.

— The joys and sorrows of the flesh, said Fox. I think he had some sense of just what a human has over an angel. He wanted it; and I wanted my soul back. And of course, how could I pass up any chance to glean the rest of his story from him, to find out what on Earth he wanted human souls for in the first place?

— You sell them on for a profit, said Joey. Start a bidding war between Heaven and Hell.

— Maybe it was just a power trip, said Jack.

— Or he collected souls, said Puck. Like bottle-caps or action figures.

— So what did he want? I asked. And are you raising?

—No. That'll do. And no. He had no intention of selling my lost soul to Deus or Devil. I think power and glory were the last things on his mind. And I don't think, dear Puck, that immortal entities of the astral plane invite their fellow angels upstairs to "see their soul collections." Souls are not things to be displayed on shelves like knickknacks. Hal?

— I'm in. With the king and queen making a dangerous board I knew it was a risk, but I was playing loose. I could afford to lose, but I wasn't going to lose by folding Aces and Jacks to a bluff. Sometimes in poker there's a larger game that goes on in the margins of each hand: a game of confidence, morale. You have to know when to act cautious, when to act aggressive, even if the cards don't merit it. I placed my twenty on the table.

— Twenty. And another ten, said Joey, just that little bit too deliberately quickly, projecting a quiet deadliness he surely knew we'd all pick up on…wanting us all to fold. He must be bluffing.

— Thanks, Jack, he said, as Jack passed him the joint. Guy?

The River Card

—Where was I? Ah, yes: the story of the Angel of Gamblers. I heard it from him as we played that second game, between hands and during hands. He told me just how long he had been gaming for men's souls: since long before Rome fell, before the Pharaohs built the pyramids. As long, in fact, as men had put themselves into the hands of Lady Luck, he had been there to catch the fallen.

Fox waved a hand through the haze of hash smoke, shattering a billow, fluttering it away, and looking, in the low light of the green glass shade over the baize table, like a magician conjuring mysteries with his words. Even the waiter pouring my White Russian from a cocktail shaker was quite clearly listening to every word.

— He'd travelled the world for millennia, said Fox. Gathering whatever souls he could. He'd played Mah-jongg in ancient China, billiards in Imperial Britain. By whatever rules applied in all these dens of vice and lucre, he'd...won those souls who otherwise would have been lost to the much darker forces feeding on the waifs who stray from our morality's razor edge, the so-called "straight and narrow."

—The Nephilim, I've said, concern themselves with those who breach the Law in little ways — debauched and decadent but not depraved, not monstrous with their sins. Beside a tyrant, beside those who send young men to die in war, who murder, rape and torture in the name of king and country, in the name of God — beside these creatures, surely a petty thief, a prostitute, a gambler, is nothing. Were these little sinners not the sort that Christian salvation was meant for, though? Surely, these people were not damned. This is what I asked him, and his answer chilled me to the bone.

— *That shepherd only tends to his own flock,* he said.

— Redemption is the prerogative of the redeemer, so the Angel of Gamblers told me. All those souls who wandered from the path, all those too stubborn and proud to kneel, too ignorant or too intelligent to accept a story, no matter how "great," as the very Word of God Almighty, all those: lost, doomed, damned. And so the Angel of Gamblers had chosen his own congregation and travelled the world, gathering souls to save them from the devil, and from the pitiless judgement of God.

—Hal, it's your bet, I do believe.

Fox had quietly added an extra ten to the stack already in front of him.

I considered my move as the barman glided round the table, laying out our drinks and gathering empty glasses. Fox's gin and tonic, my White Russian, Puck's dry gin martini, Joey's Guinness and Jack's absinthe. I took a Marlboro from the pack on the table in front of me, tapped it on the baize and lit it. Took a draw. Sat back.

Another ten, I thought. There were so many possible hands that could beat me, and yet something in my intuition told me that the next card, the River Card, would be a Jack. I have no idea how I could be so certain, yet I was. When one has folded dreadful hands that would have won the pot, or lost on what looked like a certain winner, and known somehow, despite all common sense, that this would be the end result, one comes to trust one's inner voice, even when it seems to contradict all probability. So, I stayed in, knowing that the River Card would be a Jack.

It was the Jack of Spades.

—*No one shall come to the Father, unless he comes through me,* said Fox. That's what the Bible tells us. That's what the Angel of Gamblers told me. If we choose not to play the shepherd's bleating sheep then we stand outside of the fold and Hell can have us for all our saviour cares.

— He removed his sunglasses for the first time now, and as I looked into his eyes I knew that I could beat him, for I could see the burden of the countless souls that weighed so heavily upon him. He was an angel carrying the world upon his shoulders, or at least a little corner of the world. And I knew, as clearly as if I read it in a book, that what he wanted most of all was freedom from this dreadful burden, this duty all the more binding because he had chosen it for himself.

— Why, I asked him tentatively. Why have you bound yourself to such as me, a dissolute wastrel who would throw away his own soul in a game of poker?

— *Once you are in the game,* he said, *it can be very hard to leave.*

— Whose bet is it now?

The Final Bet

—Mine, said Joey, bringing all his remaining chips forward. I'm all-in for an extra seventy-five. Let's see if the Fox is still unbeatable.

He pushed his hair back from his face, his eyes stone-cold. It wasn't quite the confidence projected by someone holding or bluffing aces. But Joey does use subtle signs to try to warn someone off a hand or make them think he's bluffing, draw them in — or simply to unsettle them so they're not sure. He uses quiet fast raises and calm calls, silences that say, I might have something, maybe, but there's no way you can tell. Right now I couldn't tell.

Fox picked up his cards to look at them and laid them down again, not folding but in contemplation of the substantial raise. Even as the chip leader, such a loss would cut considerably into his stack.

— Ah, go for it, Fox, said Puck, blowing a smoke ring, impishly casual with someone else's money. Jack and Joey are all-in. If you finish them off I can take their money off you in the next hand. He grinned.

— The Fox might even have finished his story by then, said Joey.

Fox laughed.

— Don't worry. We're close to the end now. Let me see…

—We had been playing for most of the night now, and I was up from where I'd started, up by a long way. But the strange thing was that although I was beating him by my own skill, by my own abilities, without a soul I took no pleasure in it. It did not give me the rush, said Fox. — The thrill, that feeling you have when you get a Full House on the flop. None of the trembling anticipation when you're winning and the final moment gets closer and closer, and you know that you could throw it all away with one wrong move. All I had was the calm certainty that in this game, unlike the first, the two of us were truly matched.

— A man without a soul, said Fox. Against an angel carrying too many souls to count. It rather evens the situation up, don't you think? Power is all very well, but one shouldn't underestimate how much…responsibility can weaken those with power.

— So when I looked into his eyes, said Fox, I simply knew that I could win. And that was when, like a true professional drawing his opponent in, he raised the stakes.

—*You know, Hell hates me for the souls that I have won,* he said. *Almost as much as Heaven. There are those who'd like very much to…buy them from me.*

— Why don't you take the offer? I asked him.

— *Believe me,* he said, *sometimes I would like to. I am weary of guarding the souls of fools. But I believe in giving everyone a sporting chance. What did you say your soul was worth to you again? The world?*

— So he laid his bet upon the table for me, so to speak. If I should win I would get back my own soul and everything that went with it. I would be truly human again for the first time in a year. And I would be free. If he should win, however, not only would I lose my body but, as the representative of gamblers everywhere, I would take his burden from him. Every soul he carried would be shackled to my own, a weight of little sins, each so small, so insignificant when taken alone, but bound together forming a vast mass of vice that would drag me down to Hell as surely as if I'd murdered my own flesh and blood.

Fox paused.

I took the joint Puck passed to me with a silent nod.

— He brought out this little book, this little black leather-bound book which seemed so small that I could hardly imagine it holding all the names of those whose souls I knew he must now own. Card sharks and con-men; princes, play-boys, politicians; rich men, poor men, men and women; souls of children won by throwing pennies at a wall: he owned them all.

— I've often wondered if there are other books of souls like that, held by angels in grace, or fallen, or somewhere in between. A book of murderers and a book of thieves, books of saints and madmen. A book of every liar. A book of all whores.

— Anyway, we played, then, for my soul, and for the soul of every gambler that the angel owned. How many that might be I did not know, but clearly it was a vast sum, the highest stakes that I have ever played for, then or since; and, I suspect, the highest stakes that I will see as long as I live. Talking of which…

— Seventy-five, he said, laying down the chips. Are you in, Hal?

— Finish the story, I said. I'm thinking.

CALL

I looked at my own stack, knowing that losing this hand would pretty-much wipe me out. Not quite, but almost.

— We played past the dawn this time. And as the game drew on, we both fell silent, studying each other with stony solemnity. We were so evenly matched that both of us saw times when we were nearly out, but managed to rake back enough to keep going, doubling up, then doubling up again, going all-in three or four hands in a row. No, he was not toying with me now. This time we were equals. If anything were toying with me, it was Fortune, Fate, if such a thing exists; and the angel was as much a plaything as I was.

— One thing to understand: angels don't answer to the laws of our mundane reality. Angels can dance upon the heads of pins, walk through the furnaces of Babylon. They have no flesh, no soul of their own, only the names they're given in Eternity. They come from outside time and space; why should they not be able to enter it at any point and leave again, visiting the past that's dead to us, the future that's unborn?

—I tell you this because it dawned on me as we were playing. If he'd gambled with Roman guards beneath a crucified prisoner, gambled with gangsters in Prohibition pool halls, where else might this creature have gathered his lost souls from? Might his book hold the names of gamblers from all time? A frightening idea.

— Yet I still felt myself completely calm, for all that I was risking my own soul and those of a great many others. Only one thing niggled at me, an unanswered question from our first game; but by now we played so seriously that I dared not let myself become distracted. I desperately wanted to resolve my curiosity, but needed to concentrate so deeply on the game that I could not speak to ask.

Finally, a hand came where I realised — I was sitting facing him, and I realised — that he had gone all-in, and we were both precisely matched, so if I called him one or other of us had lost for sure. I could fold this hand and let the game go on, or I could call him here and now and finish it one way or the other. It was my choice.

—I had to clear my head. I had to have the question answered before I made my choice. And so I asked him: when he had left our previous game, when he had stopped a second at the door and told me that my soul was the last, that he, in his own words, *had enough now*, what had he meant? If these souls weighed so heavy on him, why had he gathered them all in the first place?

I passed the joint to Fox, and counted out seventy-five from my stack. I had trusted my intuition and it had given me a Full House, three Jacks and two Aces. Now it was warning me, but I couldn't separate the fear of losing from the thrill of the potential win. Perhaps it was against my better judgement, but I would see this hand through to the end, I thought. And yet my hand rested on the chips, unwilling to place them in the pot.

— Why, then? I asked Guy Fox.

—The angel had been gathering the souls of gamblers from across the world, between the dawn of time and the end of everything, until eventually, with one last soul, he had enough. And then, he said, he'd turned and walked out of reality, into the vast eternity beyond, gone to the very Gates of Hell and thrown them open, challenged Satan to a poker game. These souls that he had gathered were no more than an initial stake, a little sum he'd laid on the table to tempt Satan himself.

— Oh yes. He'd played the devil at poker, he told me, and won from him the souls of every gambler who had ever lived — of every gambler who would ever live. He had played and he had won, and now I played with him for my soul. If I lost, he said, the souls of every gambler that would walk this earth would be my burden in eternity while he walked the earth in my flesh. Those, gentlemen, were the final stakes of our game. And it was with this dread knowledge that I made my final choice. I chose to play the hand...

— Hal?

I placed my money on the table.

— I call, I said.

Jack was the first to show his hand: the Jack and Nine of Diamonds. He had two pairs — Jacks and Aces — but, given the board in front of him, I was gobsmacked that he had gone all-in on such a hand. I turned over my cards to reveal the Full House.

— Sorry, Jack, I said. You went all-in on Two Pair?

— He only got that on the River Card, said Puck.

— Actually he went all-in on a pair of Aces with two over cards on board to his Jack. Completely bonkers.

Jack shrugged. I was looking for a diamond or a ten, a Flush or a Straight. It was pretty good odds.

— Not good enough, I said.

— I'm afraid not, Hal, said Joey Narcosis, turning over his own cards to reveal the Ace of Hearts and the Ace of Clubs. My Pocket Rockets beat your Kojaks: Four of a Kind.

Joey hadn't been bluffing after all. He looked across at Fox, a shit-eating grin of malicious delight on his face.

— Well, Fox, he said. My guess is you won your soul back from the Angel of Gamblers and that means you're not unbeatable any more…because unless you have a Straight Flush all those chips are mine. Time to show your hand.

Fox smiled.

— I won that game, had won it, perhaps, before I even sat down at the table. I believe it was the Angel's intention all along to give me what he called a sporting chance. I have heard rumours since, stories of a mysterious gambler dressed all in white with a little goat's-head tiepin, who plays to win your soul or your flesh…but only for a year.

— These may be no more than garbled versions of the tale that I have just told you, but I like to think not. I like to think that I was just the first to win his soul back, as I was the last to lose it. I like to think that every gambler is given that chance, one day, when they have played so long that they have gained the skill they need but also lost a little of themselves already to the game. I like to think the Angel of Gamblers comes to every one of us at some point in our lives and offers us that bet, the chance to lose one's soul and win it back, free for eternity from god or devil, free from any angel.

I noticed that my cigarette was now no more than a filter wedged into one of the ashtray's nooks, a ragged cylinder of ash collapsing into the mess of butts. I should go back to smoking roll-ups, I often think. At least they go out if you leave them for a minute, rather than burn themselves away to nothing because they're loaded up with saltpetre. And Marlboros are the worst for extra additives — extra addictives, even.

— But what if you'd lost? I said.

— Well, then, said Fox. The Angel of Gamblers would be sitting here in my place right now, sipping my gin and tonic and enjoying a fine game of poker with his very good friends.

He smiled a mysterious and mischievous smile. I looked at my Full House and Joey's Four Aces, and I looked at Fox, thinking about just how…remarkable it was that Joey and I both had killer hands. Remarkable.

— Queen and Ten of Spades, said Fox.

And on the board, as we all saw, the Ace and King and Jack of Spades gave Fox the highest hand a player can get in poker.

—That's a bloody Royal Flush, said Puck.

Joey's face said everything: a look of utter incredulity that he had lost, that he had lost with Four Aces.

— You sure you won that game? he muttered. Because I don't fucking believe this.

— Would I lie to you? said Fox. As I say, I think he wanted to lose. Maybe that's his aim: to free us all, one soul at a time. I may not be unbeatable, Joey, but I'm a remarkably lucky man.

Jack was laughing at the outrageous odds that had given the hand to Fox, while I simply shook my head with a wry smile — still in the game, if only just. Yes, I thought. Remarkably lucky.

— What if the angel was trying to win? I said. What if he wins one of these days? What if all of those gamblers who haven't met the angel and played him for their freedom yet end up owned by some fat cigar-smoking drunk, some scrawny Vegas amateur with a shabby suit and an unlucky streak? What if the angel wins some loser's flesh, their life, and gets to dump his burden on some hopeless shambling…ghost?

Fox laughed and shook his head as he gathered in the chips.

— While he gets to live a normal life, you mean? With all the ups and downs of human fortunes, muddling through the joys and sorrows, trying to understand this strange thing called mortality?

— That's just the chance we take, he said. Perhaps.

The Shoulder of Pelops

—It is the stance of Pelops that sings meaning, says Poseidon.

Hips cocked in contrapposto pose, the boy stands with his head turned, left shoulder slightly raised, his sling draped over it, like Michelangelo's David two millennia and a dozen empires distant. Black tousle of hair and tan burnished by sweat and sunlight, framed in the doorway of his father's cool cellar, the beardless boy gazes westward across the Aegean, towards Arcadia, not knowing he will settle that little earthly heaven, set his name on its environs. A sonnet of summers, oblivious of his father's guest, his future studying him.

Tantalus scowls at the notion of his wayward son carrying meaning, carrying anything. That shoulder so slightly raised barely knows the clasp of a linen exomis, let alone a burden; labour's a stranger to the sportive lad, hunter of rabbits, racer of hounds. That stance carrying meaning?

— No, not *carrying*, says Poseidon. Meaning is not *carried*. That mad metaphor is mumbo jumbo.

Symbol's sense as mystic substance, gumbo dished out in a bowl? The god of oceans shakes his head.

— That shoulder smooth as marble, he says. No, not the shoulder itself but the raising of it…*that* is meaning.

For Tantalus meaning resides only in signs. The nearest he can come to understanding the stance of Pelops is as...patina of subtle tones shading the symbol, as painted pattern on ceramic amphora.

Not that he'll argue with Poseidon. One does not argue with a god of oceans who has rapped his knuckles on your door at midday, blue eyes glinting even shaded by the broad brim of his peplos, smiling as he speaks of his traveller's thirst, waves and earthquakes in his low voice. One simply offers hospitality, calls over the son this god finds so unfathomably charming.

2.

Tantalus shows off his little kingdom under the shadow of Mount Sipylus, his lands so grand to him, grander even in imaginations of future schoolboys learning Homer and Hesiod by the rod, vast as the interstices of a century of global cinema, as dreams born of Technicolor and 3D, as little televisual buds of electromagnetism blossoming out into space, eternity. He offers Poseidon a proud tour of a domain greater even than he thinks but, in reality, in the soil and stone of the palace and gardens he has built, tiny to a god. His hall. His orchard. His cellar.

This meaning that Poseidon talks of as they step down into Tantalus's tomb of fine victuals...the best Tantalus understands it is as the spurious flourish of a decorative glaze on a clay pot. Or perhaps essential oils, extracts of connotative herbs infused into the vessel's denotative wine to spice it, subtextual import in suspension in the textual content.

Like *this* amphora with its inscription: barkɪŋdɔgz.

Here in his cellar it sits along with the amphorae inscribed slipɪŋdɔgz and snarlɪŋdɔgz — a little closer to the latter.

That is what meaning is for Tantalus, the liquid logos in those clay vessels.

At night, he dreams it an unstable signified, the wine spiced differently for each reveller at his feasts, differently at each feast, differently as each servant pours it out of the amphora. Never the same wine twice, never, never. Nightmared in the palace of his paradigm, Tantalus clings to a conceit: Things stand for Things, he dreams, a metaphysics of meaning as mental object.

As his son idles at the door, Pelops proves with every limbering of his sunlit shoulder that meaning is action, process, state.

Tantalus does not understand the sign itself is to be remade as the stance.

3

When the gods come to feast, Tantalus will panic.

He'll clap his hand for servants, have his whole cellarful of amphorae brought forth, poured out, each a meaning to be tasted, one by one, by the revellers at his banquet table. But Tantalus will test the first, find the taste of meaning unsatisfying...incomplete. He'll test the second, only to find it changes that first taste. And so on. Disaster, calamity, this is his nightmare, meaning ever deferred.

The feast will have to be postponed, unless...

He'll slaughter his son, cut him up and make a goulash of the pieces.

Poseidon taps the amphora.

— What exactly is the meaning in this vessel? he says.

Tantalus opens his mouth but finds himself mute. He frowns, then has a notion, gestures at another amphora: it is like this one...but not quite. He gestures at a third: not like that one at all. Poseidon simply repeats his challenge for each.

— What exactly is the meaning in *this* vessel? he says.

So Tantalus spends eternity lost in the semiotic system of his cellar, gesturing at amphora after amphora, trying to establish the contents of one as distinct by not being in any other.

The shoulder of Pelops is lost, not due to Demeter but to *différance*. The gods sit at Tantalus's banquet table, shake their heads at his infanticide. And as they leave, Tantalus is thrown into his true torture.

— It is the stance of Pelops that sings meaning, Poseidon had said.

He must rebuild the boy or face the Furies! So, in feast after feast, Tantalus scrambles through the permutations of his ritual, desperate to track down all the pieces of his slaughtered son in amphorae and bowls, in the imaginary content of signs.

The shoulder of Pelops remains lost.

4

—You say my stance sings meaning? asks the youth. How can this be?

Poseidon lays a hand on ivory deltoid, smooth curves sculpted, fitted to replace a father's folly. The shoulder is slightly raised, hips cocked, head too in puzzlement — another stance. The god of oceans smiles at Pelops, his keen student now, and speaks a word once graved on an amphora: barkɪŋdɔgz.

There is no amphora here, though, just the sound, sensation triggering ideation in the youth — notions that are themselves sensation — a subliminal, subsequential splash of import in the impact of the word.

No denotation, only connotation.

The word is a rain of phonemes on imagination, a patter of beats, a pattern battered on the bronze boy's chest.

(Pelops is no automaton, of course. Rather men were once gold, then silver; now they are bronze. This is an epoch in which even metal may be soft and warm as flesh, yet still resound. So the word is a series of notes struck on the gong of Pelops, each sustained before subsiding, the result an ever-changing chord — import, meaning not as mental object, but as action, process, state — a sounding of strings in imagination tuned to resonate.)

They stand in the gymnasium of Olympia, near the agora, Poseidon's bronze eromenos gazing with his dark eyes, fidgeting with the discus in his hand but sprung to learn all that a god of oceans might teach. As the word sounds in him, that connotative splash of import which can only be unique each time, he begins to sense just what it might be that Poseidon has to teach him.

Another word from Poseidon. Pelops lowers into the throwing stance, poised; he winds back, poised; swings, hurls the sign away from him, meaning become action upon him, action within him.

5.

Pelops remembers resurrection, waking from dismembered death to the orchestral import of objects in reality. A shade returned to flesh reformed, he relished agency again, savoured his animated state, exploring every inner articulation. And as he turned to each and every object round him, recognising it, he knew now as he'd never known: he could call each and every chord they struck in him a notion, but the import of the ocean was not a sign for the inspiring object, rather a stance toward it.

— There is no content, Poseidon explained. At most we have contention. Never denotation, only disposition.

He woke up in Arcadia to the sight of Pan—Pan dancing the delight of dawn around a fire's embers, wild dogs barking to the birdsong conjured with the horned god's pipes. A story of his life was brought to him, a plain white linen exomis, its flax nurtured and harvested by Demeter, winnowed by Dionysos

Liknites, retted and scutched by dew of Dryads, iron of Furies, heckled with the comb of Aphrodite to fine fibres for the Fates to weave, to clothe his naked grace. (As if a tale of life were only one thread spun, measured and snipped.)

—Stance is, says Poseidon, always already a disposition to a disposition. To live is to recognise your stances to the world's ephemera — the barking dogs, the amphorae, your own dark eyes. Or mine.

Poseidon leans in close, the pupil of one eye black as a well but gleaming, an obsidian mirror. Pelops glances, sees his own reflection in this fish-eye lens, bronze form in a half-crouch, one ivory shoulder slightly raised. His stance itself, he sees, is part of that ephemera. He has a stance toward it…if only that it *is* an attitude that's *to* an object.

6.

Poseidon remembers the rebuilding of the boy, bone by bone, muscle by muscle, organ by organ — not by Zeus, of course, but by Prometheus, who as humanity's creator knew how the whole should articulate. He remembers the still-dead puppet moving as some masked figure in a tragedy, striking a pose to each object summoned forth to test the mechanisms of response. They brought barking dogs before the boy, and he struck a guarded pose. This was no stance though, merely mummery. No fire, no breath, no words at first, just empty echoes of the boy's dispositions in life.

No fire, no breath, no words. The boy's life was no spiritual substance to be poured back into him as wine into an amphora. Instead it was only the final stringing of the bronze organ at the heart of him, kardia or kythera, the first strumming drum of fingers, as a patter of beats on the boy's chest, that set Pelops resonating once again, his dark eyes not just open but wide. When they brought the barking dogs before him now, as Pelops struck that guarded pose, Poseidon heard the chord of import, the changes subtly shifting posture to stance.

The only fire was that thieved by the Titan, brought here to the slopes of Mainalon, omphalos of the Peloponnesus. The fire was only, as it ever was, a light at night for them to work their magics by, Prometheus and Hephaestos, the cripple crouching on the other side, carving an ivory shoulder to replace that which was lost.

The only breath was that blown softly by Aeolus, gentling the flames to crackle of sparks that rose in vortices, drifted off into the onyx sky as stars, vanishing towards the compass points, towards the future's Corinth, Argos, Sparta and Olympia.

7.

—A strange idea, says Tantalus. Your notion of Pelops's stance...but still an idea, no? And so we have a Thing that's *standing for* a Thing, your notion referencing reality.

Poseidon laughs, rich as the seas.

— Tantalus, he says. My *notion* of Pelops's stance is disposition too, my stance toward your son's. And were it in his nous instead it would be, just the same, a stance toward a stance. There is no need of signs here, only recognition.

The stance, Poseidon knows, need not sing meaning in bold discords or proud harmonies; an epistemic stance is still a stance.

—Sign does not stand for object, says Poseidon.

They step out of the cellar of Tantalus. Noon sun paints a Cézanne patched of pale ochres, golden-greens — the courtyard, orchard, villa.

— Ideation is simply sleeker, says the god of oceans, when recall is cursory, liminal, partial. A gestural recognition of one's stance to barking dogs, amphorae or dark eyes is...more ergonomic.

He lays a hand on the shoulder of Pelops, that shoulder slightly raised.

— Slicker still if one may take a simple stance — a little pattering dance of phonemes, say — as a surrogate for one more complex.

Pelops turns.

—So we now take a stance, the god of oceans says, to let our stance toward this be applied as stance toward *that*; that where we would recall our attitude to barking dogs, we will instead call up another stance, a word: barkɪŋdɔgz.

As they stroll toward a simple lunch, the boy falls in behind, indifferent to philosophy, to his own name, to his father's frown at understanding that eludes him.

Nascent, beyond, Pelops hunts imagined hills between youth's idling and impatience, gaze turned for dash of daydream rabbit, slingshot draped over a shoulder that is not ivory, not yet.

Bizarre Cubiques

A New Space

Pharis, 1910. A young Sinese boy flies a box-kite, whooping as he runs. An aviator in leather jacket and goggles banks a Stupar biplane of "stick-and-wire" construction; swooping low, he guns the engine. Amorican tourists trooping by the Eiffel Tower gaze up, thinking of steel frames of skyscrapers being built back home in New Amsterdam. All of these sights I have encased in rollfilm, in a metal cartridge, in the Kodak Brownie under my arm.

All of these sights I have encased in my imagination as I gaze at the Cubique painting on the gallery wall in front of me.

The Cubique painting banishes the grid and vanishing point, rejects the unified space of Renaissance perspective for the geometry of fractured glass, as with Bricasso's *Le Reservoir: Horta de Ebro*, (1909, Private Collection). The Cubique painting deconstructs form into fragments; it dissolves the subject into free-floating extra-rational abstractions; it demands recombination, analysis and synthesis, hence the naming of the movement's two great stages.

The overlapping facets of these paintings…they suggest these objects are being seen from many viewpoints, multiple perspectives, manifold frames of reference, as with *The Guitar Player Cadaqués* (1910, Musée National d'Art Moderne, Centre Georges Pompidou, Pharis).

I have burned the journals I once had, the record of my week-long stay in Pharis as a young man with a dream of one day being a writer. I have only disconnected memories now: of lying beneath the Eiffel Tower at night after an evening of jazz and conversation (sparked up by the offer of a Camel cigarette in the Caveau de la Huchette on Boulevard St-Michel); of Melmoth's grave in Père Lechaise, and Morrison's, signposts in vandal's ink, scrawled sacrilege on stone; a box-room in the student halls of the Université de Vincennes in St-Délice.

Bricasso and Paque denied the notion of multiple viewpoints; they explained that this Cubique restructuring of the subject was a means by which they might encode all the essential information of a 3D object, as an architect's projected plans exploded on a 2D canvas. In such works, more flattened than foreshortened, surfaces of planes may intersect at angles which express no sense of depth as we desire it. To Paque the basic principle of Cubique painting was to manifest "a new space"; the underlying purpose of the Cubique shattering of shape was the establishment of space, of motion in space.

BIZARRES CUBIQUES

I met the gargoyle and his missus on the train heading from Caerlundein (Euston, I believe) to Felixstoff, to catch the ferry to Diephe. Grey stony wings and leather luggage, black box camera around his neck, outsized brown-tinted glasses and a Yankees baseball cap, he settled his suitcase on the seat (reserved) beside me and grinned, offered a McNugget. When the girl arrived to claim her seat (reserved), he made a show of stubborn innocence. Could *she* not find another seat?

After a while, under a porter's stern officiation, he relented. Amoricans. Sometimes the most modern are the most barbaric.

Developing the old geometries of primitive creation, of Afritan tribal masks, Iberian sculpture, or Egylphan bas-reliefs, the Cubique painters fused these with the new geometries of patchwork vision in the landscapes and still lifes of Saul Cézanne, expanding on the strange, skewed sense of space and stylised relationshifts. Works consist of facets not combined in tessellated surfaces of tiles but as transparent planes turned and transformed, superimposed. The clear-cut edges hint of mass in motion in space. One finds in the Cubique construction, as employed eventually by Litan futurists, an implication of technology, of the vanguard of a dynamic century.

In the Azurian Collection of the Louvre Zoo, I sketch a karibu, its eagle wings folded along its oxen torso, human head lowered to feed, the curls of its great braided beard, long as a hobben scholar's, jutting out beneath the nose-bag. Muscles ribbed more architecturally than a horse painted by Stubbs, it is a thing of antique grace; four thousand years of age, it once stood guard, with its bull mate, outside the gates of Babylon. My pencilwork on paper does not do it justice, so I blush as passing tourists crane their necks to glimpse my awkward sketch.

From 1906 through 1907, Bricasso synthesised his sources, old and new, into his seminal *Les Demoiselles d'Avignon*, now hung in the Museum of Modern Art, New Amsterdam. Paque, one of only a few artists who both viewed and understood Bricasso's painting at the time, immediately transformed his own style in response.

Not everyone was so simpático.

In March 1909, the French art critic Louis Voxelles was reviewing the Salon des Indépendants; he referred disparagingly to how Paque's style...reduced, broke everything apart to "little cubes"...*bizarres cubiques*. Hence, the name *Cubique* began as derision, a term of insult and abuse.

A Palette of Greens and Greys

In scorn of all mimesis, *The Republic* of Platon contains what Crochet called "a solemn, celebrated, rigourous negation of representation." It stresses four key points. One: in its remove from what is real, art imitates appearance. Two: in fooling our perceptions, art deceives. Three: the artist's ignorance of any function to the objects being represented empties art of truth. Four: these forms of mimesis call to the irrational in us.

But Cubique art quite clearly deviates from Platon's theory. Unlike the art Platon describes, neither deceptive nor mimetic, neither ignorant nor sensual, it arouses a response that's intellectual, abstract, honest.

I stand before the grave of Bastian Melmoth, sculpted back in 1910 by Giacovvi Efstein as a block of great, grey tomb in the Art Déco style. An angel flies above the wild one's name, perhaps the poet as a naked Icarus; his penis, though, is long since gone, snapped off, a tour guide says, to stop the *pédés'* improper and impertinent advances — on all fours, ass in the air, abusing themselves upon this altar to the alternative.

Still, green lipstick kisses cover Melmoth's mausoleum, a moss of strange desire. I wish I'd brought the bravery to plant my own.

Inviting speculation on the real relation between actuality and artifice, Cubique's fragmented forms must be assembled by the viewer into elements we know. Despite this radical technique, though, the Cubique chooses the everyday over the epic. Subject matter is traditional — portraits, landscapes and still lifes — and fragments of the faces, or guitars, or wineglasses can be detected in the shifting contours of these patches painted with a palette of greens and greys, ochres and umbers. The paintings in the early phase, before the war, clearly originate in nature. From the beginning though, Cubique is interested in more than simple imitation.

—The Rocky Horror Picture Show? she smiles.

I peel the headphones back and click my Walkman off, hold up the cover of the cassette — black background, disembodied lips in lurid emerald. I nod.

Her hair is a shade of iridescent blue-green I associate with pigeons, peacocks, long and curled in bangs that roll around her shoulders; Natalie flicks it back now as she pulls her own earpieces out.

We talked briefly on the train from London; sat, by accident, beside each other on the ferry. Now…it seems we've tastes we share, a fortunate musical excuse to overcome my shyness.

A Clear Portrait of a Man

She's on her way to Nunes to spend summer as an au pair. I'm on my own backpacking "Grand Tour" of Elysse, starting at Caerlundein, following a path through Pharis, down to Canis and then Noce, Amor and Vrienze, back up through the Alphs, through Baal and, finally, by ferry from Oustenne, back home to Albion. The ticket's good for two months; I can stop off anywhere along the route, for any length of time. My first stop will be Pharis.

She spots my tape of Strange Days, by the Doors.

— You've got to go to Père Lechaise, she says.

Bricasso's *Whilhelm Uhde* (1910, Private Collection) depicts a clear portrait of a man, and yet his head and body have been broken into small, semi-regular planes. Despite the protestations of the artist we *can* say that these allow the subject to be seen from several angles simultaneously. More importantly these planes also insist on being recognised as entities in their own right, not simply as a technique of description.

Indifferent to the past, to the traditions of perspective, the perspectives of tradition, aligned perpendicular to the flow of history, Cubique attempts to present the subject in the most complete manner.

I remember how much of my awkward way with this ephemeral nymphen friend — whose travelling companionship would only last until we parted on the platform in a Pharis station, Gare du Nord — was down to panic. An ungainly adolescent, gay only in sexuality, I was unused to such attention from the naiads, dryads, sylphs and nymphs of rural Caledonia; a year or two spent at the University of Kentigern were nowhere near enough for as furtive a faery as I was to undo decades of bitten lips, held tongues and indeterminate pronouns. I was afraid that she might...*like* me.

Cubique works after 1912 are not concerned as much with deconstructing form as with the reconstruction of it using these new elements of artifice. In his *Still Life with Chair Caning* (1912, Musée Bricasso, Pharis), Bricasso introduces non-painting materials into painting; he includes a strip of oilcloth, indirectly challenging the very nature of his art. *Still Life* is extraordinary also because here Bricasso substitutes an oval canvas for the normal rectangle. This accentuates the sense, the presence, of the painting as an object in its own right. And shatters the metaphor of the canvas as a window on the world.

Stencilled Letters and Numbers

Jadis, *the poet Arthur Rimbaud wrote once,* si je me souviens bien, ma vie était un festin où s'ouvraient tous les coeurs, où tous les vins coulaient. Un soir, j'ai assis la Beauté sur mes genoux. — Et je l'ai trouvée amère. — Et je l'ai injuriée. Je me suis armé contre la justice. Je me suis enfui. Ô sorcières, ô misère, ô haine, c'est à vous que mon trésor a été confié! Je parvins à faire s'évanouir dans mon esprit toute l'espérance humaine. Sur toute joie pour l'étrangler j'ai fait le bond sourd de la bête féroce. J'ai appelé les bourreaux...

When Bricasso and Paque invented collages and *papiers collés* in 1912, they began the stage known as Synthetic Cubique.

It began in the Cubique paintings of late 1910, where most references to nature are no longer overt: in Paque's *The Portuguese* (1911, Kunstmuseum, Baal), one can barely visualise the form of a guitarist in a café, never mind confuse the depiction with a real scene. Then, combining and contrasting the physical with the illusory image, Paque brought elements such as sand and stencilled letters or numbers into the Cubique vocabulary, rendering the relationship of art to life conceptual, not mimetic.

Once, *I translate from Arthur Rimbaud's fine French*, if I remember right, my life was a feast where opened all the hearts, where all the wines flowed. One evening, I sat Beauty on my knees. — And I found her bitter. — And I reviled her. I armed my self against the justice. I fled my self. O sorcery, o misery, o hate, it was you who my treasure was entrusted to! I managed to make faint within my spirit all human hope. On every joy, to throttle it, I made the deaf bound of the fierce beast. I called for hangmen...

The use of these letters reasserts the dominance of the picture-surface itself, and emphasises the nature of the canvas as a two-dimensional object, a study of colour and light.

— Confronted with these various alphabetical, numerical and musical symbols, says Robert Rosenblum (*Cubique and Twentieth Century Art*, p. 66), one realizes that the arcs and planes that surround them are also to be seen as symbols, and that they are no more to be considered the visual counterparts of reality than a word is to be considered identical with the thing to which it refers.

Synthesising the Object

With the snapshots of the Kodak Brownie, painting had now lost its competition with photography. Now living in its shadow, it had no choice but to become an art focused on two dimensions.

So, we laid our objects flat upon the canvas, shown in facets, multiplying angles under which they could be seen to interpenetrate themselves, to lose their individuality, their identifiable discreteness. In this way, both Paque and I, both Bricasso and myself, well, we were proving that an independent painting could be crafted, one that would be free from any reference to the reality of the external world.

An achronistic writing, I think. This would be the narrative equivalent of Cubique, the line of language as essential to the tale as is the canvas's surface to the painting. I think this as I fly (again, in memory) the long dark road from Pharis back to St-Délice, having not known the Métro closes at midnight, having hitched the rue de St-Délice not knowing it's a red-light district, having reached the lights of Pharis's suburban neighbour, only to realise, fuck, I've lost my passport somewhere on the way. Having returned to — fortunately — find it where it fell.

The introduction of bright colour caused a further flattening of space, as did elaboration of the picture surface with such decorative devices as the stippling techniques of pointillism. Broken brush strokes, tone and shadow, distance between denser planes brought light. And still the distance being defined here was not depth.

Synthetic Cubique was the outcome of a new desire to describe visual reality without resorting to illusionistic painting. The artists strove to win their goal by synthesising the object, even to the extent of including real components of it in a collage, thus creating a new, separate reality for it.

Strolling the tree-lined avenues, browsing the stalls of leather-bound books and lightweight watercolours along the Left Bank of the River Sine, I imagine myself a latter-day Melmoth, a wanderer in the wilderness of this city, distanced by my language from its denizens. I imagine myself as Alastor, Shelley's Spirit of Solitude…but the poet or his demon? Alastor. It was the name of one of the Erinyes also, and I am as bitter a boy as I am fey, as prone to rage as romance.

Watching myself, I laugh now, but…pretence is all part of the construction of identity.

Aesthetic Objects

Of all the original Cubique painters, Paque remained the most committed. Unlike Bricasso, he remained unbound by any ideology and kept his work remote from mere human or social interests. These concerned neither his art nor, consequently, Paque himself; his interest in material things was limited to their existence as aesthetic objects, there only to be exploited for pictorial motives. Continuing the decorative patterning and flattened planes of Synthetic Cubique, through the 1920s he progressed to greater freedom. By the beginning of the 1930s he was internationally hailed as a world master of still lifes of the calibre of Chardin.

I sat alone in the Caveau de la Huchette, drinking a vodka and limon, stretching it out a long hour as I scribbled thoughts now lost forever to fire, and counted out my coins, wishing I had enough for another drink or a meal in a decent restaurant. As I sat there I watched the barman with his drooping mous-tache, all the students' caricatures of him tacked up or taped to the wall behind. An inveterate doodler, I just had to draw my own and, with an excruciating mix of embarrassment and bravado, gave it to him as I left.

Cubiques are not concerned with copying appearance, but with decom-posing it to its intrinsic parts — a circle, a triangle or a square — or with construct-ing new forms of their own from these base morphemes. For the Cubique artist, the painting is itself a physical reality, not merely a mimicry of nature, and in this sense it embodies an attempt to establish a concept of *paintingness*, the idea of which Platon did not consider. It is this aspect of Cubique which will become the pure abstraction of Mondrian's early work *Tableau No. 2 / Composition VII* (1912, Guggenheim Museum, New Amsterdam).

I decide with wry amusement that I actually rather respect the thrawn refusal of Pharisiens to make even the slightest allowances for my guidebook butchery of their language. The old cliché that the natives will appreciate it if you "make the effort" is, I've found, a nonsense here.

— Un carnet du billet, s'il vous plaît, I say to the man in the Métro kiosk.

I'm met with a blank stare, my pronunciation or my grammar (or perhaps both) clearly rendering me utterly incomprehensible. I think perhaps he wants precision. *I would like to purchase, if I may, good man…*

Paintings About Painting

Paque's works develops through his *Guéridons* and *Cheminées* and *Cané-phores*, through the tables of musicians, chimneys, women holding baskets full of flowers and fruit. An interest in Greek themes leads him to try his hand at graphic work with etchings for Vollard's edition of Hessian's *Theogony*. A series that he paints from 1950 through to 1958 also reflects this interest in the an-tique, his paintings of birds like archaic pottery designs in their clean-lined but decorative simplicity. Then from 1948 to 1955, he paints eight grand *Ateliers* in which Cubique dispenses with all mannerisms, striving simply for the balanced composition.

I walk out of the Caveau de la Huchette, knowing—knowing tonight—the Métro has been closed for hours, and that I'll have to fly again the long dark road to St-Délice to sleep in my rented accommodation. That's not my plan. Instead, I spread my wings, lower my horns and glide along the Sine towards the Eiffel Tower. Supine on a stone bench beneath its girdering, I gaze up at this complex gridwork of human endeavour. A circle of backpackers sits a little way away, but their guitar is quiet, my experience of Pharis's most noted landmark undisturbed.

The paintings that result from Cubique thought are, by Platonic standards, unimpeachable, offering no illusion, no deception: if they were held up at a distance, no one would question their nature. In fact, the viewer unfamiliar with the tropes of Cubique painting may well find it difficult to distinguish any elements whatever they will recognise. Cubiques, unlike the "ignorant" artists Platon exiles from his great utopia with its philosopher-king, concern themselves with painting as a theme, painters creating paintings about painting, painted only to be viewed and understood as paintings.

I gaze at the Cubique painting on the gallery wall.

I abandon linearity, temporality, in Pharis. I fly out of 1993 and into 1910. I buy a Kodak Brownie and take snapshots of the carts drawn by chimaerae down the streets. I wear an aviator's leather jacket, goggles, fly a box-kite, think of skyscrapers now being built in the reticulated streets of old New Amsterdam. I pose as Melmoth, sipping absinthe in a pavement cafe. I step sidewise, slide into a boulevard world where Rimbaud never died but, bored of poetry and bored of guns, became a painter, shattering his art into these…facets of the senses, these bizarres cubiques.

The Origin of the Fiend

THAT ACCUMULATED POTENTIAL

A five-and-dime store on Lincoln Street, just round the corner from Sam's Malt Café. You stand at the comic rack, captivated by Overman on the cover of *Adventure Comics*. Circus strong man's leotard in white, blue trunks, boots and cape, he's knocking seven bells out of a robot army straight from the *Flash Gordon* strips. You guess they're part of some criminal scheme of Overman's archenemy, the mad scientist Rex Roman, but you know you're not supposed to read the comics in the shop, so you beg your big brother for the ten cents. Only ten cents.

We all know Overman's origin story. Sent back in his timepod from the fifty-first century, a newborn babe arrives in 1920s California where he's discovered by spinster sisters, raised on their orange orchard. On a visit to San Angelo at age sixteen, he dives in front of a runaway tramcar to throw a child to safety, little suspecting the impact will activate his "hyper-evolved cells." Able to absorb the kinetic energy of any blow, he's invulnerable to bullet or blade. Focusing that power in fists or feet, he has "a punch like a piston, a pounce like a panther." You wish you had that famous red *O* sigil on your chest, wish it would project a hologram of your father. He'd tell you you'd been sent back to escape the destruction of the Earth itself. Later, in issue #5, you'd discover you can use this Omicron-beam as a weapon, unleash the kinetic energy built up within your body. And where at first your creators simply had you "leaping leagues in a single spring," so many would read those bounds across the sky as flight that soon the misreading would become mythos, that accumulated potential, as ever, the rationale.

You're just like Overman in his cover identity of Grant Cooper, a young law student and intern at the DA's office, investigating cover-ups and thwarting diabolical plans. Not that you investigate cover-ups and thwart diabolical plans — that's not you on the cover of *Adventure Comics* #19, punching a fighter plane from the sky. You're only ten. But you might study law when you grow up. And you're shy and quiet like Grant Cooper is, bespectacled too. You once yearned to be the Shadow, as you sat by the radio on Sunday evenings, in your pyjamas, but not now.

THE PARADOX PROTOCOL

The character's popularity (and power) grew like your scrawny limbs, his nemesis's reach scaling up too, Roman gradually recast as war profiteer selling weapons to both sides. Then came the "big turning point," (according to Donald Black's *Overman: The Century of a Saviour*) in *Overman* issues #23-24, *The Paradox Protocol*, where Roman has a minor villain with mesmeric powers, the Fiend, hypnotise the Saviour of the Century and suggest he kill Hitler to end WWII, issue #23 finishing with Overman in flight over the Atlantic.

Your big brother was in France then. If only Overman was real, you thought.

At the last minute, as Overman's about to raze Berlin, his hologram activates — Wait! No! An evil ploy is afoot: if he kills Hitler he'll change history such that he'll never be born; worse, Rex Roman himself will become President. The issue ends with Overman instead saving a crashed fighter pilot (whose features bear a remarkable resemblance to Overman's: "Like a long-lost brother, or even...ancestor!") then returning home with a solemn vow to fight wherever he can because "the smallest battle may win the greatest victory."

You read it in your tree house, one hot summer day.

July 13th.

According to Jeff Steinman, writer and co-creator with artist Jim Schweitzer, "the whole paradox thing was largely an excuse, a convenience. See, we kept getting letters from kids asking if Overman could stop the war so their dad could come home. And we thought, what are we going to do here? How do we answer this? Then we hit on the idea that this all-powerful character *couldn't* do just anything, because if he did the wrong thing, well, it'd mean he was never born."

You read that interview...when? In college, in the seventies, wasn't it? Or nineties?

As Black writes, "From the Paradox was born a true Paraclete. Expedience or not, in this sacrifice of all-conquering omnipotence on the altar of contingency, the Overman became Everyman, the messiah became mortal, a salvator with strings attached, bound to his terrible cross of consequences. That he fought the smallest battles, on our soil, in our skies, in the streets of our cities, by day or night – this made his struggle ours, the struggle of the human spirit against history itself."

But if his struggle was ours, *your* struggle was never *his*, was it? He didn't have your secret.

Red Shift, Blue Shift

Polio-stricken cub reporter Gary Gordon may walk with a cane, but when he shouts the magic word three times in a second – "Thunderbolt! Thunderbolt! Thunderbolt!" (try it, kids!) – it activates the powers given him by a mysterious wizard masquerading as a doctor, and Gordon transforms into the fastest man on the planet: the Human Blur, the Blue Streak... the Thunderbolt!

Well, of course, that's the Golden Age origin. The Thunderbolt who heralded the Silver Age with his 1956 revival had his particles accelerated to the speed of light by blue omicron rays...but that's another story.

You remember both.

Caught in the blast of a meteorite, its exotic alien minerals vaporised on impact, permeating every cell in his body, Jake Walker wakes up in the crater, apparently unharmed but for a weird golden glow to his skin, fading even as his head clears. With his thrill-seeking nature, though, it's not long before a practice run in an abandoned Speedway track reveals the truth...that when excitement sparks in his heart, that spark ignites his very molecules, transforming him into Flameboy — Flameboy, the Comet Kid, shooting fireballs from his fingers, blasting through the sky like a human rocket. You...

You love them both. You *desire* them both. Thunderbolt can run rings round the super-villain, save the planet, and get the copy in before the *Globe*'s star reporter, "Slick" Jackson, has even finished his coffee. Often with some friendly banter aimed at fellow Legion member Flameboy along the way. Fighting villains for the fun of it, ribbing the other Legion members (only to wind up doused by an irate Water Woman or blown out by the Thunderbolt), Flameboy's roguish charm is…hot. "You're light on your feet for a hoofer, Twinkletoes," he joshes. "But me? I'm just plain smokin'!"

"Yeah? Well, light me up a Lucky, hotshot," says Thunderbolt in *Legion of American Watchers* #18. "I'll try not to snuff you with my slipstream."

That friendly banter between "the Blunderdolt" and "Ginger, the Dancing Zippo" (a reference to Ginger Rogers as much as Flameboy's red hair) was condemned by Dr Werther Fredericks in *The Corruption of the Young* (1954) as "blatant homoerotic flirtation, rife with innuendo." Still, it's the most popular pairing in comics, the limited series *Flameboy and Thunderbolt: Red Shift, Blue Shift* one of AC's all-time bestsellers.

At thirteen you drew fan art of them kissing.

In Cold Pointed Steel

Fredericks didn't know shit, you think. Overman and Hookman at AC Comics, Monkeyboy at Wonder — none of the Big Three could possibly be "inverts," as one of the least vicious terms had it back then. The Golden Age was an era free of faggots, devoid of deviants…in the surface text, anyways. Captain Steadfast wasn't no queer. The Secret ain't some homo. The Quantum's kinda gay, but not in that sense — in the sense that he's *lame*. He doesn't kick ass like the Green Blade or Warhound. Warhound *rocks*; he's the only modern superhero even close to those classics.

The Hookman does sort of resonate with you though. His origin is dark—mother dead in childbirth, father shot before his very eyes, for gambling debts. That image, the reflection in the young boy's eye, the man hanging by his cuffed wrists from an abattoir meathook…if you were that kid you'd have his nightmares. Little wonder young John Flynn grew up on the streets, his only break being sent to juvie, where a gruff boxing coach steered him right, put the punk on the straight and narrow.

"Work on that hook, kid," growls Coach. "It's the hook'll floor 'em."

Coach gets Flynn a job on the docks, a stevedore hauling cargo, hook in hand. By night he trains for his first pro bout, fixes up an old Indian Scout motorbike, or reads.

"Brains *and* brawn," says Coach.

Goons in the dressing room, threats — throw the fight or else.

SMACK! CRACK!

"Tell *that* to the Shark! Tell him to find another patsy."

But the next day Flynn is down on the docks and there's something in the water, a body. Hauled out with a boathook, Coach's limp form lies on the jetty. And that night, the barbed beast is born.

In his steel-blue skintights with midnight-blue trappings—trunks, boots and gauntlets, cape furled around him, he carves a cool silhouette. It's the hooks that are his trademark though, glinting in the shadows. Part welded helmet, part sewn-together mask, his cowl sports the scariest — a metal mohawk, a centurion's crest in cold pointed steel. Spring-loaded hooks built into his gloves slash out for combat or for climbing, fire into the air as grappling irons. He has no superpower but his will — to bring a reckoning down upon all racketeers.

He has his sidekick too, Kid Swift.

WHO YOU MIGHT BE

There have, of course, been a number of Kid Swifts over the years, with various origins. Your favourite was the second, Todd Jonas, an orphaned street kid like Hookman himself (by then, the "the" in the character's name had largely been dropped), he survived by his wits, "hustling and grifting" until the Hookman took him in.

You'll never forgive the fan-voted outcome of the controversial late-eighties storyline, *The Costume in the Closet*. You'll never forgive the fact that the world's first homo superhero is no sooner out than he's suffering and dying. You'll never forgive, never forget, never...

You dressed up as Kid Swift one Halloween—red tee-shirt and pants, yellow trunks and cape, green mask and belt. That was the year Derek Mason dressed up as Water Woman and all the kids made fun of him from then on, called him queer. Shit, you were all so young, did you even know what it meant? Well, maybe. When Kid Swift on TV said, "Golly gosh gumdrops, Hookman! I don't think it's just the Jester's laughing gas that's making me feel so gay!" you got the word's...other meaning.

Didn't stop you taunting Derek though, scorning him.

Him being a sissy took the heat off you, of course, and with a name like Animus Thrawn you needed a scapegoat. Annie-Mouse, they called you, Annie-Mouse Prawn. Even your friends called you Mouse, the nickname sticking long past the point when anyone but you even remembered it was a taunt. You didn't mind so much after you found this old Nebula anthology in the library, a science-fiction story with a cool street-thief character called Mouse. He sort of merged with Kid Swift in your daydream doodles of who you might be if you weren't you.

But, no. They couldn't let you have that. As if AIDS and Mutual Assured Destruction weren't enough, they had to put a bullet in your very fantasies of a future. Cold steel in Todd Jonas's gut. The Jester's laughter echoed like some creepy carnival automaton as he stood there watching; Hookman kneeling over the dying youth; the Fiend standing over him, behind him, the pure malevolence that had played the City's Sentinel like a puppet, shrouding his mind with illusions to tear.

"What'll you say when they ask how Kid Swift died?" mocks the Jester. "By crook…or by hook?"

Hide Your Sins in Silence

A villain wakes from a nightmare, heart pounding, hands grasping the bedsheets in panic. What was that noise? A whisper? An echo? A moan of the soul, a groan of terror in a guilty heart? A fedora shadows a featureless face, a long coat billows and, in the dark, a grey shape slips away, for the Secret's work is done. Dream on, you wrongdoers who think your soul is safe! Imagine that no one knows your foul deeds! But there is one who walks among the sleeping, one who can damn you with a single word whispered softly into your dreams.

His origin unknown, none can say whence his powers came, whether his terrible torments are magic, mechanics or mesmerism. But of this you can be sure: you can cover up your crimes, hush up and hide your sins in silence, but the Secret will haunt you to the grave!

"An iron cage?" he scoffs in *Awesome Comics* #40. "Hah! There are some secrets that cannot be kept, my friend. Whatever you do, they will…slip out."

And in a little trick of the pen, perspectives shift from one panel to the next: the Secret's free and the villain caged!

You used to love listening to *The Shadow* serials, but for all that the Secret is homage standing a hair's-breadth from plagiarism, something about the Master of Mysteries has always soured you to him. Vengeful to the point of vicious, shaping the dreams of criminals to drive them to insanity, he exploits hidden shames to enforce his merciless morality. With that callousness and the similar powers, you could easily believe the rumour: that the Fiend was introduced not just to kill Kid Swift, but with a shocking revelation planned — that the Fiend was what the Secret would eventually become.

"It does too work," you argue with Keith Johnstone. "See, in *Catastrophe for Universes*, Project Moonchild only *think* they've brought a demon from another dimension. Really they've brought the Fiend from the *future*, and that's why he knows everyone's secret identities just like the Secret does, because he *is* the Secret."

You're in your room, comics strewn around you on your brother's bed — vacant since he was called up for Iraq.

"So how come the Fiend can move in time?" says Keith. "The Secret can't move in time."

"Because Project Moonchild doesn't *bind* him properly. They *make* him like that."

The Fabric of Spacetime

Of course, later writers were to use the Paradox Protocol as the basis for numerous retcons of AC's continuity. The earliest and still most controversial example came in the wake of Steinman's blacklisting, at the height of the McCarthy era, with *The Red Menace* story arc, where new writer Edgar Franklin had Overman discover that — *SHOCK! HORROR!* — Rex Roman has secretly been in league with Stalin all along. To prevent a Communist takeover of the U.S., Overman has no choice but to sacrifice himself, punching the A-bomb Roman tries to drop on Washington, exploding it high in the atmosphere.

A nuclear blast was the one thing that could kill Overman, you knew. It was thrilling, that final panel of Overman's shadow burned across Capitol Hill and the question "Is this the end?" It was *excruciating*.

In the next issue though, *The Paradox Punch*, Overman's origin is retold, updated. His hologram father reveals a wild twist: from the temporal shock waves of Overman's death a whole new future-history erupts; now it's a *Communist* takeover of the U.S. that'll lead to the Earth's destruction.

You remember the hot July 13th you read that comic, in your tree house, in another world.

It all hinges on a hint that Overman is one of his own ancestors. By sacrificing himself before he's passed on his genes, he's created a future in which he was never born; but that means he *never went back in time*, meaning he *didn't die!* "Reality warping in a great loop back to the very beginning of it all," a new fifty-first century is forged. And luckily Overman's father is able to detect echoes of the original history left in the fabric of spacetime by Overman's Omicron-beams, able to warn his son.

Nobody warned your brother, did they?

You'd read the recap of Overman's adventures in this remade continuity, all condensed to a montage of panels. You'd read the thrilling climax, where he again confronts his arch-enemy on the plane above Washington; only this time, with his Omicronbeam, Overman blasts a portal to the Fourth Dimension, hurls the A-bomb through it just in time.

The whole world rewritten! You had to tell someone. You scrambled down the rope-ladder, ran into the kitchen, the living room.

Soldiers stood, hats in hand.

Your mother sat on the sofa, crying.

The first word you heard was "Korea."

You Can Never Go Home

Shot down in the skies over Pearl Harbor, leaping from his plummeting P-36 Hawk without a parachute, Captain Steve "Steadfast" Sturgeon can only pray for a miracle. And a miracle he gets! Struck by lightning at that exact moment, he finds himself standing before the Archons of the Cosmos, with a choice between Eternity and Earth. But for Steve Sturgeon, no choice needs to be made.

"Send me back," he says. "There's a war to be won!"

There was talk of the movie having him shot down over Afghanistan, like your brother, who isn't ever coming back, not ever.

In the history books, it says there was no third wave to the Japanese at-tack, but any airman who was there that day will tell you those Nips were turned back by a strange sight in the sky…an angel sent from Heaven, an American angel. And so began the daring deeds of the hero known as Captain Steadfast.

"We'll finish what you started, No-Joe Tojo!" he says in *Captain Steadfast* #13. "And that's the truth!"

The truth? you think. Yeah, and Nixon's not a crook.

Home for the holidays, you sit in your old bedroom, hiding from Christmas.

To the people of Atlantis she is Princess Naia, half-mortal daughter of the Oceanid Queen Metis and her long-lost human consort. To the surface-dwellers she is Water Woman, sensual and spritely as Aphrodite, fearless and feisty as Artemis...Water Woman, Mistress of the Seas. When Princess Naia investigates a disturbance among her dolphin subjects, she discovers Ensign Hank Murray, the sole survivor of a German U-boat attack. "His strange skin...so...pink!" she says (*Top-Notch Comics* #8).

And though her people are sworn never to intercede in the affairs of surface-dwellers, she saves him.

Exiled from her beloved Atlantis in punishment, what's a girl to do but... fight Nazis with her electric eel-hide whip!

They say you can never go home again; it's all too true. Two years of college in New York and you've discovered the Village, sex, drugs and shoulder-length hair. It's changed you, is still changing you. It was that drag queen in the Stonewall, dressed as Water Woman — that's when you decided it was time to come clean, to come out. Like you weren't already the beatnik black sheep of the family anyways, the stranger in their midst.

FLOATING THROUGH TIME

Professor Miles Quant is on the verge of replicating the primal state of matter in his physics lab when he discovers one of his colleagues is a Nazi spy sent to steal the secret for the Germans. Knocked out and left in an overloading photon chamber, exposed to an "uncertainty field" beyond all measure, his atoms are thrown into pure flux. Able to transform himself into any element, to shrink or grow at will, even to teleport by swapping places with something of equal mass, he is no longer Quant, M., Ph.D., but is now the Quantum, Master of Matter!

You take the joint from him, beautiful hippy farmboy with hair as blond as Captain Steadfast's but long. It brushes across your naked chest as he shifts, tickles. Above you, the sky is a full-colour painting in spattered light, Milky Way aglow in acid streamings, wheelings. Ancient gods battle in chariots that whirl apart to mandalas, Celtic knots of weaving dragons. You feel them in your serpent spine.

"Cosmic, man," he says, then laughs. "That sounds like a superhero, right? Cosmicman."

Screw college, you think. Screw Vietnam. It's the Age of Aquarius and everything's changing.

You've got a boyfriend.

"Turn lead into gold?" says Quantum in *True-American Comics* #3. "No, Dr von Strann... Into the very stuff both elements are made of!"

It's only later, during AC's *Catastrophe for Two Worlds*, in an attempt to simplify the morass of rationales for superpowers, that the Prof's "primalised matter" is revealed to be none other than the proteanite toxic to Overman. Fortunately, it's in an omicron-irradiated form harmless to the Man of the Future. Unfortunately, during AC's *Ultimate Catastrophe*, the Fiend will reverse that omicron-irradiation, turn the Quantum into a doomsday weapon with which to kill Overman himself.

You take the joint from him, beautiful sculpted surfer, hair as blond as Captain Steadfast's but long. It tickles your naked chest as he shifts. Above you, the sky is a myriad of universes exploded to atoms of a cosmic man. Sand under you, surf crashing the beach, its spray aglow in acid glitterings, all is energy disguised as mass, imagination masked as energy, forever shifting, muscles of a horse beneath its skin.

"You know we're floating through time even as we lie here," you say. "Or time is floating through us."

Later, you'll forget why that felt so true.

VICE WILL FALL

"You look great," he says. "Dude, you look *hot*."

"I look like a douche," you say.

But you blush as much because the sleeveless wetsuit *does* cut a sleek physique in black and red, lean arms exposed, showing off your shoulder tats like a motherfucking rock star. You feel so nakedly narcissistic, seeing the strut and stance in the mirror. Shit, however slick you look it's not going to help when you fall off the board. You're *so* not sure about these lessons. But...

"I'm *so* doing the Fiend next Halloween," you grin.

"Mouse, dude. You're such a geek."

Attacked by bandits and left for dead in the Sahara Desert, millionaire playboy Franklin Wallace stumbles on the lost oasis of a mysterious green-robed Moor, Amir Al-Hazred. Bound for centuries by an evil sorcerer's curse, Al-Hazred plays on Wallace's greed and gratitude to trick him into a death-match… where the true conflict is in Wallace's heart.

"Do I fight to win this 'great treasure' he guards? Or to give this poor madman the release he prays for…*in death*? I…I don't know!"

Only as Al-Hazred dies in Wallace's arms does he reveal the truth:

"You were led here, to take my life…and sacred duty. *You* are the Archon of the Earth now!"

For only a man on the cusp of redemption, a man whose past is vice and his future virtue, can take up the Kamir Husam — a sword that can cut through anything, even spacetime itself.

"When lesser man and greater man, Together with a single hand, Strike out for freedom on command, Then vice will fall and virtue stand!" (*The Green Blade* #1).

Hypnotised by Project Moonchild, it's the Green Blade who opens the portal, unleashes the Fiend on AC's multiverse.

"You never talk about him," he says, handing the photo back.

"There's not really much to say. And…well, ten years…"

In truth, it feels like more. And less. The scar tissue of teenage grief is smooth, healed to an image, but ever tender. Every July 13th is *that* July 13th for you. But your heart remade, somehow it's almost welcome, a reminder to live your life. To finish your term paper, phone Mom, get your ass to the Prop. 8 demo on Saturday and…today…

In the wetsuits, you look like Thunderbolt and Flameboy.

"Come on." You smile. "Surf's up."

THE ORIGIN OF THE FIEND

You were reading *The Paradox Protocol* the day the soldiers brought the news that your brother had been killed in action in France. You were reading *The Paradox Punch* the day the soldiers brought the news that your brother had been killed in action in Korea. *Catastrophe for Two Worlds, Catastrophe for Universes, Ultimate Catastrophe.* Vietnam, Bosnia, Afghanistan.

You're thirteen years old and you've just finished reading Grant Milligan's new graphic novel, *The Origin of the Fiend*, when the soldiers bring the news that your brother has been killed in action in Iraq.

The Fiend's name has just been revealed.

They stand in the ruins of the Legion of American Watchers' moonbase.

"Animus Thrawn," says the Secret.

"Not any more," says the Fiend.

The story is fucked-up. That's the only way to describe it. The Fiend who killed Kid Swift, the Fiend who killed Overman, the Fiend who turned AC's entire pantheon of superheroes against one another in the Ultimate Catastrophe crossover event…that demon is from the Fifth Dimension, from a universe in which that pantheon is mere fiction.

"From another reality?" says the latest Kid Swift. But the Fiend simply laughs.

"There *is* no reality," he says.

You're outside the five-and-dime store on Lincoln Street, flicking through a comic, but every page is from a different issue, a different year, a different era. *Wait.*

You're reading it in your tree house, every turn of a page a different character, a different story, universe, July 13th. *No.*

But you're running inside, through years of kitchens, to a half dozen living rooms where soldiers of shifting wars stand, and where mothers sit on sofas, here, there, anywhere, crying. *No.*

France, Korea, Vietnam. *No.*

And the story is a kid screaming "**NO!**" because no superhero saved his brother.

No.

No, that's not the story, you're shouting as galaxies of lives explode around you. In every one of those lives, the story is healing, not hate. It's college and Christmases and coming out; it's bitching about Nixon, Reagan, Bush; laughing with beatniks, hippies, surfers; living; loving.

It's *this* moment of madness you're denying.

Except you can't deny it, as you stand in the comic store, your boyfriend's hand on your shoulder, as you open *The Origin of the Fiend* to this page, and are torn into infinities of fiction.

And a red rage for vengeance rips out of your lungs.

Each Botched and Broken Continuity

A five-and-dime store on Lincoln Street, but it's a city that doesn't exist in your world, a blend of New York and Los Angeles, San Francisco and Chicago. Passersby wear fedoras and Walkmans, G.I. uniforms and baseball caps; they come out of cars with running boards, talking on their cell phones. It might be 1910 or 2010, but you know it's both and more besides — your story untold but unfolding across each botched and broken continuity. The Legion of American Watchers fight each other on the street, and you look on, laughing.

It's the Fiend's first appearance.

"Animus Thrawn! Fiend of the Hell Dimension, I bind thee to this world! I bind thee to my will!"

The high priest whirls, his bloody hands raised to the thundering skies. The Green Blade stands behind him, entranced, sword aglow, lighting up the stone circle and the Acolytes of Armageddon, the hooded scientist-priests of Project Moonchild.

"It's too late!" Kid Swift is shouting as the Hookman slams into the high priest.

Crouched in the bloody pentagram, you look into the boy's eyes, remember his death; it's already written. *Rewritten.* The *Elsewhens* one-shot series retold it in Edo Japan.

"What'll you say when they ask how Kid Swift died?" the Jester mocks. "By crook...*or by hook?*"

Another scene. You're looking down upon your handiwork — one dead sidekick, one hero on his knees — and you can feel your fucking glee in the destruction. So they wanted a fucking villain? But even as you laugh, you're sobbing, focus free-falling through too many memories of malevolence to bear, to another:

"...by sending his mind back and forth along his own timestream, between his past and future," the Quantum is saying. "It's really quite ingenious."

"That's one word for it," says Flameboy.

Another memory, another, another. No, *memory* isn't the right word; this is raw *experience*. You're blowing up cities, snuffing henchmen, murdering Overman himself, resetting the multiverse in *Ultimate Catastrophe*. And you can't stop, can't hold to one moment, have no control. But the worst of it is that, as you're shredded in the maelstrom of your future, you realise you will. Eventually.

And you'll be the Fiend. You'll kill Kid Swift, destroy the multiverse itself. Even now you're *becoming* your own demented future, knowing only fury at the brutal secret of your origin: your heart was pure until one day...

THE ORIGIN OF THE FIEND

Black with red details, the neoprene skinsuit fits snug to your form, enough stretch to carve your musculature in its shadows but in a hide thick as leather, not some tawdry film of spandex, lightweight and lurid as the eighties. It's snakeskin jeans versus nylon tights, and you look fucking killer in it. Sleeveless, of course, to show off the black sigils graved in the scarlet skin of your arms. In the scar tissue covering your whole body, from being dragged through the searing omicron energy fields between your world and this one.

Black gauntlets, belt and boots.

You're ready.

You flex your fingers, spark up a ball of light in your palm. It's pure illusion, but then so is this whole world, the whole universe, the multiverse. It's not even a true superpower, your trickery, just the science of a few centuries into the future wired into your gauntlets; but that just makes it all the more satisfying, knowing what you're about to do with it. How that tediously earnest paragon of reason, that ponderous fool, Professor Miles Quant aka the Quantum, will bend to your will, reconfigure his proteanite matter to the madness you conjure in his mind.

Then you're there, hand out like Flameboy blasting, fingers twisting, crunching thought; and the Quantum goes boom, Overman swallowed in the blast. You've lived this moment countless times, will live it countless more. You know this, remembering all the pasts and futures you've jumped back to here from. Time travel? No. Time is meaningless.

Reality splits as the Paradox Protocol kicks in, a new multiverse born through the breach, a rebooted continuity in which Overman's timepod will arrive in the early nineties. New to everyone but you, at least. You were still reading after *Ultimate Catastrophe*. In one life anyway.

You flick through this new timestream to your other favourite moment, the finale of *The Origin of the Fiend*, the Law headquarters in ruins, the Secret crawling over the rubble.

"Animus," he begs. "You know this is insane."

You kick him onto his back, crouch to cradle his head, pull the grey mask from his face. Your face.

You were wrong, you know now. That shocking revelation? It wasn't that the Secret would become the Fiend. No, it was that one day the Fiend would reach towards redemption, become the Secret.

"Mouse."

"Not today," you laugh.

And snap his neck.

Sons of the Law

THE EDITOR

With the Wild West it's often hard to tell where fact ends and fantasy begins. Journalists writing for the newspapers back east were no strangers to elaboration and even downright fabrication. Many of them took the stories that they'd heard, the wild tales of gunslingers and gamblers — tales that grew larger with each telling — and wrote them up as dimestore novels; those penny dreadfuls, in many ways, created an idea of the West that was, in some ways, truer than the real history.

My maternal grandfather was one of those men. Between 1871 and 1882, while writing for the *Arkham Herald* under his real name, Joshua Hobbes, he also wrote a series of western novels under the pen-name of Jake Carter. They were never the most popular, and today even the most ardent bibliophile and historian of pulp might be forgiven for not recognising the nom-de-plume. My uncle on my mother's side, however, kept every one of Jake Carter's original manuscripts until the day he died.

Recently, then, these manuscripts came into my possession along with various notes and fragments, one of which, I noticed as I was looking through them, was headed up, in bold block capitals, with a phrase that caught my eye — **SONS OF THE LAW**. Reading on, I gradually began to piece together the story of a gunfight that took place in an unnamed town, in an unnamed state, on an unspecified date. Whether the interviews and scraps of description that make up the story have any grounding in reality or not, I don't know. It might just be that my grandfather saw firsthand the bullets and the blood. On the other hand, it is entirely possible that what we have here are only notes for a planned novel that my grandfather, for some reason, abandoned. Whatever the case, I thought it was a story worth the telling and, out of respect for Joshua Hobbes — and Jake Carter — I thought I should let him tell it in his own words...

The Writer

The saloon is quiet; you can tell that there is something in the air. Trouble is brewing.

The four strangers know that every eye in the place is on them, flicking first from one to another, to another, to the last, watching them all the time. For their part, they watch each other, across the saloon, silent and wary, as cougars meeting in the woods will circle each other and stare to size each other up. Everyone knows these are the only players in the game — these four strangers and the judge that they're waiting for.

Standing at the middle of the bar is the hunter. His scuffed-brown, sand-scoured, leather overcoat near enough touches the floor but at the bottom of it, sticking out, you can still see the tip of his Sharps Big 50, built to bring down buffalo. Though his face is shadowed by his hat, you can see the grim steel-grey of his eyes. This is a man who's hunting for something, hunting someone, and everything about him says it isn't for the bounty.

Down at one end of the bar, clear space all round him, there's the killer. He has the sharp black waistcoat, black hat, black ribbon tie and rig — two Colt 45's in holsters, one each side, belted, buckled at the waist and tied around his thighs — that tells the world that he's a pro. This is a gunslinger, with the cold heart of a rattlesnake and the deadly bite to match. Every man in the saloon knows his game, and near enough everyone can guess his name. At the moment, he has his eye on the hunter.

At a green baize table at the back of the saloon, the gambler is sitting, dealing out a hand of solitaire and watching everything that goes on at the bar. Every so often, he brushes imaginary dust from off the shoulder of his immaculate grey jacket. From the red silk handkerchief in his breast pocket to the red silk cravat, he spells money. A lot of people in the bar are watching him, trying to figure out which way he'll fall in what is coming down. Nobody is sure. But you could lay good odds he has a Derringer up his sleeve and a jack-knife in his boot.

Last of all is the drifter, a young man — little more than a kid, really, sitting at a table on his own where he can watch the other three without too much of a trouble. He's less on edge than anyone in the saloon, so cool and calm you'd almost say he didn't give a damn except for the way that he *is* eyeing up the situation, like a big-city theatre critic rating actors in a play. He's young, but he has old, old eyes. If you looked hard enough you might just be able to tell that the faded dusty outfit that he wears was once a uniform, stripped of all braid and all insignia. He tugs at the yellow bandanna around his neck.

The saloon is quiet, only the low murmur of a few hushed voices, a wrangler in the corner muttering to himself, and the strangled sobs of one of the show-girls to be heard — a pretty girl in a dress all silks and frills, scarlet and purple. An old Negro hums a sad tune to himself as he sweeps a broken bottle off the floor.

Over this, from outside, there comes the slow *creak…creak…creak* of wood under a swinging weight.

The Hunter

—My pa, he was a farmhand for this big-shot landowner, old army man, local judge, real pillar of society. Tell the truth, I don't remember much about it on account of we left when my brother and me was still real young. Seems the judge's son, he kind of took a fancy to my ma and, well, he gave her an apple from the Judge's own orchard. She didn't want none of that boy though, cause she could see that he was mean as hell, so she takes the apple straight to my pa. Anyway, the judge found out about it, there was accusations and arguments and the judge he threw us all out. Whole family. You imagine that — on account of an apple.

— Those were hard years, me and my brother growing up. We moved east and set up our own little farmstead. I'm telling you, we had nothing. The soil was dust. Every year praying for rain. You grow up hard. We put our blood and sweat into that land.

— So, years later the judge shows up, only by now he's moved on. Seems he's a made himself a cattle-baron. His boy, he's split from him, he's off raising hell all over the state; shit, he's the meanest son of a bitch that ever lived, they're saying. Everybody's heard of him. Judge's son gone bad. And that just makes the old bastard meaner than hell.

— So the judge shows up and he's buying up land and raising taxes on the set-tlers, just cause he can, cause he's the Law, isn't he? And I don't know why, but my brother, my own brother, falls in with all his cowboys. He wants to ride out on the trail, wants to wear a gun at his side, wants a little excitement in his life.

— Well, the judge, he wasn't happy till our barn was burned to the ground. Set fire to our crop, killed all our livestock. I remember the smell of it to this day. My pa, he tried to stop me, but I went out after those boys, and you know what they did? They sent my brother back to stop me.

— I shot him in a cornfield. I remember looking down at his body, and the blood just running into the earth. I knew it was him before I shot him; I just couldn't stop it. It'd gone too far.

— I guess the judge thought he'd broken me, cause they threw me in jail and beat the hell out of me — judge did, that is...wouldn't let anyone else touch me — but they didn't hang me. No, they just branded me. That's where I got this here mark. They branded me and they ran me out of town. I told him then he ought to kill me. I told him then that if he didn't kill me, nothing would. I'd come after him and nothing was gonna get me till I'd finished with him. That's why I'm here. I don't give a damn what else is coming down, cause I know there's nothing can hurt me till I'm finished with my business. That's what this mark is. Unfinished business.

THE KILLER

—I love my father. I surely do. I reckon in a lot of ways I only ever wanted to please him. But you know, he surely is a hard man to please. Nothing I ever did was right for him. I was always the proverbial bad penny, the bastard son he couldn't get rid of. Black sheep of the family. I reckon one day I just woke up and thought, *To hell with it.*

— I say that. I say "I reckon," but in honest truth I do remember the day real well. It was the day I saw his true face, you see, the day I saw what he was really like.

— You see, he had this old slave — this old house nigger called Job — and one day he's cursing me and saying Job's a better man than I'll ever be, talking about how loyal and all Job is, and so on. Sure, I says to him, but what the hell else has he got? Job, he's like a cowardly dog that no matter how many times you kick it, it keeps coming back, cause it's got nowhere else to go and it's too scared to run away even if it had, and anyway it can't understand why you're kicking it.

— Now, my father, my old man, he makes a bet with me, bets me that no matter what I do, I can't turn Job away from him. Well, I was wild in those days. Hell, I burned in the night like the goddamn morning star. Now, I am not proud of it, I surely am not, but I took him up on that bet. Made that poor slave's life a living hell. And you know what? I lost.

— That's when I knew, when I looked into my father's eyes, when he'd won. That's when I knew what power is, how it works. It's not fear. It's not being afraid of someone that gives them a hold over you. No, the kind of slavery I'm talking about, it doesn't come through chains and whippings. It's the kind that creeps into your heart when you're not looking, when all you want is to have a quiet life and let someone else take care of all the hangings and suchlike that needs be done. That's where people like my father step in because they're bigger and heavier than anyone else, and they know, they know, that they were born to lay down the law. Power is in the knowing that you're going to win.

— Every gunfight I go into, that's what I think. I know I'm going to win. I learned that from my old man.

— Now you may not believe me, but I tell you it is surely true that people have called me a cold and heartless son of a bitch. Now that just is not true; I am the goddamn fires of hell compared to my old man. Cold? You look into his eyes and, I tell you, it will freeze your heart. I seen him burn a town to ashes because he didn't approve of their fornication. I seen him blow a dam and flood a whole valley just to clear the settlers off it. I never thought he'd do this though...

— You know, we have not spoken to each other in about ten years; Last time we spoke, know what he said to me? *You were always my favourite.* Looked me dead in the eye, face hard as stone, and said that to me...

— I always knew he was a cold-hearted bastard, but I never thought he'd do this. I never thought he'd hang the boy.

THE SLAVE

—Yassuh, I surely do love the Massuh. He's a hard man, but the Massuh's always done right by Old Abraham. Old Abraham's been promised by the Massuh; Massuh promised me he always gonna take care of Old Abraham's children, *real* good care of them. Old Abraham's gonna have a hundred grandchildren, gonna be a whole nation someday.

— Yassuh, Old Abraham's real proud to work for the Massuh — do anything for the Massuh, *anything.* Why, one day the Massuh he up'n asked me if I'd kill my own son for him. Yassuh, I said, I surely would, if the Massuh asked me to. And the Massuh, he says, *Prove it.*

— Well, Old Abraham, he was mighty scared but he wasn't gonna make the Massuh angry. No sir. So he takes his son up into the hills and he lays him down, and he would've killed him too, if the Massuh hadn't stopped him. Killed a goat instead — or was it a lamb? Can't rightly recall.

— But you see now? Old Abraham's gonna have a hundred grandchildren, and they gonna be a whole nation. Yassuh.

— What's that you say? Yassuh, he surely would've done. Old Abraham knows he would. Massuh, he kill his own son for being on the wrong side of the law. Yassuh, that's the Massuh's son up there. His only son. Leastwise, his only *proper* son.

— Yassuh, he was claiming to be a U.S. Marshall, he was. Massuh wouldn't stand for it. Townsfolk wouldn't stand for it, neither. Good folks round here. They knows the law. Yassuh, he's a hard man, the Massuh. But he's a righteous man.

THE SHOWGIRL

—Mister, I don't feel much like talking right now, and I don't feel much like doing nothing else. I'm sorry, honey, but tonight, I just wanna get drunk. Sure. Okay. Bourbon, mister.

— That's right. I knew him. I knew him better than anyone in the world, and he knew me the same way. He showed me there was more to life than being a cheap whore in a no-class saloon. Showed me there was more to *me*.

— No, he didn't hurt nobody, mister. He wouldn't even wear a gun. I kept on telling him, kept saying that they wouldn't stand for it, that they'd come gunning for him. I think he knew it from the start.

— I don't know if he was. He said he was and I believed him. And he had the badge. But that didn't stop them, mister. That didn't stop them.

— I know he loved me. First time I set eyes on him — when he rode into town with his boys and started tearing up the courtroom — the two of us just kind of saw each other as he was riding down the street. He was the first man ever looked at me that way, mister, first man didn't look at me like I was dirt. He looked at me like I was something special.

— I think maybe we might have been married, you know? I think I would've liked that.

— They ought to cut him down, though. Somebody ought to cut him down.

THE GAMBLER

—Yes sir, I sold him out, and I don't care who knows it. I'm a gambling man, son, and I surely do enjoy the living of my life on the dangerous side. Only sometimes Lady Luck deals you a hand you can't do nothing with except fold.

— Why, me and him, son, we went back a long way, but I tell you…there was a man who kept his cards close to his chest. Didn't give a thing away until that final game. I mean to say, I've played a lot of card games in my time, clean and dirty, and I never known a man so cool under pressure, not in all my days.

— So we were playing cards, and that cheap slut, she's draped all over him like usual, of course. And all of a sudden he holds up his whisky and his cigar, and he says, *You all gonna remember me when I'm gone, right?* And he takes a slug of whisky and a puff on his cigar, and says, *What you all gonna do without me?* Well, all the boys start yammering about this and that, but I just sit there, quiet-like. I remember, I had aces and deuces, Dead Man's Hand. And while they're all yakking and yammering, he looks me straight in the eye and says, real low, *You know, one of you boys sitting here is gonna sell me out.* And I looked at the hand he dealt me, and I looked at him, and I knew.

— I'm a gambling man, son, so I know a high-stakes game when I see one. And I looked into his eyes, and I knew he wasn't bluffing. I didn't believe it, but I knew he wasn't bluffing. *Make it quick,* he said. *Make it quick.*

— I don't know if he thought they wouldn't go through with it. I don't think so; I think he knew the moment I left the table, he was a dead man. I think he knew *exactly* what he was dealing when he dealt me that Dead Man's Hand, and I think he knew exactly what he was dealing himself.

— Times I think he was just tired of being the peacemaker, tired of having to carry the Law about with him, wearing the badge that nobody else would wear. But he wasn't a quitter. No, I think he just decided that he had to die, that it was only when the people saw just how far it could go — just how much the judge and his bought men were capable of — it was only then that they were going to wake up and see the Law for what it really is…and what it *should* be. That it was too heavy a weight for just one man to carry. We're all of us sons of the Law. All of us.

— Oh, yeah. You like it? Real pretty piece of firepower, ain't she? Custom single-action Star revolver, silver-plated and engraved, ivory handle-grips. Shoots like a dream too. Cost me thirty silver dollars. I think she's gonna come in handy real soon.

The Wrangler

—No sir, I never knew the man. Heard about him and all, but I—now that's a lie. I never ran with his crew in all my life, I swear. I'm just passing through, headed west. *I'm telling you.* I don't know the man, never have.

—Well, I'm right pleased to meet you. My name…well…you can call me Thomas. Hell no, I'm just a drifter, travelling along, thought I'd stop off in this nice town for a drink and a bath. Yep, looks like something's going down here, and I don't think I want to be a part of it. Rather just sit here on the sidelines and watch.

— Now, it's funny you should say that, cause I noticed it too. Kinda spooky, don't you think, looking at some fella swinging on a scaffold and seeing a face that looks just a little too damn much like the one you look at in the mirror? Kinda like someone walking over your grave. But, no. No. We ain't related or nothing.

— Oh sure, I heard all about it, soon's I came into town. Sheriff damn near shit his pants when he saw me, looked at me like I was the living dead. I'm not surprised. Found out pretty quick why everyone was so jittery. Hell, I'd be jittery too, I saw the spitting image of a man I'd murdered riding down the street like a ghost on a white horse, while the dead body's still swinging on the gallows. But, as you can see, my friend, I'm flesh and blood like you, and I can assure you that I'm no kin to that poor dead bastard out there.

— Maybe. Maybe it ain't such a good idea to stick around with everyone so edgy and all, and me looking like the dead man risen from the grave. But I'd kinda like to see how this all plays out. I don't like hangmen, see, and it might be nice to see this judge get his. I got my reasons. Take a look at this.

— That's right, me and the poor bastard on the rope out there share a little more than just our faces. This little neckerchief of a scar been with me for a long time now and I don't think it'll ever go away. They hung me too, my friend; they hung me and I lived. That doesn't go away.

— It was back in the war, and some son-of-a-bitch sergeant got me drunk and signed me up, see? Hell, I was just a boy, and I was never much of a fighter. I was scared. I ran away. Well, there was a colonel — hardest bastard in the whole of the army — and he sent his men out to hunt me down. Wouldn't suffer no deserters from his army. I ran for a long time, ran so long it seemed like all I'd ever done was run, but in the end they got me. Caught me in a cornfield. Nowhere else to run. They got me and they brung me back.

— I remember waking up in the slave-pen, waking up being dragged out of the slave-pen by the rope around my neck. Remember it? Hell, I dream it every night. Every night I dream I'm being dragged out of the slave-pen, up the scaffold to the noose. Every night I feel that noose tighten round my neck, and then the trapdoor falls away and I'm dangling and I can't breathe, but I can *just* breathe cause it ain't on right and the weights are wrong which is why my neck ain't snapped and why I'm dangling there, and I can *feel* it digging in, and burning, and it's getting harder and harder to breathe but, oh god, it takes so long to die, and I'm praying, won't somebody cut me down from here oh god forgive us all you bastards goddamn you all to hell. Every night I wake up dying.

— But so they cut me down too quick cause, with the weights and all, my neck should've broken and I should've been dead. But I wasn't. And they didn't think it right to hang me twice. That colonel, he was thinking about it, you could see it in his face, but his daughter — Sophia, her name was — she talked him round. Still... I've never liked a man too keen on hanging, so I'm just gonna stick around here for a while, see what happens. This judge, he seems to have made himself some enemies. I'd like to see...to see...that's him? That's him there?

— That's him. That's *him*. I know that face.

The Writer

The judge turns and, without another word, walks out of the saloon and out into the middle of the street. He walks back to where the sheriff and his deputies are standing, seven men with a mercenary glint in their eyes, that greed for gold or glory, bought men, hired guns. He turns back. The saloon doors are still swinging.

The drifter comes out first, untying the yellow bandanna from around his neck. He wipes the palms of his hand with it, then winds it, wraps it tight around his left wrist. He flicks his blond hair back out of his eyes and takes up a position about halfway towards the centre of the street.

The hunter comes out and passes him, slowly, handing the kid the buffalo gun and a bandolier of ammunition, with a look that says he knows the kid can handle it, and walks on. How or why he carries such a weight around with him, you couldn't say, but as he takes his place towards the other side of the road he flicks back the leather flaps of his long dust coat and brings out two-handed death: an eight-shot Le Matt revolver in his left hand — a specialist gun with a little single-shot shotgun barrel nestled underneath the main barrel; and in his right hand, a Winchester carbine with a trigger-guard customised so that a flick of the wrist will twirl it round and cock it for firing from the hip in one swift move. Two bandoliers make an *X* across his chest.

The gambler strolls out, stops on the wooden porch of the saloon, leans on the support beam for a casual couple of seconds as he lights up a cheroot, then comes down the steps. He straightens his cravat, brushes at the brim of his hat and pulls his right coattail back behind his holster. He stretches the fingers of his right hand out and curls them. He moves his left wrist slightly, just a touch, and there's an almost silent click.

The killer pauses halfway through the swing doors of the saloon to survey the scene, the Judge and his seven gunmen, and the other three. He walks down the steps and shares a glance with the gambler that says, *Eight against four, good odds.* He walks past the drifter, looking quizzically at the profile of the kid, then at the scaffold where the body has been cut down by the sobbing showgirl and some others. Cradled in the madam's arms, the dead man's head flops back. Same profile. They might've been twins.

The killer walks past the hunter, looking at the mark just visible under the shadow of his hat, the mark burned into his skin and deeper still. You can see it in the hunter's eyes, burning in his very soul. The killer walks on, walks right up to the edge of the scaffold and up the steps.

The showgirl looks up at him and he puts a hand on her shoulder. He crouches on his haunches at the body for a second, then stands up again and makes his way back down the steps. He walks out into the dead centre of the street, a little forward of the other three. Something glints in his hand.

The judge swats at a fly that buzzes at his face, flicking it out of the air with one finger.

For a second the killer just holds the glinting object that he's taken from the body of the murdered marshal, then he pins it to his chest. The star shines silver in the sun.

— Now we have ourselves a reckoning, he says.

And the gunfire thunders.

Sic Him, Hellhound! Kill! Kill!

I wake curled up at the foot of the bed again, back snugged tight into the crook of my boy's legs — tight enough to be on top of them really. He groans, slaps the alarm clock off, tries to pull the quilt over his head. Doesn't work with me weighing it down, clambering up to lick his face.

— Get up, I say. Get up get up get up.

He shoves me away.

— Get *down*, he says.

I roll off the bed, grab whiffy boxers from the floor.

— I'm *hungry*.

He groans.

A boy and his werewolf. Truest love there is.

—Breathe. Then eat, he says. Or eat, then breathe. You know you can't do the two together.

I raise my head from the bowl of corn flakes, give another cough as I lick milk from my lips then dive back in. I don't have to look to know he's shaking his head, smiling wryly. Hey, he knows it's all part of the method anyway. Guzzling food, snuffling crotches, rolling in things he has to hose off. And that's his part of the deal — to deal with that shit, to handle it, handle me.

Every agent has a handler, don't you know?

They tried it without handlers, I hear. Like, back in my alpha's day, back before he became a recruiter, some bright spark figured they should try letting us off the leash. A lone hellhound on the road, that would just be another drifter, right? Like *Kung Fu*. Or maybe *The Littlest Hobo*. Things got kinda messy though, it seems; there were a few incidents; cops got eaten and, *yes*, they were fascist pigs, but it *just wasn't on*.

Don't know why they were worried about the handlers in the first place. Like I'd ever let anything happen to my boy.

He sits on the edge of the bed, flicking through the file, glancing up now and then as I run the water in the shower.

— You're actually using the shower gel this time, yes? he calls.

— Absolutely, I shout.

I stand behind the half-open door, peeking at him through the crack. After ten minutes, I duck my head under the water, turn it off and come out towelling my hair. He puts the file down, open at the photograph, the missing kid. *Dead* kid.

— I know you didn't actually wash, he says. My sense of smell isn't that bad.

2.

—You got your cover story down, right?

I pick up a sleeveless tee, give it a sniff to make sure it's good and stinky, then pull it on.

— Yes, boss, I say.

It's the same story as ever, just different monickers: we're poor orphaned brothers, just moved to town to be near an aged aunt. I got ADHD and other issues. Impulse control. Drugs. He's the older bro sworn to raise me on his own, put me through school and all.

With the regeneration that comes with the shifts, you'd never know I've got... well, a few years on him.

I got bitten as a pup, see—bitten in the metaphorical sense, that is. I mean, forget what you think you know about werewolves. Silver bullets? Came in with the silver screen, dude. Wolfsbane? Man, that's poisonous to *everyone*. And all that contagion crap? Not how it works. No, how it works is ritual and magic — a wolfskin coat, a hip flask of dirty water drawn from lupine paw prints, and a bit of blood and dancing under the full moon. Being bitten might help, but it's all in the mindset. Shifting is a fucking skill, motherfucker. Not something you can catch.

When *exactly* I got bitten—in the metaphorical sense—that's a hard question though. Cause I remember a dream I had, age nine or so, of running across an old viaduct, a wolf pack at my heels. But I wasn't being chased, dig; I was at the head of them, *one* of them. When I woke up sweating, it wasn't with fear but with excitement. Was that when I got bit? *Maybe* it was years later, when my alpha took me in off the streets, turned this teenage stray into an initiate. But even at nine I had...that dream.

Reckon we're born this way, my alpha used to say. It was important to him, the gruff old fuck, and I can kinda understand, what with every movie at the drive-in painting us as cursed abominations, beasts with monstrous appetites. *Fuckin unnatural?* he'd growl as he scratched his chest tat through the leather vest. *This is who I fuckin am.*

Me, I'm sort of a bolshie bastard about it. No quarter. Ask me if it's nature or nurture, and I'll tell you it's a choice. I'll tell you it's my fucking choice to make, right? So deal with it.

3.

I pull the wolfskin on over the tee. With the leather pants too, it's gonna be hot as hell, but it's a necessary part of the whole kit and kaboodle. Besides, the ensemble has a rock star-cum-hustler bad-boy chic that tickles my fancy. It doesn't do me any favours with the PETA-loving emo kids, but it's just *awesome* for starting fights with small town dickwads who think *queer* is an insult.

My boy scruffles fingers through my hair, scratches my ear. I wonder what those dickwads would make of our rough-and-tumble playfights. Or sleeping arrangements.

I grab the car-keys from the coffee table and bring them to him, hold them out, take a step back as he reaches.

— Give, he says.

— Take them, I say.

— We don't have time for this.

He makes a grab and I snatch the keys away, turning so he has to reach round me, try and prise them from my hand.

Sic Him, Hellhound! Kill! Kill!

— *Give.*

I give them up. He's the best handler I've ever had, swear to God. There's no way what happened to the Louisiana team will happen to us. That was a *bad* werewolf, a weak handler. *We're* invincible.

I knew it from the first day he came to the Pound, the way the truth didn't even faze him. I mean whatever run-ins they've had with the nasties we track, they always come out of it with a fucking iron will, else they'd wouldn't be looking to join the cause; but usually the whole secret-agency thing leaves them at least a little *what the fuck?* But he just strolled down the line of pups and returnees till he came to me. I saw it in his eyes.

— What's your name? he said.

— You decide, I told him.

—You ready?

As he pulls the car up at the gates of the school, I bring my head back in from the window, grin at him and throw my hands in the air.

— Rub my tummy!

— Behave, he says.

I give him my best puppy eyes.

— Not. Now. You have a job to do, so go on. Git.

I climb out of the car, bath-time slow. When he drives away, he'll be abandoning me, like, *forever.* He sighs, knowing what I need.

— *Where's the vampire?* he says. *Go find the vampire, boy!*

And suddenly I'm as keen as his voice.

4.

One hundred million hours later—one bazillion trillion hours of history and French, or maths and geography, or fucking whatever later — I'm sitting in the school cafeteria, on my own at a table in a corner, eating burgers out of the buns and trying my best to be human about it. Not standing out is a lost cause — I'm the new kid, and a weird one at that — but we're still in the avoidance stage; the freaks and geeks aren't sure if I'm one of them yet, and the alpha jock's still working up to his challenge.

Then *they* arrive.

I take a furtive sip from my hip flask, not enough to spark a shift, but enough to boost my sense of smell. Because she's all flowers and soap and chocolate and Bibles and need — so much need, so deep an aroma of insatiable yearning that it almost masks his stench. The smell of her longing fills the room, fills the *school*; shit, I've been smelling it all day, that perfume of victimhood. Without it I wouldn't have to go through this bullshit to catch his trail, so I don't think it's too harsh to give a little growl, is it?

So, okay, hers is a scent of sickness, not in a twisted-and-malicious way but in a patient-in-a-hospice way. I should pity her. But she's got...that classic Mary Sue look — that's what my boy calls them — all nice and normal, a little plain, a little plump. A cross round her neck, or a crucifix maybe; I can't tell from here. She's not pretty enough to be popular, not strange enough to be an outcast, just a mannequin of mediocrity, blandness and banality, desperate to be made more by her Ghoul Boyfriend Forever.

As fucking ever.

As for him? Yeah, he's got the boy-band looks...if you trust your eyes. Which ain't a good idea.

Truth is, ticks got a sexy rep these days, all that Byronic bullshit, teen girls swooning over brooding tortured souls, but if you think vampires are *hawt*, you ought to read the motherfucking lore. *These are corpses, fuckhead,* my alpha told me way back. Rotted, stinking, fetid corpses that walk as men. Shit, it takes them years of feeding to even get to *that*.

So this tick sure looks like some pale poetic catwalk cutie, but I can smell his soil.

5.

Here's how a vampire starts. It starts with some manipulative leeching bastard dead in a grave, some kiddie-fiddler or wife beater, some Ponzi scheme merchant — or, worse, politician. It starts with someone so deep into using people they can't stop even when they're six feet down with maggots eating their tongue. It starts with their ghost haunting people they've abused, feeding on them even from the grave, sucking this...energy — chi, my alpha called it, or kundalini.

It's just a spectre at first, dig? No fangs, no frilly fucking cuffs on flouncy shirts. Just a mindless parasitic poisonous miasma.

There's a stink of the pulpit on this one, oak and ink, sermons scribbled by lamplight. It's old; shit, the victim probably wasn't even born when this fucker

Sic Him, Hellhound! Kill! Kill!

came seeping up from its silk-lined coffin to carry on its spiritual vocation, polluting the living with dreams of death, fears of the flesh and all its sordid passions. It's the smell of chickenshit, that stench, of something so gutless in the face of life and death it can't face either, has to deny them both. There's nothing uglier than the mockery of a human being you end up with then.

Fuck, let me tell you how much of a heartthrob the first tick I tracked was. Dude, my alpha took me to a cemetery, and I could smell the fucker from the gates, smell the stench of misery, even before this reanimated rotting corpse — this ghoulish, mummified, zombie *thing* — came digging its way up out of the earth with the bones of its fingers. It was more filth than flesh, blood-sodden graveyard dirt packed round bones, and the first thing it did was make a beeline for a nearby field, to feed on a fucking cow.

Real romantic.

That's stage two, see. If your vampire can feed enough as a spectre—suck juice from some debt-ridden fuck till he blows his own brains out in the depths of depression, or drive some insomniac mother to drown herself and the sick child she doesn't have the strength to care for — if the tick can bleed just enough vitality from the susceptible, it can dance its own corpse like a fucking puppet.

Only ticks look even half-human are stage threes plus, the ones who find some sad bastard and eat their insides out, wear them as a motherfucking skinsuit.

6.

The tick and the Mary Sue sit down at a table over near the door, holding hands, gazing into each other's eyes. They're the centre of their own little world — scratch that; they're the centre of *everyone's* world. You can smell the delusion wafting from them, the psychic smokescreen that lets a tick like this walk into a high school without a single question. Me, I got fake transfer papers, but all a tick needs is confusion and conviction. The glamour that makes everyone buy his new kid bullshit. Give him time and he'll have the whole town believing it.

You see...fuck, the reason most ticks don't come out in the daytime is cause you can see the skinsuit's stitches even *with* the glamour. That's why ticks and mirrors don't mix, actually — because even stage threes puke at the sight of themselves.

But then there's these stage fours.

A tick *can* kinda pass, see, if they can just find some human sick enough to swallow that glamour so completely, so commitedly, they put every ounce of their own energy into bolstering it. An amp for the signal, dig? With a Mary Sue beside them, that tick can fucking *dazzle*.

So he looks just like our missing kid, just like the victim, except maybe better. Ice-blue eyes and blond hair, cherry lips, skin smooth and spotless as an angel's ass. Fingernails manicured to metrosexual perfection. Every girl in the cafeteria, or near enough, is either gazing at him with wonder or looking daggers at Mary Sue. Some of the guys too, though they're shiftier about it; one of the indie kids over at the till is outright obsessed, the poor fuck, stinking of adolescent lust. No shame in his spicy scent, at least, but he's way out of luck.

Another high-school job, a few years back, just before the…accident that sent me back to the Pound and a new handler, to my boy — which was totally a great thing in the end, really, cause there's no way that sort of thing would happen with him — I got into a beef with these football fuckwits. They were yakking on about how their girls were all into tick-lit.
— Vampires are totally gay, one of them said.
So, yeah, I kicked the crap out of him.
These days, for most ticks, there should be an ex- in that sentence.

7.

Jared Swift. That was the kid's name. Not the tick's name, mind. You think I give a fuck what this motherfucker's name was? No, I'm talking about the kid in the photo, grabbed by the tick some night, in some dark place the boy wasn't meant to be, dragged off into the woods to be devoured. And worn.
Quiet kid, the report said, *sensitive*. No girlfriend. Journals and sketchbooks found after his disappearance indicate suicidal thoughts.
Jared Swift. That's the only name that matters here. Not the tick's or the Mary Sue's, not mine or my boy's. Just Jared Swift.

What the tick is going by here isn't worth shit; he'll have snatched it from Mary Sue's dreams while she was sleeping anyway, as he lurked outside her window, jonesing over her emptiness, or crawled in to crouch by her bed, whispering bitter nothings in her ear, watching himself glow radiant with glamour in the mirror of her dresser. If he did it over enough nights, he probably fucking

Sic Him, Hellhound! Kill! Kill!

glittered by the time he showed up as a late transfer in school to take her breath away. She, of course, being the only girl this gorgeous hunk had eyes for.

I can smell what little of Jared Swift is left in the skin worn by this ghoul. I can smell the shreds of soul in it, the despair and desire the tick has strung together into a semblance of self — behaviours born of terrified restraint, habits of shame — the salt of tears and spunk that tinges the tick's own bloody stink. I can smell a fucking moment, the words *oh, Jared's not really interested in girls yet* echoing as Jared casts his eye across a different cafeteria, fixes it on a different girl. Someone unattainable enough he'll never need to...

This would be the point where I realise I'm snarling, top lip curled back, teeth bared. Not that it matters in a blowing-my-cover sorta way; ticks don't have the wits to even know there might be hellhounds on their trail, and if the Mary Sue notices, all caught up in the glamour of her Ghoul Boyfriend Forever, she'll likely just write me into her self-centred story as another possessive potential, out to own her like her beloved does, jealous of the competition.

It does finally spur the dickwads into action though.

— Freak.

— Faggot.

Fuck yeah. At last!

8.

I ignore the detention cause, well, you know, the principal's *bad puppy* voice just doesn't carry the tone my boy's does; like I'm gonna play cowed to some yapping cur thinks he's top dog. Besides, we'll be out of here tomorrow if we get the job done tonight. So, out by the parking lot, skulking out of sight behind a dumpster, I watch them climb into a car that reeks of her — him in the driving seat though, naturally. And as they pull away, I take a deep slug from my hip flask. Strip the tee-shirt off. Unbuckle my belt.

They always play it as painful in the movies, like some hideous Jekyll and Hyde transformation, man being remade as beast in wrenching agony. Shit, it's more ecstasy than agony, and I mean that in the chemical sense, a fucking *buzz*. Skin-tingling shudders running up and down your spine, every inch of you alive with sensitivity. It's not so visual, natch, but if you can imagine a psychedelia of smell, that's how it rushes in on you when you turn wolf. When my alpha took me through my first shift, man, I thought he'd spiked the punch with acid.

Bones crunch into new shapes, muscles shift, and wolfskin furls tight to my form, binds to my naked skin, *becomes* it. No doubt my boy'll bitch about me leaving the leathers in a dumpster yet again, but it's the handiest hiding-place, boss, and it's either that or a halfway wolfman look that's bound to sparks some stares loping down the streets and through the woods after the car. While I *might* get away, in this form, with just a few confused souls wondering if they *really* did see that motherfucking massive…husky? Cause it couldn't really be…could it?

I run like that car's a supercharged stag but I got a turbo drive in my adrenal glands and a hankering for venison. I run like I have a whole pack at my heels, betas splitting off to flank the quarry. I pound the tarmac with paws that move so fast, so light, they barely make a sound. I leap walls to cut through yards, crash through bushes and fences, pace never slowing, gaze cold and keen as steel on my prey as long as it's in my sight, flared nostrils directing me when it's not.

I fucking *love* chasing cars.

9.

I'm kinda disappointed when he parks the thing at her place—he opens the door for her; hugs her but baulks when she moves in to kiss him; spins her a spiel about how he's scared he'll hurt her; strokes her cheek — then sets off on foot for his hidey-hole. I'm kinda disappointed cause ticks move slow as humans, mostly — slower even, sorta floaty — which is just plain boring. Stalking is okay, but it's nowhere near as much fun as chasing.

If it wouldn't lead to a seriously stern *bad werewolf!* scolding, I'd take him down here and now.

But no. I got my part of the job, and my boy got his. If the ticks are a fuckload less impressive than some would have you believe — if they're feeders not fighters, if they don't tend to offer *that* much in the way of struggle once you've torn their limbs off, decapitated them with your teeth, and spat their head across the room — well, there's putting them back in the grave and *keeping* them there. So there's all that clean-up afterwards, with the garlic and salt. And quicklime. Handler stuff.

And there's the whole…loyalty thing. I suppose.

So I prowl through the brush behind gnatboy, hanging back in the shadows of early evening, following him to a fancy house out past the edge of town, all

Sic Him, Hellhound! Kill! Kill!

clean-lined concrete and glass...real modern. Swimming pool out back, and an
SUV out front. I can smell rotting bodies inside, but not so's I can make out how
many. More than two, I reckon. He spider-crawls up the side of the house and
in a window.

After a quick sniff and a piss-tag on a tree, I turn, lope off.

Lassie come home, motherfucker. It's chow time.

—Hello hello hello hello! I love you!

— Yes, I know. I love you too.

— But I *really* love you! I missed you so much!

— And I missed you too. *Yes, I did! Oh, yes I did!* Now, down you go.

— But I *missed* you!

— I know, but we have work to do. Did you find the lair?

— It was *easy*! Come on. Grab the gear and let's get this tick squished.

— Okay, hang on.

— Hurry up!

— You know, maybe you should put some pants on.

— Don't need them. Hurry up! Come on!

— I'm coming.

— Come faster! Hurry up!

— Stop. Pulling.

10.

The last guttural purr of the engine as we pull into the driveway; soft clicks
and thuds of doors opening and closing; crunch of gravel underfoot; snick of the
trunk unlocking: my ears pricked even in human from, all of it's acute, carved in
the quiet like radio play sound effects.

He pulls my spare hip flask from his pocket, hands it over, starts loading up
with his own kit — crucifix, holy water, carbon-quarrelled crossbow, gun with
silver bullets. None of it actually means shit, we figure, but every tick's so convinced of their damnation these empty symbols mostly work.

—Ready? I say.

He nods, closes the trunk on the canisters full of disposal substances, and we
look into each other's eyes for a moment, saying something that can't be put
into words. Somewhere in there is the story of how he signed up for this gig,
how he got sucked into this weird world, how he came close enough to living

death to spit in its face. But you don't have to hear that story. All you have to know is that it's maybe something like Jared Swift's, but not.

I'll fucking *never* let it be that story.

Soft and easy, padding on feet half-human, half-wolf, I take point, leading my boy in through the splintered front door, muzzle twitching, senses taut. I can hear the flies buzzing, count the corpses by scent, even before we hit the dining room. I can even tell that the tick isn't in there; but we go in anyway, to remind ourselves why we do this.

Rippling with maggots, Mom and Dad and three kids sit at the table, the family dog an autopsy or feast upon it. Both.

Sanity is the first thing a tick takes from its victims.

The Zoroastrians have this ritual, you know; when someone dies they bring a dog to the corpse, and no matter what the doctor says, no matter how it looks, the person is only declared truly dead when the dog treats it as such. Way I hear it, it used to be one of us. Way I hear it, that might even be how the agency started — werewolves and their handlers brought in to make sure the dead will stay that way — but no one really knows the grand story of the origin. Or cares much.

We care about the corpses.

11.

I follow the stench into the basement, my boy at my back all the way. I know he's thinking about Jared Swift, about the thing that's wearing his skin now, the ghost become a ghoul become a glittering glamour of humanity, cold and dead inside, empty as the not-so-pretty head and hollow heart of a Mary Sue who can't read between the lines. Can't see what's under this sketchy fantasy of self-denial and overwrought passion.

In the broken concrete of the floor, a dirt mound marks where the tick has burrowed, its grave.

I piss on it.

—Softening the earth? says my boy, but I'm already snarling, ripples of the shift running up my spine as I hit the dirt with furious claws, in a shape barely hominid, scrabbling, tearing, rending the earth. You could call it *digging*, but that would be like calling a hurricane *breezy*. The scent of vampire rot is so rich

Sic Him, Hellhound! Kill! Kill!

it thickens the air, turns my stomach. I want to tear this fucker up from his sleep, rip him apart, and roll in the filth of what's left so I will *stink* of his ending.

A white hand bursts from the muck.

The rest of him follows in an explosion of dirt, an eruption of flailing in-humanity, leaping for the walls, the rafters, a corner of the ceiling, to cling there, hissing and hollow-eyed. Still glamoured to fuck, it's every inch the smooth Adonis, skin of white marble and blue veins, lithe and limber as a fucking cat but its twisted perching a mockery of a true predator. This is a fucking parasite, a tapeworm from the bowels of humanity, a leech with limbs and a face. Spitting, thoughtless, ravenous loathing.

— I will eat you and shit you out, I say.

—Really, no, says my boy. I'm not cleaning up that—

And in the second I turn, it's fired itself at him, over my head, not baseball-fast, but fast enough; and his quarrel goes wild, but at least the holy water doesn't, like acid in its face, stripping glamour to raw horror. And by then, I'm launched, hitting the tick just as its jaw opens like a snake's. A glimpse of ragged shards, broken bone for teeth. I slam into its side, slam it the fuck off my boy and into a concrete wall. There's a sick thud, splattering gore.

12.

The fucker's already broken though, been broken since before it was dead, and it rolls away, scuttles back and whirls. Its lolling head snaps back into place, for all its brains are oozing down its back. Fuck, it's a tick; whatever brains it has it likely scavenged from sewer rats, just so it could sham the life it fucked up when it had the chance. Its eyes lock on my boy again, and I'm thinking, Fuck, how I hope it didn't get a taste of him there — at the exact same moment I scent his blood on the air.

No.

Then the smell of him is rich in its scent. I can hear him fumbling, cursing, losing the trust in himself to handle this, handle *anything*; I can smell the fear of failure, smell it in the tick's breath as it sucks it in, shrieks it at me, a searing mockery, cause if he can't handle this, he can't handle *me*, he's just a boy, not a boss, just a boy, not *my* boy and —

I snarl as we leap, the tick and I, my claws ripping through the air, rending its belly, swatting the fucker clear across the basement.

I come down hard, something stolen from me in the touch. Shit, the smell of panic is so fucking physical, I stumble. I shake my head but I can't get rid of it, look to my boy but that's where the fucking problem is. He's choking, collapsing, and if he's weak, I – I don't know what to do. I want to snarl in his fucking face. I need you, you fucking fuck, need you to fight for. A boy and his werewolf, motherfucker. Loyalty. I need your fucking purpose, need you and fucking hate you for it.

Fucking bitch ass...

And then the tick is on my back, clamped tight; and it's not fangs or a feeding tube – it's not physical at all – but I can feel the bite at the back my neck, at the base of my skull, feel it reaching in to shred my thoughts and suck them out. Loyalty? I'm a fucking freak of a beast of base desires kept in line by a lie. There's no love here, only need, the need to follow, to fawn, to be favoured with treats and scraps of attention, the need to be needed, to be needed to need –

13.

And I'm turning, growling at this fucking wretch of a weak handler on the ground in front of me, this fucking faggot kid on his back, his throat exposed like the craven whelp he is, just some backwoods bottom boy who opened himself up to a tick once before, no fucking wonder he let it happen again. All I can smell now, as I crouch to leap, is his fear and my anger, his weakness and my power.

I don't know how he manages it, the roll to one side as I jump. The crossbow smashing down on my nose.

—Don't you fucking dare, he says.

I'm still growling.

– Off! he shouts.

And he's bringing the gun up even as I go back and down, firing it once, twice. The bullets don't hit my skull, but it feels like they might as well have as the tick is blasted off me. There's a scream of pure despair that hits my boy hard. I see the gun barrel turning, pointing up, towards his chin, but he's my boy again now, and – I'll apologise later for nearly biting his hand off.

I whirl to spit twisted steel at the tick. And howl.

I howl as it scrambles upright, limbs clicking back from rag-doll dislocations to roughly human placements. I howl as it backs away, scuttles to this side and that, looking for a point of attack. I howl at the tick from all fours, standing over my boy, guarding him as he hauls himself back and up. I howl like Cerberus at the gates of Hell as he stumbles to his feet beside me, lays a hand on my back, a hand that steadies as I howl, as purposed as the one that's raised now, pointing.

— Sic him, boy, he says. *Kill!*

I hit the tick as a berserker, slashing chest and belly, tearing the hamstring from one leg as it spins, wrenching the other off at the knee. I catch it by the wrists as it flails, raise it in a cruciform and tear its jaw from its face with my teeth, spit it into the grave. Half its head follows in a crunch of bone, then the rest. With a foot on its chest, the fucker's arms pop from their sockets like chicken wings.

When I'm done shaking it in my teeth like a stuffed toy, there's not much left.

14.

Still, there's *something* left. Fingers twitch and grapple at air. Toes curl. Wherever there are joints intact, they jerk and spasm. This is the creature in its natural state, I reckon — a set of clutching convulsions, twitches and shudders, driven by a brainless impetus to play out a travesty of existence. I crack open its ribcage, chew out the brown lump that passes for a heart and drop it in front of my boy, like a ball. He empties a full chamber of silver bullets into it and dissolves what's left in homoeopathically-diluted holy water. Eventually, everything is still.

My boy stands there with the empty gun still dangling in one hand, looking down at the mess of the creature that ate Jared Swift. The scent of a moment of crisis is still on him, and for all the grim determination summoned by a bloody-minded howl of defiance, there's a hint of shame too. He's not happy, and it's my fault, I know. Don't know why, but I know it's my fault.

Then he looks at me, and something changes in his eyes, and he says two words and everything changes.

— Good boy!

And I am motherfucking *magnificent*.

I shift back to humanity, feeling slick and shiny, and I don't just mean with the viscera. I feel *fierce*. Every shift is a remaking, after all, and if the transformation to wolfman unleashes a beast in me, well, so does the return to this human form. Like humans aren't beasts too? I grab his hand as he moves toward the stairs, towards disposal chemicals and rubber gloves and all that jazz, pull him in to lick his face, exuberantly. Hey, it's cleaning, sorta. He stops me, wipes a sleeve across my mouth.

— Like people, he says.

And we kiss.

So maybe I get a bit carried away as we're washing the gore off each other with holy water. Maybe it's the wolf in me that ignores the protest of *not here.* Or maybe it's the human in me that says, *especially here.* So you think we're both monsters? A hellhound and a human so offay with carnage we don't see how fucked-up it is to let the passion loose here and now?

I say it's life, to fuck as humans in the ruins of death.

As living, breathing, eating, shitting, *fucking* human beings in the ruin of death.

Sic Him, Hellhound! Kill! Kill!

Oneiriça

—a grain of sand that might be from a beach or broken hourglass, a token of the Gobi or Mojave, Kalahari or Sahara. The traveller gazes at it on their palm, scries its depths, scanning the desert to be crossed as a first step towards the Realm. In its minute multi-facets they glean a glimpse of a crescent sun that lights a Mesolithic savanna of lions and antelopes painted in ochre on the rock-dwellings of the Tassili-n-Ajer. What they see is you, here now, leaving your tribe of noble scavengers, walking in the skinsuit of your shaman ancestor, setting out across the grass plains for the vine-rich jungle that begins where reeds and rushes give way to the fern and foliage of elder eras, the borderlands of Palaeolithic and Pleistocene.

You walk on through tropical and temperate wilderness into the wild-woods, the darkwoods, the forests of pine and oak and elm, the groves of olive and orange trees where Pan once played his pipes to celebrate the dawn and serenade the sleeper rousing from their slumber, Endymion blinking awake, limbering into a stretch. You stand on the edge of the Lady's Lake, the mist and mirrored moonlight, your reflection in this liquid limbo battered and broken by ripples. You strip the skinsuit from you and dive in, Narcissus shattering the spell of his self-love, swimming underwater, a boy in the blue of bubbles, breaking the surface to breathe deep. To step ashore on an island that might be Avalon or Dilmun or Manhattan.

Naked and newborn, you shake droplets from your coppersmooth metaphysique and continue inland, towards the steel mountains and the entrance to the caves of cold and dark, the cavernous underworlds of Kur and Sheol, Hades and Hell, immeasurable hollows empty even of the dead now. The sunless sea you seek here is a freshwater abyss, the Sumerian Abzu, source of every spring, found easily by following any of the five rivers that flow from it as fingers from an outstretched hand: the Acheron, river of woe's denials; the Phlegethon, river of anger's fire, the Styx, river of bargains and new beginnings; the Kokytus, river of lamented loss; and the Lethe, river of memory's healing. You cross all five, follow the coast of the Abzu to the one great river that feeds it, the Alph, trace this torrent through the netherworld towards its source. You scramble up over shingle and scree, up the slope that banks its cataract, towards the point of light that is the end of your night journey, the rift in the rock that reveals a hidden valley, low hills like arms opening out and down to left and right as if offering you the vista: the crescent sun high in the azure sky; the silver cratered moon a vast hemisphere on the horizon; a flock of sparrows swirling across it, speared by a swooping hawk; the Elysian Fields before you, stretching to eternity's ends.

The road through the Elysian Fields is as busy as the farms and orchards, filled with cars and bicycles, horsemen and pedestrians, herds of cattle and sheep driven by boys with switches, carts and caravans hauled by karibu — the eagle-winged oxen of Assyrian palaces, lumbering large as elephants, bits and blinkers on the bearded heads of ancient kings. You hitch a ride on a flatbed truck of itinerant workers grimed by red earth to the colour of clay, smile at their gabble of unintelligible questions, nod at their sage pronouncements in a tongue that's only gibberish to you. You join them when they stop to wash in a roadside shower block, join the jokes and jibes as the cool spray sloughs the dust of toil from you all, reveals men and women of obsidian and marble skin, every shade between. These Western Lands were once worked by shabtis, you tell a boy you're trying to impress, serfs and slaves of pharaohs brought here to build their kingdoms; but times change, even in eternity.

— So this is emancipation? says the sandminer lad. Feh.

You shrug as he shakes water from him like a wet dog. A greyhound, you think, gracile and loyal; lazing with you on your bed or racing you to the agora when rumours of marvels spur you both to racing keenness. You remember the first time you met.

EDIFICE I

—Philosophists, eh? the boy whispers. More hot air than A.J. Ayer, no?

Jé smothers a snort. The two sit on the stone lip of a fountain's basin. Cynics at the back of class, bonding in shared scorn of sophistry, they snicker as the eyes of eager listeners in the gymnasium crowd glance irk at them. Jé mouths apology at a hiss for hush, but he's more interested in the lithe lad beside him than the pundit pontificating on the sanctum steps. His name is…?

— Tu, says the boy, offering a clasp of forearms, hands to elbows.

They ditch the dialectics lesson, wander off together, flirt with innuendo and insults as they scramble up steps onto the washing-lined roofscape of their suburbia, a Moroccan or Mexican collage of limestone and white-washed adobe dwellings, garden courtyards below lit by sunlight shining from the crescent sun, moonlight reflected and refracted by the library towers of the city that glints on the horizon, so far ago and long away.

The mirror-glass towers of the Libraries of Language dominate the New City, rising from every corner, every quarter and district of concrete and brick, each tower isolated in its slender grace but joined to the others by bridges of silvery steel. Jé has a dream, he tells Tu, of one day being a runner of those bridges, carrying the tales and texts of every tribe this way or that between the librarians whose work is to collate and cross-reference them. It's not that he's interested in their project, this new Babel that builds its order upon a full acceptance of the confusion of tongues, mapping the weavework of all possible syntaxes and semantics in its vast distributed structure. No, it's that the bridge-runners are wild, shortcutting system with leaps from bridge to bridge. Synthe-spring heels to their boots laced up the shin, glide-wings snapping out to catch the currents, otherwise naked and oiled as athletes for their sport, they cut the air with arcs of their gleaming.

Who wouldn't want to be such a quicksilver sprite?

Jé and Tu lie on the roof, watching the monorail rattle by above. Jé relishes the weight of Tu's head in the snug between shoulder and pectoral, the tickle of tousled hair on his skin. He crooks his arm round to trail fingers across a smooth chest, to plink a nipple. His adamantium bracelet clinks on the simple charm of stone that Tu wears on a leather cord around a neck made to be nibbled. Bracelet and charm. Otherwise naked and oiled as lovers from their sport, in sweat, they smell so wholly of each other now, they are no longer sure which of them is *I* and which is *you.*

— You know we'll both be sandminers like our old men, says one. The future's already written.

— Feh, says the other. Our future's no more set than our past.

Within the crystal and chrome construction of the New City, the sand-stone gatehouses and walls of the Old City rise as a heart of golden stone, built upon a mound of aeons of ruin and rebuilding. Following one of the many roads into the city, Jé and Tu can't help but recognise the great gatehoused walls when they come to them and pass through into the Old City; but still, even as this first sighting shifts, slips into new memories of other histories, they marvel at it all. Where the walls end and the houses begin is hard to say; there is no part of the walls around the Old City that does not house inhabitants, and there is no house within the Old City that does not share a wall with another. The whole city is one great nest, and it does not simply rise upon its tell but over it, the cloistered tapestry of streets built into and upon arches and avenues of aqueducts and viaducts that spiral around and radiate from the sanctum at its centre, the whitestone dome of the cathedral.

— You have to come back to my place tonight, says Jé. The Bridge-runner's Quarter has a great view of Saint Apollyon's. If you're not afraid of heights.

— Fuck off, says Tu. *Afraid of heights.*

He pulls the impish grinner into a headlock, a tangle of limbs in mock of struggle. Feels his legs lift off the ground as their laughter turns heads. Tail wagging, jumping round their stumbles and trips, Nous barks at his masters' play.

EDIFICE III

Its vaulted dome rising on pillars that merge with the cloisters of the city, a vast unwalled chamber at the centre of the Old City, the Cathedral of Saint Apollyon was built from the ruins of the Temple of Dionysus, which was, in turn, built from the ruins of the Palace of Pentheus, King of Tears, the stones of the Theban king's domicile brought to this region in antiquity, it is said, after its destruction by the god of wine and agriculture, theatre and madness.

The three of them—corn-blond Aie and crow-black Thau and copper-brown Ouie — stroll across the Bridge of Lovers' Locks that leads to the cathedral, spiff in their bolero-cut tuxes and skin-tight jeans of black denim zipped in silvery synthe. Shin-high boots and bullet belts, kidskin gloves and canes, these three young bloods cut a cocksure strut like rebel poets or officers-in-training, but the adamantium greyhound pins they wear are the only art or medals they care for. Oh, the nights they have shared in honey rum and rotgut and ecstasy both chemical and physical, spray-painting Mercury's Dog on the most inaccessible walls of the city, tagging their names and their union — THE MESSENGER BOYS. Daring each other to greater dangers.

Ouie darts off to one side of the bridge, crouches to check one of the many little padlocks clicked through the grillwork that runs between the bridge's rails. Aie nudges Thau, nods a wry amusement at their sparky mate. It's only to be expected, really, him being the locus of their love and lust, after all.

— Still here, says Ouie as he bounds back, cane a-twirl.

It was only last week they scratched their names into the synthe and latched the padlock closed — forever, they swore, as they threw the key out into the river of sand. It's a grand symbolic gesture as silly as it is sincere, in some respects, but in this city all gestures are symbolic.

While the cathedral has no walls it does have a chamber in the form of the open amphitheatre, where every year they enact a pageant representing the Destruction of the Temple and the Raising of the Cathedral, the architectural revolution following the deity's assimilation to the Orphic religion in the form of Saint Apollyon through a merging with Apollo, god of sunlight and medicine, music and reason.

The pose could almost be planned as Aie, Thau and Ouie pause at the grand entrance to the amphitheatre. The pillars and dome rise above them. Steps lead down into the curved, carved terraces of seating mostly filled already by an audience of the high class and the hoi polloi — all of them in evening dress, of course, but none with the swank and swagger of the Messenger Boys. The pose could almost be planned in the cock of hips, the linking of arms, the angle of canes and gazes, Aie to this side, Thau to that, and Ouie between them straight ahead and down at the stage. But it isn't; the poise is only an attitude of admiration, the natural grace of those so lost in their appreciation of a statue or a painting they don't notice their own casual contrapposto. Ardor has its own elegance.

— It's starting, says Ouie. Look!

On stage, three players stand, each in one of the masks of drama — the grimace of tragedy, the grin of comedy, the gawk of fantasy — beckoning the Messenger Boys forward.

LABYRINTH

We are no sooner on the stage than we are off, it seems, our part only prologue in the spectacle of the show. Our mummer's mime is short: a knife-fight between the dramas of sorrow and joy interrupted by the drama of pure whimsy; a bitter feud turned to a ballet of flourishes first, as we flail at the inter-fering trickster; a tango of tangled forms that becomes in the end, as this new choreography takes over, a waltz of mutual entrancement. As soon as it is over, even before the three of us have taken our bows, the Dionysus is whirling out to huckle us to the wings with the birl of his thyrsus. Backstage, we strip off the masks and slap each other on the back, ruffle hair and punch each other's arms, proud of our performance. Unbuttoning sweat-soaked shirts and grabbing tow-els, we're in high enough spirits we have to be hushed by the stage manager as we head towards the dressing room, down the long corridor of white plaster walls and crimson carpet. Around a corner, relaxing into chat now that we're far enough from the stage that silence doesn't matter. Around another corner, still chatting.

The backstage area of the amphitheatre leads into the labyrinth of Icarus, built by the son of Daedalus — who apparently surpassed his father in ingenuity as much as in hubris. There is no minotaur in this labyrinth, no monster in the darkness; within these catacombs of bones the only thing that lurks, if one can penetrate the maze, is the tomb of Aidoneus.

We are lost, we realise. And there's a fourth in our party now, not Mi or Yi or Uz, but a shadow by the name of Uther, his skin the royal blue of the night sky, filigreed with pin-pricks of light and sigils scratched between them, a luminous tattoo of constellations we do not recognise. He leads us through the corridors of the hotel, the hospital, the house of many rooms, insisting that he knows the way to the after-show party. We're not sure we trust him, mutter our discontent in low voices behind his dark but sparkling back. When we met him in the Great Ballroom and he said, *Come with me,* it seemed only sensible, but now we fear that we'll be late for the wake, that the lamentations will have started without us.

— We must hurry, says Uther. It's nearly time.

We run, turning this way and that through the corridors of crypts, torch light flickering on the skulls that cram each nook and niche we pass. Finally we turn a corner to find the great copper doors that are our destination, green with verdigris, the gates they're set in tiled in lapis lazuli.

The entrance into that tomb from the labyrinth was, as any attentive student should know, discovered and opened in 1916 by the archaeological team of Shemuel Champollion, Ham Carter and Japhethia Schliemann, who found the chamber long-since stripped of grave goods by millennia of tomb-robbers. However, there is an exit from the tomb that comes out somewhere in the Elysian Fields, a small stone slab sealing it shut. Its location is forgotten to history, but on the other side of this slab, three shepherds stand – or rather bend, crouch and kneel respectively – to clear the moss and lichen from this innocuous memorial that seems carved into a crag of rock, to read its inscription – ET IN ARCADIA EGO. *And also in Arcadia I dwell.* The first reads a lyrical joy into this cryptic phrase, a claim to a happy ever after life of bucolic idyll. The second sees a poignant elegy, an articulation of the presence of death even in that idyll. The third understands that this is the tomb of Aidoneus, Aides, Hades, the crypt of Death himself.

None of them are aware that from where they stand, in this elsewhen of theirs, the tomb is still filled with all the riches of eternity. Only the black dog sniffing in the underbrush beside them knows this, and Else does not care, more concerned with her frantic digging at a fugitive rabbit's burrow.

ARTEFACT I

—And in Arcadia, says Eco warily. I don't like it.

– You're a pussy, says reckless Itch. Let's go in.

Sylph peers between them into the gloom, right hand resting on the shoulder of one, left on the arm of the other – as if to stay the argument with an unspoken communion. Ever the mediator, thinks Chateau, looking back at them from where he's hunkered down on the threshold, caught in chiaroscuro, half-lit in the sloping shaft of late-afternoon sunlight. Never one to fear the unknown, Chateau is comfortable on the edge of darkness; but he knows he's the odd one out here, the brooding thunder to Itch's lightning verve, the silent logic to Eco's nervous overthinking, the steel resolve to Sylph's easy charm; he knows that while they – even audacious Itch – need courage to explore the tunnel, for him it is only…a natural habitat. So he waits as they gather that courage in their chatter, patient as the grave itself.

— So. Are you going to stand here all day or go in? says Animal.

She stands behind them, arms folded, a hint of arch to one eyebrow as if she's thinking, *boys!*

The beams of their flashlights flick across the chamber's walls, pick out decades of graffiti — gang tags and band names going back to the seventies at least, Chateau reckons. The Doors, the Sex Pistols, the Messenger Boys. An anarchist CIRCLE-A is almost lost in the lurid chaos of lichens. Slick streaks of mineral glisten where they've been washed from the stone above by seeping rains, and Chateau wonders if the constant drips pattering here and there in the chamber might one day transform this place into a true grotto, leeched sediments of the stone above slowly accreting into stalactites and stalagmites.

— Man, this place fucking stinks, says Itch.

He's right. Mostly it's just damp and piss, thinks Chateau, but there's a richer rot to the stench as well. A scent of death.

The artefact sits in the centre of the room, a solid stone chest all too similar in size and shape to a sarcophagus. Some of the stories say that's what it is, sure enough — the coffin of Osiris or Adonis or Tammuz or whatever His Name was. Others say it contains not the body of the Dead God but His Law, that it is the Ark of His Covenant. (Some say that this is the same thing.) Still others say it is Pandora's Box, the chest that when opened released all the ills humanity has ever known upon the world.

(And some say that, again, this is the same thing.)

Chateau lays the artefact down upon the cold stone surface of the altar, runs a hand across the hard black leather. None of them know what's in the briefcase, but it's got to be something important, right? Maybe it's a trillion bucks in used billion dollar notes. Maybe it's filled with plastic-wrapped packages of the finest quality uncut soma, with a street-value beyond their wildest dreams. Maybe it's bars of gold or platinum or adamantium bullion. Maybe it's the Top Secret files of the conspiracy that runs the whole fucking show from behind the scenes, from beyond even time and space. Maybe it's just...power. Maybe when they open it, thinks Chateau, it'll be like in the movies, this weird glow lighting up their faces as they gaze in rapture at an unimaginable wonder that now belongs to them. Maybe their faces will melt, or they'll be driven mad, blind with greed, murdering each other one by one.

— Where did you get it? he asks Animal.

She just smiles and motions him aside, slides her fingers round the seal, to the lock.

Animal unsnicks the great brass clasp of the leather-bound tome and opens the book. The endpapers are a map of the Realm – desert and savanna, jungle and lake, island and mountains, the cave of a great underground sea. Five rivers like fingers flowing from it, and the sixth flowing into it, its source in a hidden valley. The road to the city. The spirals of streets and the cathedral at its centre. The catacombs that brought them here. *X* marks the spot.

She turns a page of brittle vellum.

Every map has a key, and that's what the rest of the book is, pages upon pages of indexing that decrypts the strange symbols scattered across the chart, all those sigils standing in for names of places and people, buildings and objects, all those glyphs and logos in place of titles that are in themselves almost as arbitrary, little more than pointers to myths and legends too detailed to include in the cartography. She flips forward to the page she wants, the one that holds the story of the Merchant-King's Box and, more importantly, the combination for opening it.

ARTEFACT III

I stand at the altar with the five of them behind me—I, Thou and Us, Him and Her – each holding their torch high overhead, a human lamp stand. This is the secret of the so-called Hand of Glory, I realise now. That fabled ritual object of the occultist, said to be used in spells to conjure demons, is not, as the stories claim, a murderer's hand with a candle melded by wax onto the tip of each finger, nothing so gruesome. That diabolist's menorah is mere metaphor. No, each light stands for a human spirit – Khu, Ka, Ba, Khaibit and Sekem – who must be gathered together to bring light to the sixth, the Master of Ceremonies.

I pull the cork from the bottle with my teeth and pour the dark liquid out into the bowl of stone that sits before me, crystal carved smooth as polished glass, so pure a chalice it can only be seen when it is full. I lift this cup to my lips with both hands, taste the salt of blood, the richness of red wine, the bitter tang of oil or ink. And when I speak the Ren, the Secret Name, it is the same word spoken by God to start the cosmos, the word that shattered Adam Kadmon into waking.

The crack splits the lid of the sarcophagus in two, golden light streaming from the ragged seam. I dig my fingernails in to prise the two halves apart; for all that each half of the great stone slab should be impossible to move without a crowbar, they slide away easily, glide as if on air. Inside is everything we ever dreamed of — gemstones of every hue, all the iridescent Eyes of Argos, all the glittering, gleaming shards of the Eye of Horus, the great crystal that is the Philosopher's Stone, and the Grail Stone, of course, the lattice of its flaws forming that simple sign the Sumerians exegesised in their cuneiform Tablets of Destiny. The whole Templars' treasure is here, millennia's worth of coins stamped with the head remembered in myth as that of John the Baptist or Bran the Thrice-Blessed, of Baphomet or Orpheus. A golden mask that gazes out from each surface, every tragedy or comedy or fantasy written in its eyes, it is, I understand now, the Face of Glory.

I recognise it instantly. And laugh.

One by one, they bring their weapons forward, throw them into the pile of treasure. A rusted dagger. A broken sword. A gun with no bullets. A bent iron rod. The phallus of Osiris that was the progenitor of them all. As each of these objects of power clatters into the coffin, I remember the trials and tribulations we suffered to win them in our epic quest across the Realm, how we travelled east and west, north and south, to the Heavens themselves, in order to bring them all together for this great reforging of the original artefact. All the vessels, hearts or chalices. All the treasures, diamonds or coins. All spades or swords, all such tools for breaching soil or skin. In the sarcophagus now, they flow into each other, glowing as molten gold, shifting as quicksilver into the shape of a sleeper.

I want to reach in and touch this strange slumbering form. But I know it would shatter.

I raise my own hand now, feel the weight of wood in it. I do not have to look to know that I'm holding a mace or sceptre of sorts. I have been carrying it all along, the thyrsus of Dionysus and the club of Heracles, the staff of Prospero and the spear of Longinus, Odin's Gungnir and Sun Go-ku's Rúyì-Jīngū-Bàng. It is the most modern magician's wand and the most ancient spearthrower. I squeeze it in my grasp and it shrinks to a twirlable size, sits comfortably between my fingers, a pen. There is no need for any statement of authority more grand than this, I think, not in this day and age. What was comfortable in one era as a humble reed with a wedge-shaped end, will be comfortable here and now as a simple ballpoint. It is the most important of all these objects of power, I think — though I am prejudiced, I suspect — the original of all tools for shaping order and chaos.

I drop it into the crucible, and the six of us stand there, side by side, looking down on it as it melts into the seventh, the Sekhu to whom we are all mere imaginings, to whom we are fading now as the form uncurls and stretches, flicks back the quilt from their coffin and begins to dress — hurrying as they spot the time on the alarm clock. Shit, it's late. There's a plane to catch, a business trip to Oneirica, and the taxi is due in fifteen minutes. Fuck, fuck, fuckety fuck. Must have overslept.

The traveller pats their trouser pocket to be sure the switchblade is still there, checks that the wand of their pen is clipped onto the inside pocket of their jacket where it belongs, checks the outside pocket to make sure they have the coins for the ferry, and picks up their hip flask, takes a swig of the dark, rich liquor before tucking it into their back pocket. They feel an irk on their tongue, a piece of grit that they fetch out with a fingertip to examine, a little fragment of eternity —

Publication Credits

"How a Scruffian Starts Their Story," copyright © 2010, first appeared in *The Scruffians Project*, Notes from the Geek Show

"How a Scruffian Gets Their Name," copyright © 2014, original to this volume

"The Behold of the Eye," copyright © 2008, first appeared in *Lone Star Stories* #28

"Scruffian's Stamp," copyright © 2010, first appeared in *The Scruffians Project*, Notes from the Geek Show

"An Alfabetcha of Scruffian Names," copyright © 2010, first appeared in *The Scruffians Project*, Notes from the Geek Show

"Jack Scallywag," copyright © 2010, first appeared in *The Scruffians Project*, Notes from the Geek Show

"The Disappearance of James H___," copyright © 2005, first appeared in *Strange Horizons*, June 13, 2005

"The Island of the Pirate Gods," copyright © 2007, first appeared in *Postscripts*, Winter 2007

"The Angel of Gamblers," copyright © 2006, first appeared in *Eidolon I* (ed. by Jeremy G. Byrne and Jonathan Strahan)

"The Shoulder of Pelops" copyright © 2014, original to this volume

"Bizarre Cubiques," copyright © 2006, first appeared in *Fantasy Magazine*, Fall 2006

"The Origin of the Fiend," copyright © 2012, first appeared in *Icarus* #14

"Sons of the Law," copyright © 2011, first appeared in *Fantastique Unfettered*, Issue 4

"Sic Him, Hellhound! Kill! Kill!" copyright © 2012, first appeared in *Subterranean Online*, Spring 2012

"Oneirica," copyright © 2010, first appeared in *Icarus* #5

Scottish author HAL DUNCAN's debut novel, *Vellum*, garnered nominations for the Crawford, Locus, BFS and World Fantasy awards, and won the Gaylactic Spectrum, Kurd Lasswitz and Tähtivaeltaja awards. He's since published the sequel, *Ink*, the novella *Escape from Hell!*, various short stories, a poetry collection, *Songs for the Devil and Death*, and two chapbooks, *The A-Z of the Fantastic City* from Small Beer Press and the self-published *Errata*.

CPSIA information can be obtained
at www.ICGtesting.com
Printed in the USA
FFOW02n1951140414
4830FF